Dangerous Gifts

Haywood Smith

St. Martin's Paperbacks

This book is dedicated to the two
"M's" in my life:

Marjorie Dooley Smith, my
wonderful mother-in-law (Luckily
for me, the nicest man I ever met—
my husband Jim—had the nicest
mother!), and Michaelyn Koss, my
niece who is not only beautiful
inside and out, but also a brilliant
writer and an inspiration to her
Aunt Haywood.

ACKNOWLEDGMENTS

No one achieves success in a vacuum. My books have been published only because many, many people have helped me every step of the way—especially the readers who took a chance on a new author and spread the word that they liked my work.

So first, I want to thank my readers, with a double helping to those who have taken time to write me. What a joy it is to go to my mailbox and find something besides bills inside! Thanks, readers! Every time I sit down to write, I think of the women who will be reading the stories I create: women squeezing in a few chapters during break at the office; women sitting up with sick kids; women at the doctor's office or stuck in traffic or waiting for their kids at practice or the gym; women who lock the bathroom door, run a hot bath, and get pruney with a good book; or women who crawl into bed after a long, hard day and try their best to get through a whole chapter before falling asleep. I know how precious time is to every one of my readers. So I do my best to give them a lot of fun, some fascinating history, a big dose of old-fashioned romance, a lot of magic, and an upbeat ending with every book. You, readers, are my inspiration.

There are a few special people I would like to thank by name for their help. One of them is Dr. John Akin of Atlanta, first and foremost for the surgical skills that saved my son's life twenty-five years ago—along with the lives of countless others in the years before and since. More recently, thanks for helping me with the technical aspects of the surgery described in this book. As always, you were there when I needed you, ready and willing to help. I just hope I kept the facts straight.

My deepest gratitude, also, goes to all the wonderful people at *Romantic Times* magazine—particularly Kathryn Falk and Kathe Robin—whose generous support and encouragement have helped put wings on my dreams.

As always, I owe a tremendous debt of thanks to my editor, Jennifer Enderlin, without whose guidance and creative input my books would not be what they are. Thanks are due, as well, to all the dedicated, supportive people at St. Martin's Paperbacks, especially to the following: to Matthew Shear, a wonderful publisher and Blackjack player; to Walter Halee for his encouragement, cooperation and always-enthusiastic P.R.; to Ann Twomey and her staff for my beautiful covers; and to patient, always cheerful Dee Dee Zobian for tying up all the many loose ends.

I would be remiss if I did not say thanks to my husband Jim for never complaining or saying "I told you so" when I end up working a week without sleep to make a deadline because I put off getting started when I should have. And for seven years of asking, "Where are we going for supper?" without a trace of sarcasm. But most of all, for not "forsaking not the wife of thy youth," even when I became a writer.

Last, but by no means least, I am grateful to my incomparable literary agent, Damaris Rowland, and her associate Steven Axelrod, for believing in me. Thanks, Damaris, for your expertise, your unfailing understanding, and· your uncommon good sense. You keep my creative streams flowing and in their banks (pun intended). Couldn't do it without you.

PROLOGUE

Her husband was dead; Claire knew it the moment she looked down and saw the mud-spattered courier gallop his lathered mount across the drawbridge and into the frozen bailey below.

She stood transfixed, watching the messenger dismount and hasten to the main entry to hammer urgently with the bronze door knocker. Odd, that no sound reached her when the heavy metal ring struck against the stob.

Time seemed suddenly suspended in an eerie lull of crystalline clarity so silent she no longer heard the click of William's wooden blocks nor the crackle of the fire across her chamber nor the whistling winter wind that funneled through the narrow window where she stood. So silent and strangely colorless, yet every detail magnified somehow. She did not even hear her own heart racking heavily inside her chest.

And then it came: the distant screams of her goodmother's raw, agonized keening grief from the great hall—sounds more animal than human.

Icy fingers of terror closed inside Claire's chest, a terror that left no room for grief but squeezed the very breath from her lungs and set her pulse at a frantic rhythm.

William. He was all that mattered now.

Her son had been life's greatest gift, but as with all of life's gifts, a terrible price would have to be paid. As mistress of this great house she had once served, she was rejected by her husband's family as well as the servants who had been her friends. And since her husband had left to liberate the Holy Sepulcher, she had lived as a virtual prisoner in her chamber, with William her only comfort.

A series of dangerous gifts and unpredictable retribution—that was what her life had become. And now, her husband was dead, leaving her without a protector.

Retribution, dark and demanding, had arrived at her door.

Her fingers strangely slow to obey, she closed the wooden shutters and locked them, then turned to her son. Everything seemed labored and sluggish, as if the world were suddenly moving underwater.

William was sitting quietly on the bearskin rug a safe distance from the fire, his pudgy three-year-old's hands laboriously stacking wooden blocks until they tottered and fell, then stacking them all over again in grave concentration. He had no idea that the sword which had hung over their heads for the past two years was about to fall.

Dear God. What would become of them now?

She feared little for herself, but what would become of *William*?

With no one but her to safeguard William's legacy as the rightful heir . . .

All Claire could think of was the sullen, resentful

gleam of malice she saw in her brother-by-law's eyes every time he looked at her son. Sir Robert was a greedy man devoid of scruple, and now only William stood between him and the lordship of the rich lands of Compton.

She had to take her son to safety, but where? How? She had no money and no kin besides her husband's. Her parents had lived and died as faithful servants in this household, and Castle Compton was the only home she'd ever known.

Claire flew across the room and scooped her son close against her, taking courage from the solid weight of his pudgy body in her arms.

"Ow, Mama!" William protested, pushing her away. His big brown eyes looked up at her with annoyance, then widened in concern. "S'a matter, Mama?" He cradled her cheeks in his little palms just as she had so often cradled his in her own. "Why you weepin'?"

"Sometimes mamas weep, just like their little boys," she managed. Claire drew him close more gently, burying her nose into the sweet, soft brown curls that covered his head. She breathed in the unique, musty scent of honey and milk and woodsmoke and little boy.

Without so much as a word of warning, the door to her chamber flew open and a sobbing Lady DePeche burst in, her arms outstretched for William. "My son!" she wailed. "My firstborn! Dead! Lost to me forever!"

William recoiled from this unprecedented display of emotion in his usually reserved grandmother, but the dowager tore him from Claire's arms with surprising strength. She crushed the child to her and rocked back and forth on rigid legs like a madwoman. "Your father's dead, William. Gone from us forever. And all for

nothing. He never even made it to the Holy Land."
Her eyes turned toward heaven. "Dear God, why?
Such a senseless waste. I told him not to go, and now
he's dead. Dead!" She regarded her grandson with desperate intensity. "Oh, William, William! You're all I
have left in this dark and hateful world." Her outburst
dissolved into wracking sobs.

"Good-mother," Claire protested, as frightened as
William by Lady DePeche's lack of control. "You're
hurting him. He can't breathe. I pray thee, ease your
hold upon him, lest he smother."

The dowager didn't seem to hear her, but William
managed to wiggle his face free of his grandmother's
bosom. Flushed with alarm, his eyes huge and terrified,
the toddler struggled to get loose, looking to his mother
for help.

"I told him not to go," the dowager resumed.
"Begged him. Bullied him. Sacrificed my very dignity
in an effort to stop him, but he wouldn't listen. No."
She turned blazing eyes to Claire. "Sacred vow, indeed. Other men have healthy sons without making
such vows." Abruptly, her hysteria shifted to cunning
suspicion, her words dripping hatred. "You had something to do with that, didn't you?"

Claire felt the force of that hatred like a blast of
demon's breath. "Nay, my lady! Like you, I pleaded
with my lord husband to stay. I swear it. A child needs
a father, and I told my husband so, but he would not
be persuaded." Fear left her with scarcely the breath
to speak. "I truly think he believed William would die
if he broke his vow."

"Lie all you want," Lady DePeche spat out, "but
it will do you no good now. He's not here to protect
you." Her eyes narrowed. "I've often suspected that
you bewitched my son. Why else would a man of his

age and stature marry my *maid*?'' An unholy light lit their depths. ''Of course. You bewitched him. It's the only explanation.''

Claire's heart lurched. Lady DePeche was a powerful noblewoman and well-known benefactor of the Church. Her word, alone, would be enough to convict Claire of witchcraft and send her to the stake.

What would become of William then?

She hastened to defend herself, knowing even as she spoke that her words would hold no weight with her good-mother. ''Nay, my lady. I did nothing to encourage him, and you know it.'' She hastened to remind her good-mother, ''He told you why he married me. Don't you remember?'' She struggled to keep the terror from her voice. ''His first three wives were great ladies, God rest their souls, but all died in childbirth, along with their babes. Can you blame my lord husband for saying he wanted the strength of my Norman peasant blood to mother his sons?'' A tight edge of desperation crept into her tone. ''And I did give him a son. A healthy son. I am the mother of the heir.''

''A *servant*,'' the dowager spat at her. ''That's all you were and all you'll ever be.''

Sir Robert's voice sounded behind them. ''I agree.''

Both women turned toward him.

Claire recognized all too well the look of contempt in his eyes. She had seen it every time Sir Robert looked at her or her son. But now that glitter was heightened by a gleam of evil triumph.

With the Lord of Compton dead, only William stood between Sir Robert and the family's fertile holdings in Suffolk.

Sensing the danger both she and William were in, Claire struggled once more to wrest her son from his grandmother's arms, but Lady DePeche was too strong for her. "No!" The dowager tore free of Claire's efforts and backed out of reach, ignoring William's shrieks for his mother.

"Of course," Sir Robert mused, "now that my brother is dead, it falls to me to assume the burden of his responsibilities until our dear William reaches his majority." He shot the child a patently insincere look of sympathy. "Assuming the dear boy *does,* in fact, reach his majority." Sir Robert turned a soulless smile to Claire. "Such a dangerous, pestilential world we live in. We lose so many of our precious children."

The threat was so blatant, even Lady DePeche blanched white. She glared at her younger son. "I buried your father and six of your brothers and sisters, Robert, but by a just and holy God, I shall not bury my grandson." Her chin lifted in defiance. "Despite the stain of his mother's common blood, William is rightful heir to the lands of Compton, and I swear by my hope of heaven, I shall not let you harm him, even if it costs my very life." She stepped forward in challenge. "Or *yours.*"

Lady DePeche adored her only grandson; Claire was certain of that, at least. It was a small comfort, but the only one she had, now. Yet how could even William's grandmother protect him from his own uncle, especially since the law would make Sir Robert guardian?

"How touching, Mother. Such fierce devotion." Sir Robert leveled a scornful glare at the dowager. "Pity you never cared for me that way."

"I would have, Robert, if only you'd given me the slightest cause," his mother answered with scalding candor. Her voice hardened. "But you never did. Even as a child, you were spoiled and cruel. Your whole life, you've lied, manipulated, connived, and taken shameless advantage of the privileges of your birth without once contributing anything of value to our family.''

For the first time since her betrothal, Claire and her good-mother were in absolute agreement. Claire's husband had been a big man in spirit as well as body, but his only sibling was small, inside and out.

Lady DePeche regarded her younger son without sympathy. ''Your brother was the soul of honor. With the exception of his infatuation with this—'' She shot Claire a brief, scornful look. ''—serving wench, he did nothing unworthy or irresponsible in his entire life. Unlike you, who have been a constant vexation since you took your first wailing breath.''

Sir Robert would hate Claire even more for hearing this. She had to get William out of here, and quickly. She'd been fond of her elderly husband and would mourn his loss, but at this moment she wanted only to seize her son and run, as far and as fast as she could.

Castle Compton had once been her home. Since her doting husband's absence, these walls had become her prison, but now they closed down into a death trap.

She had to get William away from here. He was her only joy, her whole world, her heart.

The dowager, though, clearly had no intention of letting him loose. She tightened her arms protectively around her grandson, who had suddenly gone quiet as if he too sensed the danger. ''I've often wondered, Robert,'' Lady DePeche said wearily, ''how you and your brother could have shared the same blood.''

''It's your blood as well, Mother,'' Sir Robert retorted evenly.

Lady DePeche shifted her arms to cover William from his uncle's glare of open hatred. ''I won't let you harm him. Do you hear me?''

''Let me?'' Robert arched a narrow eyebrow. ''I am the one who shall do the letting from now on, *Mother*.''

The subtle emphasis was pregnant with contempt. "Norman law makes me the boy's guardian as the closest surviving male relative. You would do well to remember that."

Claire prayed there was some shred of decency in her brother-by-law. "Sir Robert, I beg you," she entreated, "if you have any love for your brother's memory—"

"Love?" He let out a derisive snort. "Love is the greatest lie of all, you ignorant wench." Then he faced her with consummate satisfaction. "Now get out. You have one hour to pack your things and go. The jewels, of course, stay here, but I want you out within the hour, and forever."

Stunned, Claire could only stare at him in mute denial.

When she did not react, Sir Robert stepped to within a few inches of her and ran his hands roughly over her breasts, murmuring, "I said, pack your clothes and go."

The shock of his filthy touch brought her back to life. She backed toward the dowager, then whirled and in a last, desperate effort, took hold of William.

A feral grimace distorted Lady DePeche's face. "Take your hands off him!" she roared. "He's mine, now. Mine!"

William began to scream. "Mama! Mama! I want my Mama!"

A surge of supernatural maternal energy enabled Claire to wrench her son from his captor, but the moment she turned to flee, Sir Robert struck the side of her head so hard she lost her breath and staggered, seeing stars.

The momentary lapse was all he needed to snatch her screaming child from her. He fairly hurled the boy at Lady DePeche. "Get him out of here!"

"William!" Claire lunged after her son, but Sir Robert struck her again, this time with even greater force. After a blinding flash of pain, she opened her eyes to find herself lying on her back, her head aching where it had hit the cold stone floor.

William and Lady DePeche were gone.

Sir Robert calmly walked over and straddled her shoulders, looming huge above her, the oily smell of his body polluting her every breath. Claire averted her eyes from the dark hairs and flaccid member dangling between the gausses under his tunic.

"I said, pack your things and get out," he repeated icily. "If you refuse, I shall see that before another sunrise, William joins his father in hell, and you with him."

Claire cared little enough about her own safety, but William's . . . Sickened, she tried to rise. "You wouldn't dare!"

Sir Robert kicked her back to the floor, then resumed standing with his legs spread above her. "Ah, but I would." He smiled, his narrow nostrils flaring. "A pity, everyone will say, how your husband's death so unhinged you that you would leap from the parapet with your child in your arms, taking both of you to your deaths."

To her horror, she saw his member twitch and begin to stiffen at the mere prospect of killing her and her son. She knew then that not only would he make good his threat of murder, he took unholy pleasure at the very thought. And he held all the power.

A jolt of dread shuddered through Claire as she realized she was at the mercy of her brother-by-law.

"Make up your mind," he said harshly. Then he added in an almost offhand manner, "Getting rid of both of you *would* be a bit of a bother, I must admit. 'Tis bound to raise some awkward questions, as well, especially with Mother.'' His narrow face hardened. ''Nothing I couldn't handle, though, I assure you.'' His dark brows lifted. ''The choice is yours. So what shall it be, *sister*? The heights or the highway?''

''I . . . I . . .'' Claire tried to speak, but her throat had gone dry as cotton.

Her brother-by-law bent down closer, his odor so strong she gagged. ''I advise you to go. And if you ever make any claim on the boy,'' he said almost pleasantly, ''or try to return or communicate with him in any way, or even repeat so much as one word of what has been said in this room today, I'll kill your dear little William before you have a chance to set eyes on him. Do I make myself clear?''

She nodded.

''I didn't hear you,'' Sir Robert chided.

''I understand,'' she managed. Rage and frustration boiled up within her. ''And I'll go, but only if you swear not to harm my son.''

His features congealed; he placed his foot between her breasts, pressing down with increasing force until the veins stood out on her face. ''I shall swear nothing,'' he said softly. The harder he pressed, the thicker and more rigid his member became. Claire wondered if he would give in to his unholy lust and crush her already shattered heart, but just as she started to lose consciousness, the pressure was released. ''Get out,'' he spat, stepping away from her.

Claire closed her eyes, her heart as dead as the stones beneath her. Losing William to this monster . . . if she could have willed the life from her own aching heart, she'd have done so. No. Better still, if she could will anyone to die, it would be Sir Robert—as lingering and horrible a death as possible.

At least he was mortal.

The thought triggered a ray of hope in her grief-fogged mind: he *was* mortal. If he should die, the threat to William would die with him, so she must stay alive and ready to reclaim her son. She must stay alive! That would take money.

Grim determination helped her struggle to her feet. "I said I'd leave, and I shall."

Sir Robert turned, clearly surprised by the resolution in her voice.

"But I shall expect a reference at least." She lifted her chin. "I served here well and faithfully for many years, until . . ." Claire faltered. She dared not mention her marriage.

"Ah, yes. *Until* . . ." A disturbing light brightened Sir Robert's eyes. "Why, I'd be delighted to write you a reference, Claire. I feel it my duty. After all, I think it's only fair that any prospective employer should know how you bewitched my brother and seduced him into marrying you."

Claire hadn't thought she could feel more desolate, but now she did.

"The lady of the house," Sir Robert continued with alacrity, "would be particularly interested in that bit of information, don't you think?"

There would be no reference.

Almost frantic, Claire tried to think. At least she had experience. But if she said she had experience . . .

She did what any prospective employer would do: She looked at the smooth skin and spotless, neatly trimmed nails of her hands. Then she turned them over and looked at her soft, unblemished palms. Six years as lady of Castle Compton had erased all evidence that she had once been a servant. No one would ever believe she had worked as a servant.

Sir Robert wouldn't have to kill her. As a woman alone in the world, without decent work . . . she would starve.

Sir Robert must have read her mind. "Delicious," he said seductively. "Such suffering. Such misery." Still facing her, he relaxed into a chair beside the fire. "If it were up to me, I would cast you out the way you came here, naked and empty-handed."

"I was *born* here," Claire choked out.

"Yes. Well . . ." He waved his hand. "Church-going Christian that I am, I suppose I must overlook that particular impulse, no matter how appealing I find the idea of your walking out of my life forever without a stitch on." He frowned with mock concern. "I suppose I should do something to make up for such an unworthy thought. Some act of Christian charity."

Christian charity, indeed! If God were truly just, Sir Robert would have been struck dead for what he'd done this day, Claire fumed.

"I think I shall allow you to take along your maid and your mare, as well as your clothes."

What was he up to?

He drew a fat purse from his belt and hefted it in his hand. "After all, our Lord did say that true religion lies in caring for widows and orphans. Since you are both, my generosity should earn me double recompense." He hurled the purse at her so hard Claire scarcely managed to catch it.

By the heft and feel, she judged the pouch to contain a small fortune in coins. She frowned, puzzled.

"Consider it payment." His face smoothed in final triumph. "For your son."

And then she understood. If she took the money, Sir

Robert and the dowager would doubtless tell everyone, William included, that Claire had sold her son and abandoned him.

That was the final, most killing blow.

But it was a blow she must endure to keep herself—and the hope of one day reclaiming her son—alive.

Sir Robert rose and started for the door. "You have one hour." When he opened it, she saw the armed guards in the hallway. He stopped on the threshold, his smug smile as cold as a winter star. "You have your money, you thankless bitch," he said loudly enough for the guards to hear. "Now take your things and go." He closed the door behind him.

Claire sank to the floor.

Dear God, but the darkness had descended upon her swiftly and completely, taking away the only thing that gave meaning to her life.

Where would she go? What would she do? Without William, the world was as dark and hateful as Lady DePeche had said it was.

But she had to go to save his life.

So within the hour, she left both her heart and her hope behind as she and her maid rode through the gate of Castle Compton into a world that had no place for women alone.

ONE

Two years later (January 1097)
A thousand miles away in a Carpathian
mountain monastery

Four hundred ninety steps to the top of the tower. Palmer had climbed the spiral stairway often enough to know exactly how many treads there were: seventy times seven. The number had significance, as did every other feature of this isolated community of men.

Panting heavily in the rarefied air, he eased himself into the shelter of a merlon and waited for his heart to stop battering against his scrawny ribs.

So weak, even after seven long months of rest and care.

God, how he hated being weak, never knowing when the fever would strike him down.

Fully ten minutes passed before his pulse and breathing eased enough for him to stand, but when he did, it was to see the sun break through the blanket of winter clouds, illuminating the stark, snow-capped peaks all around him.

He stepped to the edge of the parapet and opened his arms to the cold, cutting wind. As always, it seemed to purge him. He closed his eyes and let the stinging breath of these dark, desolate mountains slash through his clothes until his skin went numb.

If only he could numb his mind as easily, to silence the guilt that had been eating away at him for more than a year.

Palmer opened his eyes and looked down.

Rain-swollen and turgid a thousand feet below him, the Váh reflected an errant shaft of sunlight that pointed like a silvered arrow from the bottom of the gorge.

What would it feel like to step out into space, then tumble down and down and down into those cold, raging waters?

One step. That was all it would take.

Oddly unafraid, Palmer stared into the precipice and tried to imagine the rush of wind and rock hurtling past him. He could almost hear the river calling him, promising oblivion—an end to torment. That was siren song enough.

A familiar voice intruded from behind him. "It's a lie, you know."

Palmer froze in place, annoyed at the interruption despite the sense of detachment that had overtaken him.

"What you're thinking," the voice continued in the familiar accents of their common homeland, "it's no solution, Palmer. You know that."

Now only an arm's length away, Brother Urbi made no move to pull Palmer to safety. Thin as an alpine snag and twice as tough, the little monk could easily have taken advantage of Palmer's weakness to overpower him, but instead, he attacked with logic, not force, going straight for the heart of the matter, as always. "Talk to me, Palmer."

Palmer felt the subtle heat of the monk's presence move in close behind him. "The nightmares have come back," he confessed, "worse than ever. I dare not close my eyes for what I'll see."

"I feared as much," the monk acknowledged.

A tense, thoughtful pause stretched between them.

The mere mention of Palmer's nightmares was enough to bring on a flood of hideous memories. The stench of blood and smoke and excrement filled his nostrils. His ears rang with the screams of helpless women and children.

He had been just as guilty as the rest that fateful day in Hungary.

When the main body of Peter the Hermit's Crusaders had reached the village of Semlin and discovered the bloodied armor and clothes of their advance forces hanging from the town walls like grim trophies, Palmer had assumed the worst along with the rest of the fighting men. He'd been just as eager as any to strike down these foreign infidels who had dared attack the Army of God. But like the others, he had no way of knowing their men had merely been beaten, stripped, and sent on their way by the frightened townspeople.

What a fool he'd been. What an idealistic, sanctimonious fool.

True, none of his fellow Crusaders had spoken the language. But Palmer had long ago abandoned the cowardly comfort of that excuse. He, along with the rest of them, had assumed the worst and attacked the village with the righteous zeal of avenging angels, Palmer at the forefront.

Perhaps he could have lived with that, if that had been all there was.

But what came next . . . the raping, the burning, the looting . . . the massacre of women and children. How could any man worth his soul come to terms with such brutality . . . ever?

When he'd seen their victims' crucifixes, he'd tried to stop the madness, only to be skewered in the gut, stripped, and left for dead by his own frenzied troops.

It was only when he'd regained consciousness under the gentle care of Semlin's priest that the truth had been confirmed: No infidels lived within the walls of Semlin, just frightened Christian townspeople who had feared the invading hordes of ragtag foreigners flooding their homeland and consuming their already scarce food.

The same Christian townspeople who had found Palmer, an enemy, in the burning ruins of their town and brought him to the priest to be nursed back to life.

Palmer turned tortured eyes to Brother Urbi. He could manage only a single word, but it was a word that said everything. "Semlin."

"Still?" Brother Urbi sighed. "I had hoped—"

"Your hopes are poorly spent on me, sir," Palmer said bitterly. "Where was your God at Semlin?" he accused.

"Grieving," Brother Urbi said softly, meeting Palmer's anguish with level compassion. "Living every atrocity through His children who bore them."

"But why did He allow such a thing? How could He have let it happen?"

"He let us *choose,* Palmer," Brother Urbi said urgently. "Such evil exists only because we have the freedom to choose. That was His gift to us—"

"A dangerous gift," Palmer said grimly, "at a terrible cost."

"Aye, but He willingly paid the cost for that gift with His own blood on the cross."

"I used to believe that," Palmer said flatly. "Now I believe nothing."

"He's already forgiven you, Palmer. Why can't you forgive yourself?"

"Only death will free me from the guilt I bear."

"And what if Saint Paul had said the same thing?" Brother Urbi challenged. "Before his conversion, he hunted down and killed as many Christians as he could find. What if he had let the guilt of those crimes cripple him as yours has crippled you?"

"Paul was a saint," Palmer shot back. "I am not."

"Yet you have repented your sin, my brother, and made penance, as well," the monk reminded him. "You have done much good as a healer. But forgiveness can only be found at the cross, not in good works."

"If that's the case, then why go on living?" Palmer shot a sidelong glance at the monk. "I've been to the cross a thousand times since that day, but my guilt remains." He turned back to peer into the gorge. Again, the depths seduced him, whispering of oblivion.

"My brother, I know your torment is real," his mentor said quietly, "yet this suffering is mortal, temporary." He hesitated, his silence pregnant with compassion. "But suicide . . . it will not end your pain; it will only send your soul to *eternal* torment, for hell is everlasting."

Much as Palmer would wish it otherwise, the man had a point. His gaze rose from the gorge to the mountain peaks.

"When I was just a lad," he said, as much to himself as to his friend and counselor, "I used to dream of faraway places like this." A dull throb of homesickness pulsed within him. "I was always climbing into the tallest trees, trying to see what lay beyond the safe, serene borders of my home."

So much had happened since then, Palmer felt as if

he were looking back on someone else's life whenever he thought of the headstrong, idealistic boy he had once been.

Suddenly, he was weary almost beyond breathing.

Not today. He couldn't jump today.

He turned to find Brother Urbi's gaunt features tight with concern.

"Would to God I'd never left there." Palmer sighed. His shoulders sagged as he surrendered the notion of ending his anguish by destroying his mortal body. Brother Urbi was doubtless right: hell would bring anguish eternal. At least here, on earth, he could help others even though he could not help himself.

Palmer let out a long sigh of resignation.

Taking that as a sign that the immediate crisis had passed, Brother Urbi grasped Palmer's elbow and urged him to safer footing. "Come. Let me get you something hot to eat. You'll feel better after some warm food and a little rest—"

Palmer shook his head. "You have been kind to me here, all of you, and I am most grateful," he said, "but the time has come for me to leave."

From the day he had been brought here, too ill and fevered to stand, they had both known this moment would come.

Palmer had sought oblivion from the brothels of Bohemia to the poppy dens of Zara, but what little comfort he'd found had never lasted long. Chased by the ghosts of Semlin, he had healed those he could along the way, but always, the ghosts had caught up with him and hounded him to move on in an endless, useless quest for peace.

This had been his longest respite, but now it too had ended with the return of the nightmares.

Brother Urbi acknowledged his decision with a nod. "Where will you go, my brother?"

"I do not know." Palmer shrugged. "Somewhere." He offered his mentor a bitter smile. "Anywhere."

The monk stilled, his gaunt, wind-polished features composed. "Have you considered going home, my brother?"

Palmer wasn't easily caught off guard, but this took him by surprise. "Home?" he repeated.

"Aye. Home." Brother Urbi's piercing dark eyes met his in challenge.

"Home is the *last* place I would go. The shame of what I've done . . ." Palmer felt himself shrivel inside. "How could I face my mother, her friends? My enemies?" He shook his head. "They'll hear the truth about Semlin eventually, and my part in it—if they haven't heard already. Once they know, I'd never be able to lift my head as a man again."

"I disagree," the monk said gently. "Home might be the one place you can find what you're looking for."

"Absolution?" Palmer couldn't suppress a caustic smile. "No one can grant me that, not even your God."

"He's your God too, Palmer, and He's already forgiven you, but you will have no peace until you forgive yourself."

"So you have told me again and again." Moved by a debt of honesty to his friend, Palmer added, "For your sake, I'd like to believe you. The trouble is, I have nothing to believe you *with*. We both know that."

"Your faith is not dead, Palmer," his friend countered. "It too is immortal, and will one day make itself known to you again."

"God forbid, my brother. God forbid." Palmer turned and took the next step of a journey that had already taken him two thousand miles to nowhere. "Farewell. We shall not meet again."

"May the Holy Spirit go with you to comfort and protect you," the little monk called after him in benediction.

Palmer knew Brother Urbi meant well, but he also knew the blessing would do no good, for the Spirit of God could not coexist with the demons that had pursued him for more than a year.

As was his custom, he left without looking back.

THAT SAME EVENING IN THE NEW FOREST OF WESSEX, ENGLAND

Cold, wet wind blew snow into Claire's sodden cape as she followed the narrow road through the forest. It set the bare branches of the trees aclatter above her head, making her even more wary than usual. A woman alone could never be too careful.

"Not more than a mile down that road," the priest had said when she'd sought him out after discovering there was no provision for travelers in Linherst.

Claire looked up to the bare branches that sounded like as many dancing skeletons and crossed herself, her gesture born of superstition instead of faith. Surely she had been more than a mile already. Had she missed a turn, perhaps?

She scanned the surrounding grove of ancient oaks, certain she saw something flitting in the shadows, but it was just her imagination. She had imagined all manner of perils since Marissa had died at Michaelmas, leaving her truly alone in the world.

"You will know the place by its wall," the priest had said in Linherst. "A most impressive wall, worthy of the finest castle, although it's not a castle, really. More a fortified compound.'' He had patted Claire's arm in reassurance. ''The widow who lives there is a fine Christian woman—''

In two years of nomadic exile, Claire had suffered abuse at the hands of many a ''fine Christian woman,'' but on this cold winter's night, she had no other options. If she did not find shelter from the wind and drenching, driving snow, she might well freeze.

''. . . Dame Freeman too is alone,'' the priest had rattled on. ''I am certain you may rely on her hospitality.''

Claire hoped devoutly that she could. Her frozen fingers had already gone numb, despite her riding gloves.

Then she saw it, looming through the trees ahead in the deepening dusk. A wall. As she approached it, Claire looked up in awe.

Every inch of twelve feet tall and five feet thick, the massive fortification was made from huge stones and mortar so precisely cut and laid, the outer surface was smooth as the face of a frozen lake. She followed the base of the wall for a hundred yards before she came to the undefended opening.

Odd, that there was no gate in such a formidable wall.

Claire nudged Frieda's flanks with her heels and directed her mare to the gateless entry. Sure enough, inside the huge enclosure she saw a rambling brick structure whose crumbled stucco was softened by a healthy coat of ivy. The cottage was not roofed with thatch, but with arched red tiles now blanketed with snow. Yet that was not the cottage's most unusual feature; it was the windows—on either side of the stout wooden door, two generous openings glazed with diamond-shaped panes of real glass emitted a welcoming glow from within.

Claire had never seen glass windows in a house before, only in churches.

This healer must be wealthy beyond imagining, yet her name declared her merely a freedwoman. It made no sense.

Suddenly apprehensive, Claire halted her mare and scanned the dusky compound. Despite the snow and failing light, she made out an impressive array of outbuildings neatly arranged among acre upon acre of dormant gardens laid out in precise shapes.

Everything inside the walls looked alien, somehow, as if she had stumbled upon a foreign country.

A chilling gust of wind convinced her to take her chances. Summoning up her courage, she approached the house.

The wind shifted fitfully, wafting a gust of chimney smoke her way, and she smelled the welcome scent of food mingled with burning wood.

Claire's stomach let out a hungry gurgle.

She was ravenous, and the cottage looked almost magical with its glowing windows and snow-covered roof.

Frieda shivered, and Claire realized the poor animal was quaking from the cold. That goaded her to action. One of the outbuildings was bound to be a barn, so there would be shelter for Frieda, at least.

She leaned forward and rubbed the patient animal's neck. "Just a few steps more, sweeting, and you shall have shelter and rest." As if she understood, Frieda bobbed her head, then ambled the last few yards to the front door of the house.

When they reached the entrance, Claire dismounted and tied Frieda's reins to a wooden railing beside the entry stair. She climbed the stairs with some misgiving.

What if this woman turned her away?

Ask her! an inner voice scolded. Give her a chance to say no before you start worrying.

Claire inhaled deeply, then reached for the heavy brass ring that served as a knocker. It took both hands to operate, but produced a satisfying summons.

Then she waited.

No response.

She leaned toward the window for a look inside, but from where she was standing, all she could see were blotches of subtle color arrayed along the rafters and lit by the light of a fire.

"Hello, the cottage! Is anyone there?"

When no one answered, she knocked again, longer and louder this time.

After repeating the procedure several times, she was just about to give up and take refuge in the barn when the door was thrown open, releasing a gust of warmth redolent of herbs, spices, wood smoke, and food.

"Well, there you are!" exclaimed the white-clad, white-haired apparition silhouetted in the doorway. "Have you been knocking long? I was preparing a decoction in my apothecary and didn't hear you until just now." She motioned Claire inside. "Come in, child. Come in. I'm so glad you've come to me at last."

"Dame Freeman?" Claire croaked out, taken aback by the woman's unexpected familiarity.

"Aye, but call me Nonna, child. Everyone else does." She seized Claire's upper arms briefly and kissed her briskly on each cheek. "Thanks be to God! After all these months of waiting, here you are!" She looked past Claire through the open door to Frieda. "And a horse! Blessing upon blessing! Now we'll be able to go where we're needed much faster."

Claire recoiled, feeling as if she had stepped into someone else's dream—a very confusing dream. She could run, but where would she go? The wind had turned even colder, and the clouds obscured the moon, leaving the forest pitch-black.

"Whatever are you standing out there for?" the woman asked her. "Come in, come in, before we both freeze." Again, Dame Freeman motioned her inside, but Claire held back.

"I—I'm sorry," she stammered, "but I'm afraid you must have me confused with someone else. I . . . that is, I didn't even know I was coming here until—" Claire halted, trying to collect her wits. "If you're expecting someone else, of course, I shall understand completely if there isn't room—"

"Nonsense," her hostess exclaimed briskly. "I'm not expecting someone else. I was expecting *you*." She fingered the fabric of Claire's soggy cloak. "Gracious! Soaked through! Why, you'll catch your death standing in the doorway." Despite her snow-white hair, Dame Freeman fairly snatched Claire off her feet and into the warm, cluttered room.

A pungent cacophony of scents assaulted her from the innumerable sprays of dried herbs, spices, and flowers hung from the rafters.

"Mercy, but I'm glad you're here," her captor continued. "Not that there was ever any doubt as to your coming, of course. It was merely a question of when. I hadn't dreamed you'd have a horse, though. That's a bit of unexpected good fortune, I can tell you." Did the woman ever stop for breath? Chattering on, she steered Claire toward a sturdy wooden chair by the fire. "What lovely brown eyes you have, my dear. So kind, but sad, in a way."

Abruptly, she shifted to more practical matters.

"Listen to me, rattling on, when you're cold and wet and tired. And I know you must be hungry. We'll eat in a moment, but first, there are a few things I need to clear up." She unceremoniously shoved Claire into the seat, then circled to kneel in front of her. "Give me your hand, child."

Caught off guard both by the command and the silence that followed, Claire surrendered her hand without protest.

"My, what large hands you have for a woman," Dame Freeman commented cheerfully. "I suppose your feet are large, as well."

"Oh, really!" Claire sputtered. She tried to reclaim her hand, but Dame Freeman's roughened grip was too strong for her. Embarrassed, Claire tucked her enormous feet deeper within the concealing folds of her skirt and cloak. She was more than a little sensitive about her height and large bones, particularly her feet. "I can't imagine how the size of my feet—or the condition of my hands—could be any of your business."

"I wasn't insulting you, child. It was a compliment. Large hands and feet hold up better to hard work." Dame Freeman peered at the back of Claire's hand. "Mmm. Good skin color. No ridges on the nails or splinter hemorrhages underneath. Knuckles are large, but not arthritic. No scars. Healthy nail beds."

Claire took advantage of the opportunity to study her hostess at close range. It was hard to tell just how old the healer truly was, for though her hair was white, the woman's bright blue eyes and expressive features sparkled with the glow of a young girl's. The fine wrinkles that radiated from the corners of her eyes and bracketed her mouth were common in older women, but the lines of her face were not so deep as those of a woman of fifty.

Before Claire could reach a conclusion as to her hostess's age, Dame Freeman turned her hand over and frowned. "Oh, dear." She shook her head. "No calluses." She added absently, "Whatever is He thinking, sending me a girl with such soft hands?" Obviously the question was rhetorical, for she did not await a response. "Ah, well. The horse more than makes up for that, I should think." After an indulgent pat, she allowed Claire to reclaim her extremity.

Dame Freeman smiled in reassurance. "No reason for alarm. You're intelligent; I can see that in your eyes. That's all that matters, really. The rest, you can learn."

"Dame Freeman," Claire protested, "I have no idea what you're talking about." Something was wrong here. "You couldn't possibly have been waiting for *me* . . . not for months, as you said. Why, I wasn't even directed here until this afternoon—"

Undaunted, her hostess only smiled and shook her head. "Everything will be clear to you soon enough, my dear." She leaned forward intently and stared at Claire, looking up her nose, peering into her eyes, examining her skin, and generally crowding her beyond endurance. "Have you ever done any real work before?"

The irony of that particular question would have made Claire laugh if she hadn't been so discomfited. Instead, she had the sinking feeling she had stumbled on a madwoman, and whether or not Dame Freeman was harmless remained to be seen.

A spark of pure panic goaded her beyond good manners. "Forgive me, good woman, but I have endured quite enough of this. What in the name of heaven gives you the right to inspect my hands?" She felt her cheeks flush hot with indignation. "And how dare you question me so personally, as if you were selecting an apprentice?''

"But that's it, you see! You do understand, after all. I knew you were bright.'' Dame Freeman beamed. ''I asked God to send me an apprentice, and He sent you!''

Sensible at last of Claire's agitation, she drew back, her expression apologetic. ''You'll have to be patient with me, my dear. I get rather wound up when God answers my prayers so neatly, although it shouldn't really surprise us when He keeps His promises, now should it?'' She laughed like a girl. ''I'm forever expecting everyone to see things the way I do, and when they don't...'' She chuckled. ''You see, it never ceases to amaze me what unexpected methods God uses in matters such as this, but then again, if we could understand how He did everything, He would hardly be God, would he?'' She settled a benign smile on her guest.

Taking advantage of the rare lull in her monologue, Claire blurted out, ''This is preposterous. I know nothing of any apprenticeship. I came here for shelter, nothing more.'' In spite of her growing desperation, she forced her voice to calm. ''Please excuse me, good woman. I seem to have stumbled upon the wrong house. All I would ask of you is shelter for my mare and me in your barn. We shall not trouble you further.'' She eased sideways, praying for a clear path to the door and escape.

''Piffle,'' Dame Freeman declared. Then she paused. ''Unless...'' Those bright blue eyes peered into Claire's. ''Forgive me, child. Perhaps I was mistaken. Are you visiting family here, then, or on your way home, perhaps?''

''No.'' Claire faltered. ''My husband died two years

ago, and I have no blood kinfolk to take me in, but—"

"I see." A hint of smugness colored the older woman's response. "Perhaps you are making a pilgrimage, then? Or traveling to a specific destination?"

"No, I . . ."

Dame Freeman eyed the elegant cut and fabric of her visitor's apparel. "Or had you planned to enter the contemplative life?" The question acknowledged Claire as a woman of substance, for only the nobility could afford a convent dowry.

"No . . ." The money Sir Richard had thrown at Claire wasn't nearly enough for the bride-price of a convent—not that she'd ever considered entering a convent. Sir Richard's blood money had only been enough for Claire and Marissa to scrimp along for almost two years, searching for work and a place to settle. But paying for Marissa's burial had all but emptied the purse now tucked behind Claire's girdle. "I was not going to a convent. And I have no money."

"There you have it, then, by your own admission." Dame Freeman let out a solid, satisfied breath. "No home. No family. No destination. No money. No trade." Her eyebrows lifted in appraisal. "Do you still think I am waiting for someone else?"

Claire had to admit, it all was rather convenient. "But—"

"A match made in heaven, if you ask me," her hostess asserted, her sparkle returning. "Isn't God's economy a beautiful thing to behold? You need a home. I need an apprentice. Now, what could be tidier? And He threw in a horse, as well." Dame Freeman's grin was dazzling.

"True, I have been looking for a place to settle," Claire confessed, "but I hardly think it wise to base such an important decision on mere coincidence.''

''Piffle. There *are* no coincidences.'' Dame Freeman didn't bother to pursue the argument, as her mind was quite obviously made up. ''Your bed is ready, but that must wait until you've eaten.'' She crossed to the kettle bubbling over the fire. ''I hope you like chicken stew.''

It was Claire's favorite.

Another coincidence.

Disconcerted, Claire rose and backed toward the door. ''My horse . . . She's colder and hungrier than I. Pray, excuse me while I put her in the barn.''

''How thoughtless of me,'' Dame Freeman responded. ''Of course the horse must be attended to, and straightaway.'' She frowned. ''But you mustn't go, my dear. You're wet through and chilled to the bone. Stay here and eat.'' She ladled up a steaming bowl of stew and tore off a chunk of fresh bread. ''I'll stable your horse and cover her with a nice, warm blanket, then feed her a bucket of oats.'' Before Claire could object, Dame Freeman thrust the bowl of stew into her hands, snatched a heavy white cloak from its peg, and hastened out into the night.

Feeling as if she'd encountered a human whirlwind, Claire subsided into the chair. Madwoman or not, though, Dame Freeman seemed to be an excellent cook, for the stew looked and smelled irresistible. Claire tore off a polite-sized chunk of bread and dipped up a mouthful of hot stew.

It was the best she'd ever tasted. By the time her hostess returned, the bread was gone and the bowl was empty.

''Let me get you some more, dear,'' Dame Freeman insisted.

Embarrassed that she had wolfed down everything

so quickly, Claire said, "No, thank you. But it was wonderful."

"It is, isn't it?" No false modesty, here. The older woman took the empty bowl and refilled it. "Eat just a little more. You'll sleep better, if you do." She tore off another chunk of bread and insisted Claire take it.

Tempted by the spicy aroma of the stew, Claire took just one more bite. Then another.

Dame Freeman winked at her in satisfaction. "I've been fattening that hen for weeks, but for some reason, today just seemed to be the day to put her to the pot." Her face glowed with irony. "Another convenient coincidence, wasn't it?"

Her mouth full, Claire could only nod.

"Tell me, child," Dame Freeman asked, "can you read?"

Read?

Claire fairly choked on her food.

Why, she couldn't think of a single woman, base or noble, who *could* read. Eyes narrowing, she shook her head and tried her best to finish the food in her mouth.

"Never fear," Dame Freeman said. "I can teach you. Reading and writing aren't so difficult, really. Of course, the Latin might take quite a bit longer."

"Latin?" Claire gasped out, but Dame Freeman rattled on without seeming to notice.

"Aye. And then the Greek. But don't worry about those now. The reading can come later, but we won't have to wait until then to start learning." Her large, expressive hands motioned to the roots, herbs, and blossoms hanging from the rafters. "Nature provides most of my cures. The recipes have come down through the centuries with my people, passed from mother to daughter. We'll start with the plants in this room. Before you know it, you'll be able to name every one and tell me where it grows and how it's used."

Claire had no idea how to respond, so she sat mute.

Part of her wanted to run for the barn, get her horse, and take her chances on the road. But another part of her saw a certain elegant logic in Dame Freeman's proposition.

Stay here and learn to be a healer?

Addlepated as it sounded, the prospect ignited a tiny spark of hope in Claire's mind.

A home, and something dignified to do with her life. She might actually have something to do besides scrubbing floors and scouring after other people's waste . . . something useful and helpful to others.

But could she learn? Reading, and *Latin*, and all those plants . . .

As if she could read Claire's very thoughts, Dame Freeman reassured her. "Don't worry, child. I'm no wizard, and no scholar. If *I* can do it, I know you can." The older woman sobered. "There is only one condition—a boon that I would ask in return for providing you with food, shelter, and a trade."

Claire's stomach tightened. Now, the truth would out. She braced herself for the worst.

Dame Freeman looked away, her cheeks coloring. "I would ask only your promise that . . . that you would care for me when I can no longer care for myself." An exquisite pain limned her features when she leveled her gaze to Claire's. "You needn't answer me now. Take all the time you need to reach a decision. But if you choose to accept, I would ask that you do so with your whole heart, upon a sacred vow."

Claire didn't have a whole heart to give, but something in Dame Freeman's expression touched a common chord inside her.

Another woman, alone.

Perhaps God had ordained it, after all. If there was a God . . .

Looking around her, she wondered what it would be like to call this place home. The cottage's wooden floors gleamed with age and care, and despite the cluttered impression of the main room, she quickly realized that every bottle, tool, and implement had its place—an arrangement that strongly appealed to her own sense of order. She peered through the open doors on either side of the fireplace and noted two cozy bedchambers, each with its own lofty bedstead, mattress, and colorful hangings.

Dame Freeman followed her gaze. "The east bedchamber shall be yours. It has a fine featherbed, and a window with glass, so you can watch the sun rise."

Her own room? Claire had never in her life had a bedchamber all to herself. Even when she was mistress of her own house, either her husband or her maid Marissa had shared her quarters.

"I know it's a lot to think about, my dear." Dame Freeman rose. "Why don't I just leave you in peace to mull things over?" She yawned behind her hand. "I must confess, all this excitement has left me a bit weary. I must bid you a good night." She covered the kettle and shifted it to the edge of the fire to simmer, then headed for the bedroom at the far side of the hearth.

Halfway there, she paused as if she'd forgotten something.

Claire waited for her to speak, but the older woman merely stared into space. The silence lengthened uncomfortably before, with a slight quake, Dame Freeman came back to herself. She turned and regarded Claire as if seeing her for the first time. "Who . . . ?" Her frown of concentration wilted into a mask of subtle agony that stole the sparkle from her eyes. With shaking hand, she threaded her fingers absently through her snow-white mane. "Now what was I about? It was important, but I can't seem to . . ."

Suddenly, she looked old. And very, very frightened.

In spite of her reservations, Claire's heart went out to the older woman.

"Oh, yes." Abruptly, the spark of intelligence rekindled Dame Freeman's confidence. "I remember now." She smiled. "Silly old woman that I am, prattling on and on, when I haven't even asked your name. What is it, child?"

Claire surprised herself by responding without hesitation. "Claire. My name is Claire. Claire Commeronne DePeche." Already, she was behaving like an apprentice!

"Claire." Dame Freeman nodded in approval. "It's a good, solid name, and it suits you."

Solid?

Always sensitive about her height and large frame, Claire flushed at Dame Freeman's blunt assessment, but the older woman took no note of her reaction.

Dame Freeman granted Claire a weary smile. "Make yourself at home and sleep well. I know I shall." As she entered her bedchamber, she added, "And don't forget to think about my proposition. Pray about it, too." She granted Claire a parting smile. "I'm certain we'll come to an agreement." With that, she left Claire alone to ponder the most important decision she had made since leaving Castle Compton.

TWO

Claire dreamed she was floating on a cloud, basking in the heat of the sun. Soft. Warm. Safe.

Part of her remembered dark journeys of nights past—searching endlessly for William through fantastic landscapes in shades of gray. But this dream was different. This was sunlight, perfumed by the scent of spring. Too good to be true. Yet when at last she told her dreaming self that it was time to wake, she could not. This peace, this warmth, was so intoxicating, she willed herself to drift on—until a harsh sound from beyond her door drew her unwilling consciousness back to reality.

Eyes tightly closed, she stretched.

Still she was warm, held secure in blissful softness, surrounded by the subtle scents of a meadow in the sun.

Was she awake, or dreaming?

She opened her eyes to a dim cavern of damask bed-hangings illuminated by tiny shards of brilliant light.

Where was she?

Claire scrubbed her eyes with the heels of her hands and yawned.

Ah, yes. She remembered now: the healer's.

She drew the smooth linen sheet to her nose and inhaled. Roses.

How long had she slept? A very long time, judging from the heaviness in her arms and legs. She could not even form a fist.

After so many months of huddling next to Marissa along the roadside, sleeping on stone ledges at monastery guest houses, or passing anxious nights in noisy, filthy inns, she scarcely knew how to react to the immaculate cleanliness, quiet, and security of this house.

The tantalizing aroma of last night's stew wafted into her room.

Claire pulled back the heavy bedhangings to the brilliant light of a still, sunny winter's midmorning. Outside her window, cold sunlight set the snow aglisten, transforming the walled compound into a magic place, all clean and bright and peaceful.

She should have felt guilty for sleeping half the day away, but strangely, she didn't. The sunlight streaming into her very own window warmed not only her room, but the weary recesses of her heart.

She could easily become accustomed to such a place.

The very air was special, permeated by the herbs and spices drying along the rafters overhead. Claire looked up and saw bunches of clover, dill, sage, roses, and rose hips hanging there. Nonna had taken advantage of every available space to dry her healing herbs and flowers.

Claire couldn't remember feeling so secure since her parents had died. Afraid that this fragile sense of well-being would evaporate any moment, she crawled back into bed and pulled the covers up to her chin.

She *could* stay here. Nonna seemed kind, despite her eccentricities.

Considering the matter, Claire tried to think of every possible drawback and how she would react.

What if she and Nonna didn't get along?

She dismissed that idea as too preposterous. Nonna, despite her obvious peculiarities, seemed genuinely good-hearted and generous. And she obviously had a practical streak, just like Claire.

No. Getting along would not be a problem.

But the healing . . . and the learning. What if Claire was too slow?

That, indeed, was a risk. But Nonna had promised to pace her teaching to Claire's abilities, so that shouldn't pose a problem.

The only real question left was one Claire couldn't answer: Was she strong enough and smart enough?

After two years of living rough and rootless, she wasn't so certain.

She'd always had a good memory, though, and she loved solving riddles.

Inside her, a still, small voice whispered, "Stay."

I would ask only one thing in return . . . promise that you will care for me when I can no longer care for myself.

Could she promise with her whole heart to care for Nonna? Claire's word was all she had left to give. If she promised, she would do it. But Claire wasn't sure she could promise forever.

Perhaps Nonna would agree to a trial period . . . for both of them.

Yes. A trial. Six months, perhaps a year—time for both of them to make up their minds about each other.

Claire snuggled deeper into the featherbed, reveling in its warmth. She would stay, at least until the darkness caught up with her.

She must have dozed off, for when next she opened

her eyes, a smiling Nonna was standing beside the bed with a covered tray in hand.

"Ah, good," the older woman said. "Awake at last." She pulled off the napkin covering the tray and laid the square of fabric across Claire's chest. "I was afraid I was going to have to eat this myself." She nodded to Claire. "Sit up, dear, so I can put this in your lap."

Shamed by her laziness, Claire sat up and slid her legs over the side of the bed. "Oh, no, Nonna. It is I who should be serving you. After all—"

Nonna pushed her firmly back against the pillows. "Nonsense. Put those feet back under the covers. Today, you are my guest. You won't be my apprentice until I say so." She laid the tray across Claire's lap with a wink. "But don't get used to this. Once you've had a chance to rest and regain your strength, we'll begin to work in earnest, from sunrise to sundown." She backed toward the door. "Just call me when you're finished."

Who did Nonna think Claire was, she wondered, an idle aristocrat or an invalid, to be served her meal in bed?

It was lovely, though, to be able to eat in warmth and comfort. Even as mistress of Castle Compton, she had enjoyed no such privilege.

The mere thought of Castle Compton was like a black cloud blocking the sun. Claire forced her thoughts away from that pain. She must decide if she truly wished to stay here.

Eating the stew slowly and savoring every bit of bread, she considered Dame Freeman's offer.

If she stayed, she would have a home, security, companionship, and a useful occupation. If she did not stay . . .

Claire thought for a long time before realizing that there wasn't a single reason why she shouldn't accept.

Unless things were not as they seemed.

Finishing her stew, she placed the tray beside the bed, then eased back against the pillows and drew up the covers. First, she must reassure herself that Dame Freeman was not concealing any sinister motives.

Then, and only then, would she accept.

Who could say? This might just be the new beginning she'd been searching for.

No sooner was the decision made, than she drifted off into peaceful, healing slumber.

Another night passed before she woke again. Outside, the sun was not yet risen, but Claire felt compelled to get up and dress. Her arms and legs had grown stiff, and she needed to walk around to stir her blood. When she finished dressing and combing her hair, then plaiting it, she crept quietly into the main room.

Nonna was already up and dressed, grinding herbs at her apothecary. "Good morning," she said softly. "I trust you are rested?"

"Almost too rested." Claire's words seemed overly loud in this peaceful, cluttered room. "I woke up stiff as an old woman."

"Then you've rested enough." Nonna washed her hands in a basin, dried them, then crossed to the pot boiling on the fire. "I hope you don't mind leftovers. Yesterday's stew is today's soup, but the bread is fresh." She picked up a cloth to open the oven beside the fire and gingerly removed a dark brown oval of fresh rye bread. The pungent aroma set Claire's stomach growling loudly.

Nonna ladled up a bowl of soup for each of them, tore the bread in two, and retrieved a dish of butter from the windowsill. "Your mare has two milk cows and three nanny goats to keep her company in the barn." At Claire's surprised expression, she went on, "Don't worry. I've already fed the mare and milked the ladies for this morning." She nodded wisely. "Many remedies require milk, butter, or cheese, so we shall share the dairy chores."

She drew two spoons from the ledge and put them beside the bowls of soup. "Whatever food we don't use ourselves, I give to Father Kendall for his own table, but he rarely keeps anything for himself."

"Father Kendall?" Claire sat beside one of the bowls. "Is he the village priest?"

"Aye." Nonna sat opposite Claire, swinging her legs over the bench as easily and unselfconsciously as a child would. "You've met him, then?"

Claire nodded. "He was the one who sent me here."

Nonna beamed. "I might have known the Holy Ghost would use him to show the way. He's a good man, Father Kendall." She bowed her head without warning, crossed herself, and before Claire could close her own eyes and bow her head, rattled off a blessing. That done, Nonna pushed up her sleeves and dove into the hearty meal.

In spite of her natural reservations, Claire found herself liking this no-nonsense woman. Suppressing a smile, she used her spoon to smear fresh butter on the hot bread and popped it into her mouth.

Delicious.

She could scarcely imagine what it would be like to live with someone who said exactly what she thought and always told the truth, just as Claire had always longed to do, herself.

The prospect was so exciting, it almost lifted the

heavy weight of sadness she had borne these past two years.

THE FOLLOWING AUGUST, 1097

Palmer stretched out his legs in the late summer sun and stared across the Channel toward England.

His homeland, so close he could smell its sweet green grass on the wind that blew into his face.

Could it really have been only three years since he'd first set foot on foreign soil? It seemed like seven hells ago.

It *had* been seven hells ago.

But he would go back to England, and soon. Only a few more bits of silver, and he would have his passage.

He couldn't even remember his mother's face. The harder he tried, the more elusive and insubstantial it became, like the image of a ghost.

Maybe she really was a ghost. He'd been gone a long time. A lot could happen in three years.

Palmer shuddered and wondered if his quaking was an omen, or just another reminder of the fever that had dogged him since that hideous day in Hungary.

Not that it mattered. What would be, would be. He had long since given up worrying about the future. The present was agony enough.

Wearied from thinking, he narrowed his eyes and tried to make out the cliffs of his homeland. But as usual, his mind granted him no peace.

Why had he ever left England? He'd been so foolish when he'd first crossed these waters. Everything had seemed so exotic, so exciting. And he . . . what a dolt he'd been! Green. Arrogant. Full of romantic notions.

Armed with only his sword and a faith so reckless he'd actually believed himself invincible, along with the rest of the ragtag army of peasants and outcasts who'd followed Peter the Hermit's dream of conquest.

The Army of God, mobilized and driven by one man's vision to liberate the tomb of Christ.

Now the mere thought of it brought the taste of wormwood to his mouth.

How quickly the Hermit's dream had turned into a nightmare. Since the massacre in Hungary, Palmer was too ashamed to look upon the cross of Christ, much less face his God.

"Eh!" A coarse voice accosted him from the quay a dozen yards away. *"Tu!"* The bandy-legged dockman pointed at Palmer. *"Homme des guenilles! Ici!"*

You! Raggedy man! Here!

Palmer had only a limited understanding of French, but this insult was more than familiar. Stung by the Norman's contempt, he nevertheless forced himself to his feet. A barge had landed and needed unloading. *"Oui?"* he answered. Just a few more coins, he told himself, and he would grovel for no man.

"J'ai des travaux forcés," the dockman barked, *"Si tu en as besoin, suis moi!"*

Hard labor though it might be, Palmer did need the work, so he followed as instructed.

"Allons!" The dockman leapt onto the barge and swaggered up the mound of sacks. When he reached the top, he planted his feet and began heaving the heavy sacks of grain onto the dock, one by one.

Palmer mustered all his strength, straightened to his full height, and made his way to the dock.

Just a few more coins.

He dragged first one heavy sack to the far side of the loading area, then another, stacking them neatly.

Burden by burden, he only allowed himself to think about one sack at a time. He could do this, one at a time.

Soon. He would be back in England soon.

And once he got there . . .

Palmer couldn't think about that now.

For now, he concentrated on lifting the next sack of grain, and the next.

TEN MONTHS LATER—JUNE 1098

Fifteen months after she had first sat at Nonna's table, Claire read haltingly from Homer's account of the Greek wars.

"Very good," Nonna commented when Claire paused to decipher a particularly difficult passage. "Who could have imagined that in such a short time, you would be reading not only English and Latin, but also Greek?"

Claire certainly hadn't expected it. After two slow and frustrating months spent mastering the basics of her native alphabet, her reading had gradually evolved from a duty into a fascinating challenge. Once she began to master the skill in earnest, she couldn't wait to sound out every word and letter she could find, even the foreign ones carved in strange, plain letters above the lintels on some of the buildings in Nonna's compound. When at last Nonna had shared some of her journals, Claire had felt like a butterfly let loose in the Garden of Eden.

And then there was the matter of her Latin lessons. As with English, her first few lessons had made her feel thick as a hangman's hide, but when she began to see the order and symmetry of the ancient tongue, she understood why it was the language of scholars, clergy, and kings. But Greek . . . Challenging though its odd alphabet made it, the language had a passion and nuance Latin lacked, so she stuck with it, despite real difficulty mastering the new symbols.

So, by the time Claire's first anniversary in the compound had arrived, she was reading easily in her native tongue and with some degree of competency in Greek and Latin.

It had taken some time, though, to reconcile herself to Nonna's bizarre obsession with bathing, washing their clothing with alarming frequency, and boiling their instruments, bandages, and apothecary tools before use. When Claire had asked why, Nonna simply answered, "It has been the custom of our people since the time of the Romans."

"And who were these people, these Romans," she had pressed, "that you should follow blindly in their ways?"

"Ancestors, husbands of our healing sisterhood," Nonna replied, "who wrote of their discoveries in the chronicle of our generations, each one adding to the wisdom of our traditions."

When Claire had looked unconvinced, Nonna smiled. "One need not know why certain cures or methods work, my dear. The fact that they work should be proof enough. Despite the superstitious teachings of our time, I have seen for myself that strict cleanliness promotes good health and discourages disease."

So Claire had gone along, suspicious at first, then with the same zeal as her instructor. The truth was, she quickly came to enjoy being clean, having clean clothes and clean sheets to sleep on. Even in the colder months, when she'd had to make do with cloth and a basin of tepid water by the fire, she liked washing away the grime of living before going to sleep. And in summer . . . who wouldn't enjoy bathing in the spacious marble pool within the small stone house made solely for that purpose? Claire loved it, even though she had to stoke the furnace underneath with wood or peat aplenty in order to heat the water.

She finished the Greek passage and rolled shut the vellum scroll. "That's it for today. I'm getting cross-eyed."

"I am so proud of how diligently you have studied your Greek. And of your progress in reading and Latin, my dear," Nonna, always generous with praise, was quick to say.

Claire's cheeks warmed with pride. "In truth, I find myself liking Latin best of all. It's far more consistent and orderly than English. The way we speak . . ." She exhaled sharply. "Our native tongue is as tangled as a skein of yarn after a kitten's been at it. I fear I'll never unravel all the exceptions and inconsistencies."

"Nonsense," Nonna protested. "Why, you're already reading and writing better than I." She gave Claire's hand a reassuring squeeze before settling comfortably into her own chair. "You're a natural scholar, the brightest student I have ever taught, and I have taught my share."

Claire had always known she had a knack for remembering things, and she'd always loved puzzles and riddles, but never in her wildest imaginings would she have thought of herself as a scholar. "Who have you taught besides me?"

Nonna's gaze flicked briefly toward the graveyard at the far corner of the compound. "Quite a few, child. Quite a few."

Claire had seen the markers in the little burial ground, where four simple stone crosses—one weathered and three unweathered—stood in stark contrast to an array of stone sarcophagi. "Who were they, Nonna?" she made bold to ask. "Your students, I mean."

Nonna's kind blue eyes lost their focus. "Apprentices, for the most part. Young women like you—widows or spinsters left without any means of sustenance." A soft smile transformed her expression into that of a mother fondly remembering her children. "There was Catherine; she had blond hair and beautiful hazel eyes and laughed like a running brook. And Marie—quiet, patient Marie. She was so good with the dying. So gentle. And there was Aethelred, of course—stout as a tree, but how she loved little babies. And Clara, so timid she could scarcely speak, but the cleanest woman I have ever met." A brief stab of loss marred her nostalgia. "And Palmer, of course, my one and only."

Claire picked up on the name immediately. All these many months, the two of them had lived and studied together, yet neither had asked about the other's past. But Claire could not resist this one opportunity. "Palmer?" she repeated. "Was he your husband?"

Nonna chuckled. "Of course not, silly girl. My husband was . . ." Her brows drew together. "He was . . ." Her features tightened. "Dear heaven, surely I haven't forgotten my own husband's name. He was . . ." Nonna's eyes glazed as if she were in a trance, and she stared blankly into nothingness.

That happened more and more often lately, and it frightened Claire. Regretting the question that had brought this on, Claire shifted the conversation back to safer ground. "Your apprentices . . . what happened to them?"

Nonna turned to her and started, the spark of intelligence returning to her eyes. "Forgive me, my dear. I must have been wool-gathering."

"Your apprentices," Claire repeated, still curious about the elusive Palmer but unwilling to upset Nonna further. "You haven't told me what happened to them."

"Ah, yes. My apprentices." Herself again, Nonna sighed. "Such good girls, and so willing. I only wish . . ."

Fearing she was about to drift away again, Claire prompted gently, "Did they die?"

"Aye." Nonna let out a long, hard breath. "One by one, the Good Lord called them home. They perished from the very illnesses we sought to heal." Claire could sense Nonna's thoughts reverting to the past. Again, her teacher stared sightlessly past the apple trees. "I wish I knew why. They were so young, so eager. It makes no sense that they should die, yet I should linger on, only to . . ."

"Only to what, Nonna?"

Nonna looked at Claire as if seeing her for the first time. "What?"

"You said, 'only to . . .' " Claire repeated. "Only to what?"

"Gracious, child." Nonna wagged a cautionary finger. "You must have been daydreaming. You're not making sense. Not that I blame you." She grinned, rising to her feet. "It's far too pretty a day to stay cooped up inside." Nonna reached up to retrieve her gardening basket from its peg on the rafters. "Let's take the rest of our lessons outside. You can try to name all the herbs and flowers in the east bed."

Claire nodded, hiding her concern behind a bright smile. "Good idea." These past few months had made it all too clear why Nonna had asked for Claire's promise to care for her when she could no longer care for herself.

Slowly but surely, Nonna was losing her mind. Word by word, memory by memory, something was eating away at the essence of who she was.

Claire put her arms around Nonna and gave her a long, reassuring hug. "Fear not." She drew back and met Nonna's wistful blue eyes with a look of calm resolution. "I will never leave you, no matter what happens." Dredging up the words from her childhood memories, she quoted from the Holy Writ. " 'Whither thou goest, I shall go . . . Thy people shall be my people, thy God, my God.' "

"Precious girl." Nonna returned Claire's hug. "How I wish you truly *were* my daughter-in-law, as Ruth was to Naomi." She pulled back and stroked the downy hairs away from Claire's forehead, just as her own mother had done. "If you were my daughter-in-law, I could leave all this to you." She scanned the immaculate compound of gardens and tidy outbuildings, some of which had remained locked since Claire arrived. "The Roman general Flavius Stilicho and Caesar Honorian granted this house and land to my ancestors. Generation after generation of Freemen have held this land against all invaders: Celts, Vikings, Saxons, Jutes, and now Normans." She shook her head. "I cannot bear to think that it will fall into the hands of strangers when I die."

"Posh!" Claire tightened her hold on her mentor's arm. "It's too pretty a day to talk of such morbid things. And you have many years yet before you think of dying."

A grateful smile erased Nonna's melancholy. "Ah, Claire. Whatever would I do without you?"

"You'll never have to wonder, Nonna," Claire answered in all seriousness. "For I shall never leave you." She struggled to put her feelings into words. "You have loved me like a daughter, given me a home, taught me to read and write, and instructed me in the ways of a healer, all without asking a single question about my past." At the mention of her past Nonna bristled predictably, prompting Claire to say, "I know, I know. You've told me often enough that the past is past, and no one's business but my own."

"Aye." Nonna couldn't resist. "It matters not who you were before you came here. The woman you are now . . . that's the Claire who's earned my love and trust a dozen times over. Nothing else counts for anything."

Claire's eyes welled with gratitude. "God bless you for that, dear Nonna." She hugged her teacher again to hide her tears. "If I live to be a hundred, I could never begin to repay you for that love and trust. And for all the rest."

"You already have, child," Nonna said with a mother's pride, "a dozen times over." She straightened, all business. "Now. Find the pennyroyal and tell me all about it."

"There." Claire pointed without hesitation to a foot-high patch of rambling stalks whose oval leaves almost hid the tiny blue flowers sprouting close to the stem. "Tea made from its leaves calms a troublesome stomach," she recited, "but this herb should never be used on any woman who might be with child, for it can cause her to lose the babe, particularly during the early stages. For chest congestion, a stronger tea will break up the phlegm and promote coughing, which expels the noxious humors."

"Very good," Nonna praised. "And . . . ?"

Claire prodded her memory. "Oh, yes. When a child

dies in the womb or a woman fails to expel the after-birth following delivery, oil of pennyroyal will help her expel the stillborn child or the afterbirth.''

''Perfect.'' Nonna sat on a sun-warmed bench. ''And what about those?'' She pointed to a mass of spikes graced by purple flowers.

''Clary,'' Claire identified. ''Boil six seeds in a bit of water until the seeds become soft, then place one in the corner of an irritated eye to draw out any foreign objects. After removing the seed and irritant, wash out the eye with the remaining cooled infusion. Tea made from dried clary leaves or flowers will soothe the stomach. Oil rendered from the flowers has a salutary effect on the skin and a pleasant, pungent aroma.''

''Excellent. Soon I shall have nothing left to teach you.'' Nonna turned toward a patch of Saint-John's-wort only to halt, indecisive. Her brows puckered.

Oh, dear, Claire worried. She's forgotten the name . . .

Unwilling or unable to face her lapse, Nonna stood to her feet. ''Pray excuse me, child, but I just remembered some work I needed to do inside. Why don't you stay out here and enjoy the sunshine? We've studied enough for this day.''

Claire nodded. ''Would it be all right if I explored some of the outbuildings?'' she made bold to ask. ''There are several I've never been into.''

Nonna's hand fluttered across her brow. ''As you wish, my dear. This is your home, too.'' She turned and headed back to the house, her step not as steady as usual.

Poor Nonna. How long would it be until . . . ?

Claire shut away the awful question by turning to the stone outbuildings she hadn't yet explored. Passing the bathhouse, the washhouse, and the *latrina* she had once found so amazing but now took for granted, she headed toward a small structure tucked against the north wall. As always, the door refused to open. This time, though, Claire was determined to find out what secrets lay inside.

Not that she'd found any secrets in any of the other locked buildings—just neat stacks of marble or clay tiles, floor slabs, lumber, and building stones—obviously stockpiled for repairs—or heaps of broken swords and helmets piled beside provisions locked away from intruders.

But this building was different. Its roof was made from the same clay tiles she had found in the storehouse, with deep eaves that protected from the elements an unbroken course of high clerestory windows.

The ladder. That was how she could get in.

She found the wooden ladder propped inside the brick barn and barely managed to get it back to the locked building without damaging any of Nonna's precious plants. Once it was propped firmly against the wall, she climbed up and wiggled her waist across the windowsill.

What she saw inside caused her to gasp. That single breath drew in so much dust that a fit of sneezing overtook her, causing her to kick the ladder free.

Trapped half in and half out, she focused past the shafts of dust-dappled sunlight to the room below, where every surface held a lifelike carving in wood. Why, they were so real, they almost seemed to breathe. An owl graven in white wood swooped down with talons extended toward a tiny field mouse. A hare carved in rich oak vaulted in mid-spring. Tiny partridges, nut-brown in walnut, peeked out from beneath their mother's outstretched wings. A cherrywood fox stood fixed, his ears alert.

Claire had never seen such convincing statues, even in the great cathedrals.

Too curious to be frightened, she crawled onto the sill and lowered herself into the studio. The drop was farther than she calculated, but she rose in a cloud of dust uninjured and sneezing uncontrollably.

Desperate for fresh air, she wrestled the bar from the doorway and slowly pushed it open, to the screeching complaints of its rusted hinges. Outside, she bent and sucked in clean air, praying for the sneezes to stop.

A worried Nonna appeared at the back door of the cottage. "Are you all right?" she called. "I thought I heard screams."

"Gskx!" Claire did her best to suppress the sneezing. Eyes pouring, she rounded the corner so Nonna could see her. She waved, gasping out between sneezes, "I'm fine. Gskx! It was just the hinges shrieking. Gskx! Gskx!" She motioned toward the open doorway. "May I clear away the dust in there?"

Preoccupied, Nonna frowned slightly, then shrugged. "As you wish, but I shouldn't think you'd want to bother . . . not the way you're sneezing already."

"I'll be fine!" Claire called back, not in the least convinced that she would. But dust or no dust, she wanted time alone to explore the studio's treasures.

Pulling the kerchief from her hair, she tied it over her mouth, then set about putting the long-abandoned studio to rights. It took hours, but by late afternoon, she stood in the center of the now-clean room and marveled anew at the polished luster of each artfully crafted image.

Most impressive of all were the only two human renderings—a masterful bust of Nonna and another of a kind-featured, bearded older man.

A self-portrait of Nonna's husband? Claire wondered.

She didn't know who the artist was, but the statues conveyed much about their maker.

First, she decided he must be male, for there was a certain raw energy in the owl and the fox that was decidedly masculine.

Definitely a man.

A man with a sense of humor.

She studied the cunning execution of the baby partridges peeking out from beneath their mother and the benign expression—if a bird could have an expression, which this one did—of the mother bird, herself. The carver had given her an almost human look of surprise.

And the owl . . . for all his gruesome talons, the owl would never make a meal of *this* mouse, for the clever little rodent was halfway down his hole already.

Reverently, Claire picked up the owl and noted with awe how the artist had used the grain of the wood to make the feathers look so real she almost expected the creature to hoot.

"Hoo! Hoo!"

The unexpected sound came as such a shock, she almost dropped the exquisite carving. Whirling toward its source, she found a flaxen-haired young peasant woman standing in the doorway, her expression contrite.

"I'm sorry." The interloper curtsied to Claire. "Pray, forgive me, good lady. I had no idea you'd be so frightened. Truly, I didn't, or I would never have hooted that way."

Her heart still pumping wildly, Claire set the owl carefully back on its pedestal. "I overreacted." Suddenly self-conscious, she smoothed her dusty dress before addressing the stranger. "I've met quite a few of the villagers since I came here, but I don't recall meeting you." She approached the girl with hand extended. "I'm Claire, Mistress Freeman's apprentice."

"And I am Ardra." Blushing, the girl took Claire's hand and executed another clumsy curtsy.

"How now?" Claire hastily drew her aright. "You owe me no such honor, child. I am merely a woman, and a stranger to these parts."

"But you are a great healer." Ardra gazed at her in open admiration. "Nonna told me so. She said that already you are a greater healer than she."

"Nonsense." Whatever had possessed Nonna to say such a thing?

And who *was* this person?

It occurred to Claire that perhaps Nonna had taken on another apprentice. The prospect caused her heart to contract. She had grown accustomed to having Nonna to herself and wasn't at all sure she would like sharing either Nonna's wisdom or her company. "Have you come for healing, then?"

"Nay," Ardra replied blithely. "I'm never sick. Ask Nonna." She scanned the neat array of tools and statues in the studio. "I've always wondered what was in this building. Of course, I was very small then, but I do remember that Palmer was quite mysterious about the place. He used to hole up in here for hours, sometimes days at a time. And he never let anyone but Nonna inside." She stroked the fox's back. "So lifelike." She offered Claire a wry smile. "Little wonder he kept his work hidden, though. I daresay the bishop would burn them all as graven images, and Palmer along with them." She said it casually, but the words made Claire's blood run cold.

Still, she wasn't about to miss this chance to find

out who the elusive Palmer was. "Tell me, please, who was Palmer?"

Ardra cocked her head. "He's Nonna's son, of course." Her bright eyes clouded. "I'm surprised she never told you about him."

"We never speak of the past," Claire explained, unsettled by the girl's inquiring gaze. "Hers, or mine."

To her relief, the girl smiled. "Fair enough." She crooked her young mouth. "Of course, when one is only twelve, one hasn't much of a past to be mysterious about. But I do have my secrets." Ardra stepped close to Claire and confided, "I too would be a healer, but my mother has forbidden it."

She shot a sidelong glance, lowering her voice conspiratorially. "Just because my mum's a midwife, she expects me to be one." She let out an impatient sigh. "It isn't as if she needed me to follow in her footsteps." Ardra frowned. "My twin sister Corly loves absolutely everything about delivering babies; she can hardly wait to become a midwife. I don't know why Mum insists that I do it, too."

Relief flooded through Claire even as she inwardly chided herself for being so selfish about Nonna. "Does your mother know you're here now?"

Ardra shook her head. "No. I only come when I can steal away. No one was here the last few times, so I left."

"What would your mother do if she found out you'd come here?"

"Probably beat me well, then shout at poor Nonna like she did the last time she caught me. I was only eight, then."

"She shouted at Nonna?" Claire had been under the impression that everyone in the village revered their healer.

Sheepish, Ardra nodded. "I don't know why, but she's never liked Nonna. Last summer when I got up the courage to tell Mum I wanted to apprentice here, she switched my backside so hard I couldn't sit for days without weeping."

Her mouth tightened into a stubborn line. "But I don't care what Mum says, or how many times she beats me, I *will* be a healer." She turned imploring eyes to Claire. "Please help me, Dame Claire. Nonna said she could not go against my mother's wishes, but you . . ." Claire saw all the hope in the world in Ardra's young face. "Please help me reach for my dream. I swear, I'll never tell a soul."

The last thing in the world Claire needed was to come between a mother and daughter, and the local midwife, at that! But there was something so poignant in Ardra's heartfelt plea that she couldn't deny the girl outright. Not yet, anyway. "I'll think about it. That's all I can promise."

Ardra fairly exploded. "Oh, thank you, good lady! God bless you!" She kissed Claire on each cheek, then crushed her in an enthusiastic embrace. "I knew God would make a way, and now He's sent you!" She released Claire and scampered toward the door, her feet scarcely touching the ground. "I'll be back whenever I can creep away. We can start then. And bless you."

"Wait!" Claire called after her. "I didn't say yes. I only said I'd think about it!" But she found herself talking to an empty doorway.

By all the stars in heaven, what had she gotten herself into?

Claire subsided into the studio's only chair.

She'd found out who Palmer was, but what should she do about Ardra?

Claire hoped, devoutly, that she would not see the girl again soon, especially not here. She and Nonna had enough problems to deal with, without adding Ardra's illicit ambitions to the list.

THREE

In the coming weeks and months, Claire's days were filled from early dawn to late at night, leaving blessedly little time for bitter memories. She deliberately pushed herself to the very edge of her endurance, collapsing at night so exhausted that even her most stubborn nightmares could not trouble her sleep. And she liked the work. Besides memorizing every healing plant in Nonna's gardens and many in the forest, she mastered the art of using them in poultices, infusions, decoctions, and essential oils.

Best of all, she now accompanied Nonna on sick calls, in the beginning as an observer, then as a helper, then—when the problem was not complicated and the treatment clear—as a healer in her own right.

At first, the villagers had regarded her with suspicion, but as the weeks passed into months, they slowly came to accept her presence and even her touch. Everyone, that is, save one. Linherst was a small village, yet Beta had somehow managed to avoid crossing paths with Claire and Nonna. So far, Claire had caught only fleeting glimpses of the woman as she did her best to avoid them.

It was mid-July in that summer of 1098, and Claire and Nonna had just completed a sick call in town when Claire spotted the heavyset woman at the far end of the village's high street.

Claire nudged Nonna's side. "Nonna. Look yonder."

Nonna followed Claire's line of sight to the stocky woman who was storming their way, her eyes downcast as she pulled her reluctant twins along behind her.

"Ah. Dear Beta." Nonna's words dripped sarcasm.

"She hasn't seen us," Claire said through a fixed smile. "Should we escape? I quake to think what might happen if Beta bumps into us by accident. She's gone to a great deal of trouble to avoid meeting me so far."

"Thank Providence for that, my dear," Nonna murmured wryly. "But I refuse to quit the street just because she's coming." She busied herself with the supplies in her basket. "Pay her no mind. For some inexplicable reason, she sees me as her rival, and now you as well, no doubt."

With that, the midwife—now only yards away—looked up and saw them. She halted, her expression as disgusted as if she'd been confronted by a leper.

Ardra smiled and tried to wave, but her mother snatched her wrist and dragged both twins across the muddy street to disappear between two reed dwellings.

Nonna was patently relieved. "That was close."

"She's a widow, too . . ." Claire mused, her eyes still trained on the house behind which the midwife had disappeared. "All three of us earn our bread by helping others. All three of us, widows." She shook her head. "We should be allies. It makes no sense for us to be enemies."

Nonna drew her alongside. "It makes no sense to me, either, but unfortunately, Beta has other ideas, no matter how hard I've tried to make peace with the woman." She gave Claire's arm a squeeze. "I once made the mistake of attempting to convince her to wash her hands before she touched anyone or anything." Nonna sighed. "She called me a sorcerer, so I reminded her that God commanded the Hebrews to wash their hands before eating and to bathe themselves after touching the dead, the sick, or anything unclean, but she remained unconvinced." She shot Claire a wry smile. "You may try to befriend her if you wish, but I've given up."

Claire did try, but she had no more luck than Nonna in the months that followed. By the time October arrived, she'd given up and accepted that Beta was determined to remain an adversary.

Seven busy weeks of harvest had just been completed when Claire, snug in her bed this chilly night, heard a faint knock on the front door. Bone-weary from helping put up the bounty of Nonna's gardens, she turned over and closed her eyes.

Tonight was Nonna's turn to answer sick calls. If she needed Claire, she'd wake her. Still, a twinge of guilt kept Claire from falling asleep right away. Her bedhangings open to the crisp night air, she could clearly hear through her chamber door the sound of Nonna unlocking the front door, pulling it open, then gasping aloud.

That gasp brought Claire immediately upright, tingling in alarm. Afraid that Nonna might be in danger, she crept from her bed as quietly as possible and retrieved the poker from her hearth. Armed with that, she tiptoed to her chamber door and peered through a crack in the wood to see Nonna dragging in a small, emaciated man clad in filthy tatters.

Claire let out a sigh of relief, put down her poker,

then opened the door. "Nonna, you should have called me." She hurried to help. "You'll throw your back out, trying to drag that man all by your—"

"Go back to bed!" Nonna's uncharacteristic harshness stopped Claire abruptly just two steps into the room. "I don't want you anywhere near this man." She glared up at her astonished apprentice. "Do as I say! Close the door behind you, draw your bedhangings, and go to sleep. Is that clear?" Seeing Claire's injured expression, she relented only slightly. "This man is dying of a highly contagious fever. You must stay away from him, or we're both likely to catch it, and then who will be left to care for us? No one." The harshness returned with an added note of desperation. "Do as I say, Claire. This minute! And don't come out until I bid you!"

"Forgive me," Claire responded, ashamed of her disobedience. But there was something frightening in Nonna's manner: fear . . . not fear of disease—Nonna had never feared illness, no matter how contagious— but something else, something dark and fathomless and sinister.

Silent alarms sounded deep within her. Dear God, she realized, the darkness had caught up with her, only this time, it had struck at Nonna.

She backed away numbly, then turned and did as she'd been told. An hour later, though, she was still wide-awake with worry and could not keep herself from getting up to peer through the crack again. What she saw stole the breath from her lungs.

Nonna had put the stranger in the cot reserved for the ill or injured and was now sitting on a stool beside him, hugging herself and weeping, her mouth wide open in a silent scream.

Something horrible had happened. But what?

Torn between her duty of obedience and concern for

her friend, Claire watched for what seemed to be an eternity. She recognized all too well what she was seeing; she too had once wept that way. But Nonna hadn't chosen to share her grief, and a true friend would not intrude on such intimate suffering. So Claire returned to her bed. Shutting away her own painful memories, she concentrated on praying for Nonna to a God she wasn't sure existed.

Half the night had passed without sleep before she rose again to peer through the crack. Nonna was no longer at the stranger's bedside. Instead she sat hunched at the small table they used as a desk, her back to Claire. Claire heard the rustle of paper, then saw Nonna lift a carefully folded letter. From this distance, she couldn't make out the name written on its exterior, but she couldn't help wondering if the stranger had brought the letter, and with it, tragic news.

Claire's heart skipped a beat. Palmer! Was it news of Palmer, terrible news?

At that very instant, as if she had sensed Claire's presence, Nonna turned and peered intently at the very door she hid behind. Again, Claire's breath caught in her throat, but she could not pull her gaze from Nonna's face. Fear and suspicion played across the healer's features, giving way at last to a look of lifeless resignation. Like a wounded animal lying down to die, Nonna clutched the letter to her bosom and crumpled to the floor, curling on her side as she wept again in silent agony.

Claire returned to her bed, but did not sleep at all that night.

The sun was well up before Nonna summoned her from her chamber.

"You can come out now, my dear." When Claire

emerged, Nonna said evenly, "Our visitor died in the night. Alas, he was far too ill for me to be of any help." Nonna took the lid off a small kettle of porridge and ladled the hot mixture into a bowl for Claire. "I ate hours ago. As soon as it was light, I rode to the church and had Father Kendall send someone for the body. He'll be giving the poor soul a decent burial, even now."

Troubled by the unexplained contrast between last night's grief and today's composure, Claire could not keep herself from asking, "Who was he? Someone you knew?"

A flicker of warning flashed in Nonna's eyes, but it was gone in a wink, replaced by absolute calm. "Aye. I knew him. He was an old friend from the village who had traveled . . ." Her pause was pregnant with what she did not say. ". . . abroad these past few years. Poor man. A great pity, that he should reach home only to die."

Claire knew better than to pry, but after what she'd seen last night, concern for Nonna overrode good manners. "Why did he come here? Has he no family?"

"No." Nonna added a generous dollop of butter and cream before setting the bowl of steaming porridge on the table, then she poured them both a cup of rose-hip tea and set them on the table.

Claire sat and briefly bowed her head, pretending as always for Nonna's benefit to say a silent blessing. She closed with another empty gesture, touching the middle finger of her right hand to her forehead, her stomach, her left shoulder, then her right. It was little enough to do to keep from offending Nonna's deep religious convictions.

When Claire opened her eyes and began to eat, Nonna had settled across the table and, in one of her most endearing traits, resumed the conversation as if she'd never been interrupted. "I suppose I was as close to family as the poor man had. Years ago, I nursed him and his family when a plague last visited our village." She took a sip of tea. "And I stood with him at their gravesides after the Lord called all of them home save him. Poor man. He left soon after that, and who could blame him? Linherst held naught but grievous memories for him, after that." She paused, suddenly pensive, then brightened. "Tom the Carter. *That's* who he was. I knew I'd remember his name eventually." She wagged her hand toward Claire. "Remind me to tell Father Kendall, so he can enter it into the parish records."

Her good spirits baffled Claire. "You do not seem too troubled by his death." She said it without accusation, almost as a question.

Nonna stilled. "Ah, Claire. How often must you hear it before you can believe it? Death is not a punishment for the believer. It is a deliverance." She shook her head and smiled. "In death, Tom is reunited with his wife and children, just as one day I shall be reunited with my dear husband and . . ." She fell silent, her eyes averted as if to conceal something.

"Your husband and who?" Claire prodded, hoping Nonna would mention Palmer at last.

To Claire's surprise, Nonna looked her straight in the eye and said, "And Palmer, my son who followed Peter the Hermit to liberate the Holy Sepulcher." A flicker of pain disturbed her composure only momentarily. "I have not spoken of him before because the pain of his absence is too great."

Nothing more. No mention of a letter.

Nonna waved a hand at Claire's porridge. "Enough of this chatter. It's time for you to stop talking and start eating, ere the whole morning is lost. We've a long day ahead of us, rendering essential oils from the petals we dried. Finish your porridge, dear, before the wax gets too hot.'' She made no move, though to leave the table.

Her questions unanswered, Claire waited expectantly while Nonna picked up her cider, took a sip, then gazed out the window. ''Speaking of Palmer,'' she said almost breathlessly, ''I've received a letter from him.'' She then paused for what seemed like a long time, her brows knitted anxiously.

The letter must have told her something important, Claire thought, for Nonna to take so long to collect her thoughts. She had no idea how important until Nonna finally spoke.

The healer inhaled deeply, then looked her square in the eye and blurted out, ''How would you like to be my daughter by marriage?''

''What?'' Claire almost dropped her cup. ''Your son . . . is he coming home, then?''

Nonna's blue eyes darkened. ''No.'' She peered into her cup. When at last she looked up, there was an uncharacteristic awkwardness in her face. ''No. But as I said, I've had a letter.'' Another deep intake of breath. ''I wrote him, you see, and told him that God had sent you to me. I told him how much I loved you, and how faithful you have been. I sent the letter to Normandy with Aelreth, the holy man, when he left last summer to join the Crusade.'' Her smile was less than convincing. She took another sip of tea.

''Tom brought the reply only last night,'' she explained. ''He told me he'd happened upon Palmer during the Crusade.'' Again she looked away. ''When Tom grew ill and decided to abandon the quest, Palmer asked him to bring the letter to me.''

Her eyes and expression cleared. ''Ill as Tom was,

Palmer knew he could trust him to deliver the letter, and Tom did, with the last of his strength, God rest his soul.'' She crossed herself. ''Fearing that he might not survive the Crusade, Palmer has proposed to marry you by proxy, waiving any dowry.'' Nonna looked to Claire with open pleading. ''That way, you would be my daughter by law, as well as by affection. Then, if I should die, no one could force you to leave this place. It would all be yours.''

So Tom *had* brought a letter! But Claire's memories of last night did not go along with Nonna's story.

Yet why would Nonna lie? What possible motive could she have?

Confused, Claire tried to digest the stunning proposition.

''You needn't make an answer right away—''

''Would such a thing be possible?'' Claire asked. ''I thought such marriages were allowed only to kings and princes—''

''Nay,'' Nonna interrupted. ''I took the letter to Father Kendall this morning. He sees no impediment, as long as both parties are free and willing.'' She actually blushed. ''He promised to send the letter to the bishop this very day for approval, along with his own endorsement. As soon as the bishop gives his permission, the ceremony can take place.''

Nonna studied Claire with something akin to desperation. ''Just think about it. It's all I ask.''

Claire's insides tingled with apprehension. Too many things didn't add up.

Marriage! Claire had never even considered the possibility of remarrying. She had no dowry, no blood kin, no connections . . .

And she knew not the first thing about Palmer Freeman.

No. That wasn't true. She had seen his work, so she knew he had the eyes and the skill of an artist. More than that. There was poetry in his sculptures.

But was that enough to commit for a lifetime?

"When Palmer comes home..." she ventured. "What if we don't like each other?"

Nonna's blue eyes welled with tears. "If Palmer could meet you, I do believe he'd be smitten from first sight. But as for your feelings for him ..." She looked down, then back at Claire with a wry smile. "We've both been married, so we both know that allowances must be made, with any man." She took a deep, hopeful breath. "It might take you a little longer, but if you could know him as I do, you would love him. I'm certain of that."

How could Claire answer the pleading in those eyes? To deny Nonna's son would be to deny Nonna, but what woman in her right mind would accept such an offer?

Nonna saw her son through the eyes of a mother's love. That did not mean what she saw was accurate— not when it came to a wife.

Still ...

Nonna had raised the one argument against which Claire had no rebuttal. What *would* happen to her if Nonna should die? As long as Palmer lived, Claire would have no right to stay here. She would be set adrift again, an outcast.

Claire couldn't face that. Not again. "I'll do it."

"What did you say?" Nonna breathed.

Claire cleared her throat. "I said, I'll do it. I don't have to think it over."

"My dear!" Relief erased years from Nonna's face. She leapt to her feet and drew Claire into a crushing embrace, sending rose-hip tea everywhere. "God bless you! I promise, upon my soul, you'll never regret this. Not for one day."

Claire had no idea how Nonna could be so certain. She only wished she could be, herself. "I'd like to have the ceremony as soon as possible."

Nonna thrust her to arm's length. "Are you sure?"

Claire's smile quavered only a little. "As sure as I can be."

"I shall ride to town and ask Father Kendall to send a courier right away. The moment the bishop's permission is granted, we'll have a wedding." Nonna reached up to the rafters and drew down a circlet of dried flowers and herbs. "I made this bride-wreath in the small hours of the night, after Tom died." Suddenly shy, she placed it on Claire's head, then lovingly smoothed the dark bound braids that bracketed her neck. "What a lovely bride you'll be."

"A bride without a groom . . ." Claire commented dryly.

"Oh, we'll find someone to act as proxy." Nonna waved her hand, her face flushed with joy. "Perhaps that nice young deacon who's just been assigned to Father Kendall . . ."

Claire couldn't help laughing. "Nonna, he's a priest in training, a celibate. The poor boy is likely to faint if you ask him to act as groom in a wedding."

"You have a point," Nonna admitted. She headed for the barn, calling back, "Never fear. We'll come up with someone. I'm off to Linherst."

Claire watched Nonna go with more than a little misgiving. For good or ill, she had made her decision to marry a complete stranger. If only she could be sure it was the right decision.

FOUR

Two weeks later, Claire stood, a married woman, at the altar in Linherst beside Palmer's proxy, a nervous and clay-caked Clyve the Potter.

The final word of Father Kendall's benediction was scarcely spoken before Clyve anxiously pleaded, "I can go now?"

The priest's nostrils flared. "Not until you've made your mark in the record."

The deacon hastened to bring the heavy parish record, its pages open and already annotated with the ceremony.

Clyve took the quill provided and laboriously marked an X where the priest indicated.

"And now the bride."

Unexpectedly nervous at this first public use of her newly acquired writing skills, Claire took the quill and carefully etched her name in the space Father Kendall pointed to.

"Now, the witnesses."

"Dame Freeman." The deacon laid the book on the altar and handed the pen to Nonna, who signed rapidly in a clear, strong hand. The deacon signed next. And last, the priest.

It was done.

She was married, to a man she'd never even met.

"*Now* I can go?" Clyve pleaded.

"Aye, Clyve." Genuine affection softened Father Kendall's response. He clapped the potter's muscled shoulders. "You've done well this day, my son. I'll say a special prayer for you at Mass."

Mightily relieved, Clyve escaped through the transverse exit.

The deacon retreated to lock away the register, leaving Claire and Nonna alone with Father Kendall.

"Pray thee, stay as long as you wish, ladies," he invited. "But I fear I must leave you now."

"Thank you, Father, for everything." Nonna rose and extracted a small bottle from her pocket. She pressed it into his hand. "A small token of my appreciation."

Syrup of poppies. Claire instantly recognized the color and consistency of the priceless liquid.

The priest stared at the bottle for several seconds, his expression pensive.

"Christ did all He could to alleviate suffering," Nonna said to him softly. "It is no sin to seek relief, my friend."

Father Kendall's eyes welled with tears. Then, to Claire's surprise, he briefly embraced Nonna and gave her a chaste kiss on the forehead. "Bless you, cherished friend."

"And you, my friend. And you." Nonna hugged him back, then the two parted.

The priest left abruptly, perhaps to hide his tears.

Claire searched her diagnostic knowledge, only now seeing Father Kendall's sallow complexion and general lack of strength as symptoms. Of course. "His liver." She looked at Nonna, then to the door from which the priest had exited. "Poor man. A painful way to die."

"Aye. And none deserve it less than he."

"If people got what they deserved in this life," Claire said with more than a hint of bitterness, "I might be able to share your faith."

"But you do not." Nonna said it calmly. She sat on the step leading up to the altar and looked up, scanning the painted beams and illustrated windows of the little church. Then she turned to Claire and smiled. "Sit, my daughter."

"You knew." Claire settled beside her.

"Aye."

"And all this time, I've been pretending to pray, crossing myself for your benefit."

Nonna chuckled. "It pleased me to see you going to so much trouble just for my benefit. But we are kinswomen now. There need be no pretense between us any longer."

Grateful, yet surprised by Nonna's statement, Claire nodded.

Nonna let out an audible breath, ending with a sad smile. "Pitiful, wasn't it?"

Claire didn't follow. "What?"

"The wedding." She chuckled. "I feared Clyve would bolt any minute. And the deacon . . ." Nonna shook her head. "He acted as if he expected the devil himself to materialize, on the spot."

Claire joined her in laughter, the day's tension broken. "Oh, aye. Thank goodness we finally managed to coax Clyve into acting as proxy, though. I was right about the deacon. I thought the lad would expire on the spot when Father Kendall suggested that *he* might be pressed into service."

Nonna cocked her head. "Was·it anything like your first wedding?"

Claire had been afraid Nonna would ask that. Ever since she'd consented to the marriage, she'd had to fight to quell the memories that contrasted so sharply with today's hurried ceremony. But she owed Nonna so much. What purpose would it serve to deny her the truth—at least, as much as Claire could bear to relate? "No. My first wedding was very different."

"How?"

"So many ways. It's hard to say." Claire looked down. "There was feasting. Celebration. A holiday for everyone, and lots of food."

She could feel Nonna's eyes probing her. "But you did not celebrate."

"No." Disturbing, how easily Nonna could look into her soul. "I went along because I had no choice. My parents had been servants, as had I, but they were dead, and I had no kinfolk. When my master took a fancy to me, I did everything I could to discourage him, but he would not be dissuaded."

"Men," Nonna said matter-of-factly. "Always wanting what they can't have."

"That must be true, for when he couldn't catch me for his mistress, he proposed marriage." Claire shook her head. "Everyone but my master was horrified, including me. Given the choice between marriage and dishonor, though, I chose marriage."

Nonna sucked in a sharp breath. "No wonder you did not celebrate. 'Tis a dangerous thing to marry so far above oneself."

Claire nodded, the pain blooming harsher and harsher within her until it tightened her voice. "It was a choice for which I paid dearly, especially when my husband died."

"Oh, child." Nonna's strong arms drew her close and held her. "Forgive me for dredging up past hurts.

We have each other now. That's all that matters."

"And Palmer," Claire felt compelled to add.

Nonna stiffened. "Aye, Palmer."

Since this was a time for confidences, Claire felt free to ask, "What was he like as a child, Nonna?"

She felt Nonna's muscles relax. "Restless. Fearless. Endlessly curious. Always trying to see what lay beyond his reach or behind every closed door." She stared into space, turning inward. "He was fascinated with everything. Saw shapes and faces in the most common bits of wood and rock. Collected everything and turned his treasures with a dab of color or a few whittles into droll little frogs, or mice, or flowers. So clever with his hands." Gentle laughter warmed the space between them. "And strong-willed . . . he thought he could do anything, and all it took to start a war of wills was to tell him no."

A cloud passed over Nonna's features. "And then, when he was older, after his father died . . . Such a tall lad, he was, all bones and shoulders and knees, but dead determined to grow strong as any knight. He learned to make swords and fight with them. Such grand dreams, he had." Her unfocused gaze turned inward, she lapsed into pensive silence.

Claire wanted to hear more. Nonna had painted a compelling picture of the man who was now her husband, but she had yet to determine his true nature. "Did he? Grow strong as any knight, that is."

"Aye. Day in and day out, he turned heaps of stone into hedges, dug in the gardens, rode his father's palfrey bareback until the two became as one, and trained with the sword he'd made and his father's bow. And then one day . . . I don't remember exactly when it happened . . . I looked at my son and saw no longer a boy, but a man. A man who grew more and more restless with the narrow borders of our lives. And that was when I knew he would leave me.'' Nonna's voice broke, and she dropped her face into her hands. ''Forgive me, but I cannot speak of him any longer. The pain of loss is too great.''

Now it was Claire's turn to offer comfort. She embraced Nonna and rocked her, gently. ''He'll come home, Nonna, in God's good time.''

Nonna looked up at her with tear-swollen eyes. ''And if it is God's will that he not come home? How does one live, knowing that her only child has died alone on foreign soil? Dear God, the pain of losing a child . . .'' She buried her face into Claire's shoulder and wept.

''I know.'' Nonna's words had sent a cold chill straight through Claire, but she forced herself to remain above the grief that welled within her own heart. ''Dear Nonna, I know.''

It would change nothing, though, to weep the day away. Claire forced herself to remain resolute. ''Let's make a pact. I'll not ask you about Palmer, and in return, you won't ask me about my first marriage. What say you?''

Nonna sniffed, then straightened. ''Aye.'' With shaking fingers, she dashed away the tears that covered her cheeks. ''A bargain it is.''

''Here.'' Claire pulled a square of fresh linen from her pocket. ''Blow.''

Nonna complied with such vehemence that both of them ended up laughing.

''Well, if your God is listening,'' Claire observed, ''He doubtless heard *that* well enough.''

''Aye, He's listening,'' Nonna managed. She shot

Claire a wry but grateful smile. "He sent you to me, didn't He?"

Claire smiled in spite of herself. "Perhaps He did." She stood to her feet and helped Nonna up. "Come. Let's go home."

"*Our* home." Nonna brightened.

"Aye." Claire threaded her arm through Nonna's elbow. "*Our* home."

"I have a very special wedding gift for you there, my dear," Nonna said as they exited the church.

"Nonna, you've done too much for me already. You needn't—"

Nonna cut her off with a smug, "Oh, it's not the sort of gift you're thinking. It's even better." She gave Claire's hand a squeeze. "My gift to you shall be the secrets of our heritage, and there are many."

"Secrets?" Claire's interest was piqued.

"Aye." Nonna lowered her voice. "Hidden escape tunnels and underground archives and secret hiding places and all manner of surprises." She added with glee, "But best of all are the chronicles of our people, an unbroken chain of journals, observations, and experimentation handed down from healer to healer since the year of our Lord four hundred sixty-four."

Claire halted. "Four hundred sixty-four? Why that's . . . that's more than six hundred years ago."

"Six hundred thirty-four, to be exact." Nonna might be losing her memory, but she could still do her sums.

Six centuries of healers . . . all their failures and their wisdom at Claire's disposal . . . The prospect filled her with gratitude and awe. "Let us hie us home, then, Good-mother." Claire hurried Nonna toward their waiting mare. "For no one loves secrets better than I."

Laughing like two carefree girls, they set out toward the forest.

SUMMER, 1099

Ten months had passed when Claire lit another candle to counteract the silvery midsummer's darkness, then settled back at the kitchen table to read, enjoying the cool peace of the evening breeze. Reading was her favorite pastime now. Whenever she could steal the time, she was drawn back to the chronicles from the archive, though she hated the pitch-dark, eerie dampness of the huge stone tunnels that connected all the buildings in the compound and led to the hidden library.

Almost halfway through the first volume now, she settled down to read the precise hand of the Greek-born healer who had been wife of the original Freeman settler in this place.

Decade after decade of experience in healing. And the science! The most interesting, and disturbing, thing she discovered from the early journals was that the civilization of Nonna's ancestors seemed far more advanced than that of the present.

The first journal was filled with wonder after wonder of construction, astronomy, and medicine, not to mention detailed building plans, diagrams, and formulae—each more fascinating than the last. And the women of the clan, literate healers all, had recorded their customs, cures, treatments, and failures for future generations, along with anecdotes of family life that fascinated Claire most of all.

Every night, she could hardly bear to tear herself away to sleep, for her chances to read during the daylight had all but disappeared now that Nonna had gratefully handed over to Claire her responsibilities as healer.

Claire glanced at the closed door to Nonna's room. Her good-mother slept often now, an escape Claire did not begrudge her.

In the months since the wedding, Nonna's good days had been reduced to good moments, and those few and far between. Now that summer was well upon them, her good-mother had retreated to a gentle silence most of the time, her only activities eating, sleeping, or sitting in her chair, either in the shady side of the garden, or in her room, looking through the window. She rarely spoke, but smiled, instead, her eyes telling Claire what her lips would not.

It was company enough. Even as she was, Nonna was still Nonna, and Claire had plenty of work to fill her days. And the chronicles to fill her nights.

Claire turned back to her reading, quickly losing track of the time. She had no idea what the hour was when she heard the sound of an approaching cart.

She closed the book, listening intently.

Footsteps, erratic spurts.

Something urgent was on its way. A serious injury?

Claire smoothed the stray tendrils into her bound braids, tied the plaits together behind her neck, then whipped off her soiled apron and donned a fresh one. A quick scrub of her hands, and she was waiting in the doorway, lamp held high, when the cart reached the house.

Judging from the strain with which the cart was drawn, the load inside was heavy. Not until he raised his head upon reaching the light of her lamp did Claire recognize Little Red, Roderick the Pitchman's eldest son.

Breathless and sweat-stained despite the cool summer's night, Little Red carefully tipped his cart to earth in front of the door and limped toward Claire.

"What's happened?" She met him halfway. "Is it your father?"

"Nay. A stranger. He's in the cart," Little Red panted, bracing his hands on his thighs. He lifted pleading eyes to Claire. "Please. You've got to save him."

"I'll do my best." Claire hastened to the rear of the cart.

Inside, a long, lanky dark-haired man writhed in delirium.

"Help me get him inside," she instructed. "Take care, though. Don't jostle him." As gently as she could, she slid the ailing man halfway out of the cartbed. "I'll take his feet. You grasp him under the arms."

Weary though he was, Little Red lifted the muttering stranger and bore the greater part of the load. Fortunately for all concerned, the man promptly lapsed into limp unconsciousness and did not put up a fight.

It wasn't easy, but Claire and Little Red managed to carry their substantial burden up the front stairs and into the house.

"Let's put him on the cot, over there." She nodded to the sturdy grid of taut leather straps crisscrossed over an iron cot that stood in a shallow pan of stone.

Both she and Little Red straightened in relief when their burden was safely laid out. The stranger was a tall one. His feet overhung the end of the cot by fully six inches.

Her eyes on the dark stranger, she picked up a clean sheet, then motioned toward the nearby worktable. "Hand me the basket on that table, please."

As Little Red obliged, Claire made a quick assessment. High fever. Pupils normally reactive. A sizable knot, bits of bark, and several deep cuts on the side of his head. But the man's hair was free of lice and clean where blood had not matted it. Septic breath. Rigid abdomen. "Do you know what happened?"

"Aye." Little Red shifted his weight from foot to foot. "I can tell ye, but only if ye swear not to tell anybody else, especially me family."

Little Red was hardly one for mischief. What secrets could he possibly have? Claire looked up and saw that he was twisting his hat into a tight spiral of felt. "Your secret's safe with me."

"All right, then. Well, you see, I was on me way back from the pitch market at Bitterne—me sire let me take the pitch all by meself, this time. But along the way home, I was set upon by thieves. They beat me senseless and stole me money, leavin' me for dead. I don't know how long I lay there." He nodded to the stranger. "But it was him who saved me. Took me back to Bitterne, hired a room, and bound my wounds. Fed me like a babe, he did."

The boy's voice thickened. "I told him what had happened. Said I couldn't go back to Linherst. I was too ashamed. The price of a year's work, gone." He looked at the unconscious man. "When I mentioned Linherst, he said he had lived here, once. And then he did the oddest thing."

One ear to his story, Claire continued her examination, checking for broken bones. "And what was that?"

"He gave me money to replace what was stolen, every penny of it. Told me to go home to me family."

"That explains what happened to *you*," Claire said briskly. "I asked you what happened to *him*."

"Oh. Well, ye see, once I was fit enough to be on me way, he offered to walk along with me for a bit, when damned if—" Little Red colored. "Beggin' yer pardon, Dame Claire. When lo, but them same ruffians set upon us. Me friend, here, would've made short work of 'em, but they had a third man with 'em this time, who crept up behind us and laid him out with a stout branch of oak.'' He winced as he said it. "It would've been all over fer us, if a mounted squire hadn't happened along and put them to rout."

The lad shook his head. "The squire chased the ruffians away, then came back and helped me load me friend into the cart. He rode along with us as far as Linherst. I got here as fast as I could."

"And his name?" Claire saw the perplexed look on Little Red's face and pointed to the unconscious stranger. "His, not the squire's."

"Oh, aye. That was another odd thing," Red confided. "I asked him, but he said he didn't have one. Not anymore. Told me just to call him Brother."

"Hmmm." Claire studied her patient. "He isn't dressed like a monk, but one never knows." She rolled up her sleeves. "Well, let's see what sort of shape he's in." She unbuckled the man's thick belt. As she removed it, a purse of coins fell to the floor. "No vow of poverty, there," she observed to no one in particular. Claire laid aside the purse with his belt, then untied his chausses, placed the folded sheet across his loins, and pulled the chausses down to his ankles. "Please take off his shoes and chausses, but try to move him as little as possible."

Coloring violently, Little Red nevertheless did as she asked him.

Claire worked with practiced precision to cut the seams of the ailing man's bloodied shirt before gently sliding the back of the shirt out from under him, then removing the front, leaving him exposed except for the folded linen across his loins.

Despite his lanky thinness, the man was large-framed and muscular. Hard work had callused his hands and developed the muscles of his arms and chest. And his thighs and calves were well-defined. But when she looked at his belly, Claire didn't like what she saw.

Angry flesh radiated from a taut white scar on the abdomen. A sword wound, from the look of it, and not a new one. "You say there was a fight. Did he take a blow to the belly?"

"Aye," the lad replied. "A vicious one. I tried to stop it, but—"

Claire silenced him with a reassuring pat. "I'm sure you did your best. But from the look of it, that blow must have ruptured this poor man's bowel. I fear that unless something drastic is done, he will die a painful and lingering death."

Little Red's hands stilled. "Something drastic?"

Claire rose. "Surgery. I would need to cut him open, stitch up the tear in his bowel, then try to clean out the poison before I closed him up. Even so, he might die, but I'm afraid he hasn't much chance, otherwise."

"Cut him open . . . ?" Little Red looked aghast. "Have you ever done it before?"

Claire had been afraid he'd ask that. "No," she said evenly, "but I have helped Nonna twice with similar situations."

"What similar situations?" Quite clearly, the boy did not believe a woman capable of such gory business.

Claire suppressed her irritation. Precious time was being wasted, but she had to convince Red, for she'd need his help. She put water on to boil. "Last year when the ironmonger's forge exploded, the apprentice's belly was ripped open and the bowel torn. I helped Nonna when she repaired it." She continued speaking as she collected her surgical instruments, tied them in a clean square of fabric, dropped the bundle into the kettle, tossed in a razor, then gathered powdered sulphur, thyme, garlic, chamomile, comfrey, and a bottle of walnut-hull extract, another of anti-infective infusion, plus a precious cache of solvent made from distillation of spirits.

"And last winter," she went on, "when the wolves attacked Gareth and Lorna's cow, we repaired the bowel and sewed the animal up just the same as we would a human."

"I remember, now that you mention it." Little Red's coppery brows drew together. "The cow lived and the boy died, aye?"

Claire nodded. "I'm not a miracle worker, lad. All I can do is my best." How many times had she heard Nonna say just the same thing?

Claire arranged the supplies on a clean cloth beside the sickbed, then fetched two basins and towels. "As I said, without the surgery, this man will quite likely die. With it, he has a chance at life. But only a chance."

Little Red sobered, showing a hint of the man he would one day be. With great gravity, he told her, "Do it, then. I want him to have that chance."

"Very well." She poured some of the anti-infective infusion into the basins, then added boiling water. "We'll have to clean him first, but let's allow this solution to cool. That should help bring his fever down."

"We?" The word was a high-pitched squeak.

"Aye. We."

"Clean him?" Red scratched his scalp. "But he's already so ill . . . won't it finish him off, all that water?" He scowled at the unconscious stranger. "Shouldn't we bleed him, first?"

"Roderick!" Claire looked at him askance. "I've

worked on your family more than a dozen times in the past two years, and Nonna before me. Have you once seen either of us bleed a patient?''

"Nay, but . . ."

"But you all recovered, didn't you?''

"Aye.''

"It is not our way to bleed patients.''

Claire frowned at the boy's dirty, broken nails. "Here.'' She handed him the bottle of infusion. "Use some of this with that brush over there to scrub your hands until there's not a speck of dirt anywhere, then bring the bottle back, and we'll begin.''

Obviously unconvinced, the boy nevertheless did as instructed. He returned with his hands scrubbed almost raw.

"Now,'' Claire said resolutely. "Help me turn him over.''

FIVE

Little Red took one look at the man's bare buttocks and blushed scarlet. "But he's. . . . . I mean, shouldn't ye cover his . . . ?"

"Calm yourself, boy." Claire handed him a cloth and basin. "This isn't the first time I've seen a man's arse, and it's not likely to be the last." She nodded at the prone figure. "Please wash his arms and legs. I'll do the rest." Claire applied her cleansing solution to her patient's well-muscled buttocks and scrubbed away with vigor. When she realized Red hadn't moved, she looked up and saw that he was gulping like a fish out of water. "We haven't much time, Red," she coaxed. "Get to work on his arms and legs."

Still blushing, the lad began to wipe down the stranger's leg as if it were made of blown glass.

Claire laid a staying hand on the boy's arm. "You can't hurt him," she said quietly. "He's unconscious. But we must get every inch of him as clean as possible, and the cool water will help to bring his fever down, so please try to be thorough. He needs a good scrubbing."

Still dubious, Red nodded and proceeded to scrub away.

That done, they turned the stranger back over, careful not to twist his inflamed torso. In deference to Red's modesty, Claire made certain the sheet covered the patient's nether regions.

She'd seen plenty of men's privates while helping Nonna, but even she was not brazen enough to say so. Blushing herself at the mere thought, Claire retrieved the steaming bundle of surgical needles, silk threads, and instruments from the pot. She laid them beside the patient, gingerly untied the cord, and spread the tools of her trade in neat array.

One thing at a time, she told herself as Nonna so often had. Don't think too much, just do first things first. All you have to remember is what to do next.

Her own mother had said almost the same thing often enough: "You can't peel but one turnip at a time."

While Little Red scrubbed away on their patient's already washed arms and legs, Claire cleaned the cuts in the stranger's head with aqua vitae, stitched them neatly with a curved damascene needle and the fine silk thread for which Nonna had paid a king's ransom, then sprinkled the wounds with a mixture of powdered comfrey, chamomile, garlic, thyme, and sulphur. Only then did she bathe the man's torso, discreetly but thoroughly washing beneath the sheet.

"Very good," she announced when their patient was as clean as they could make him. "He's ready." She motioned to Red. "Please scrub your hands again, then use the tongs to fetch the razor from the kettle. Then I'll need the stack of clean cloths bundled on the table yonder. And the basket of boiled wool beside them. Oh, and that brown bottle of walnut-husk solution."

"The razor?" His eyes glued to the array of lethally sharp instruments, Red picked up the tongs. "I . . . I won't have to watch ye cut him, will I?"

"Not if you don't wish to." Claire looked to the lad with compassion, remembering her own traumatic introduction to the sights and smells hidden inside the human body. She'd fainted or rushed outside to be sick more times than she could count before those same sights and smells had become useful information instead of horrors. "You can help me best by fetching things and handing me what I need."

Relieved, the boy did as she asked.

Meanwhile, Claire emptied the basins, swished them out with boiling water, then brewed more infusion and carried it to the bedside to cool. If the bowel had indeed ruptured, she would have to use the infusion to rinse the poison from the abdominal cavity.

She took down four stout, buckled leather straps from their hook beside the fireplace.

Red handed her the walnut-husk solution, eyeing her with some misgiving. "Here's the bottle. And the cloths and wool."

Claire took the basket of wool. "Set the cloths on the table by the bed, please." She pulled off four lengths of clean wool and used them to cushion the thick leather, then strapped the insensible man's wrists and ankles to the metal frame of the surgical bed. Still, he did not stir.

"Why must ye do that?" Red inquired.

"If he thrashes about during the surgery, it could kill him," she said matter-of-factly. When that was done, she poured walnut-hull solution onto a clean cloth, then laid it beside the patient's scar.

Again, Red's freckles became more prominent as the color ebbed from his cheeks. "Ah, I see." He paced nervously near the foot of the cot.

Claire couldn't blame him for being uneasy. She was nervous, too.

Perhaps she should scrub her hands once more, just to be sure they were clean. She picked up the wooden brush and repeated the ritual of cleansing that Nonna had drilled into her for months on end. But as she did, a sudden wave of fear washed over her.

Could she do this, really? She'd said she could, but . . .

Always before, Nonna had been there, encouraging, instructing, making available her decades of experience and wisdom.

Now, it was only Claire. A human life would be in her hands, and hers alone.

For the first time since she had come here, she envied Nonna her faith. How much easier it would be to think that God was in control. But Claire no more believed that than she believed she could raise the dead.

The responsibility for this man's life was hers, and hers alone. If she cut him open and he died, she alone would bear the blame.

We can only do our best, Claire. Nonna's soothing voice spoke within her. *People look to us for help, even when there is none. Our job, then, is to offer them what little hope there might be. And the truth.*

Claire had done that. She'd told Little Red the truth. Now, she must do her best to give her patient even a slender hope for life.

She let out a sigh of resolution. She knew what had to be done. The knives, tools, and scalpels gleamed dully blue-gray.

She nodded toward the low stool beyond the head of the cot. ''Please place that stool beside the bed, even with his abdomen.''

When Red obliged, she sat on the stool.

Claire inspected the irregular mass of scar tissue surrounded by angry flesh. A messy job of healing, that.

She decided to go in at the site of the old injury, excising the entire misshapen scar. If he lived, her patient would wake with a much less disfiguring wound.

She picked up the razor and scraped away the curly chestnut-brown hairs near the scar, giving her a clear field for the incision. Then she wiped the area with distillate.

He was ready, but was she?

She had to be. She could not sit back and watch him die.

Her hand steady now, she took the scalpel. Then, without hesitation or fear, she cut with precise pressure a shallow, six-inch-long arc on either side of the scar.

Blood welled at the eye-shaped incision, and she blotted it away with the astringent walnut-hull extract, then pulled the skin back to expose a paper-thin layer of whitish fat. After incising that and slowing the bleeding with more solution, she carefully cut through each layer of the rigid, infection-angered plates of muscle beneath.

When she completed the opening through the last plate of muscle, then gently retracted the layers, she found the lining of the abdominal cavity intact.

She picked up the instruments used to keep the incision open.

Seeing the odd-looking implements, Red, who had been careful not to look at the wound, piped up with a shaky, "What are *those* for?"

"They keep the incision open, so I can see what I'm doing."

"Ummm." The young man's color improved only slightly.

Using the two silver instruments, she carefully pulled the incision open as wide as she could without straining the tissue.

Claire assessed the opening with a critical eye. No mistakes yet. The patient was breathing regularly, his heartbeat strong.

This was the ultimate irony, this contradiction between the human body's stubborn resilience and its fragility. Under certain circumstances, a tiny cut could kill. Yet here she was, cutting through living flesh, and this man's body lived on, heart beating, lungs breathing, blood flowing.

She prayed silently that he would continue to live, not knowing to whom her prayer was offered, but compelled to offer it.

Now for the difficult, dangerous part. Her touch as light as a breath, she cut into the lining of the abdomen, fully expecting to find an unwholesome disaster within.

To her surprise, there was no odor of putrefaction, just the distinctive smell of internal bodily fluids.

Gently, gently, she eased aside the intestines in search of the cause of her patient's state. That's when she saw it. Nestled among the shining coils of intestine, and still attached to the original scar tissue, was a closed, distended abscess, the largest she had ever seen.

A network of weblike adhesions anchored the fragile walls of the abscess to the surrounding tissues. The thing could have been there for years, lurking inside until something—in this case, a blow—tipped the scales toward a slow and agonizing death.

Claire's heartbeat galloped, and her hands went cold.

"What's wrong, Dame Claire?" Little Red's eyes widened. "He's not . . . ?"

"He's alive," Claire answered, her words coming in tense, breathless spates. "But it's not a torn bowel. There's an abscess—" Seeing the boy's look of confusion, she clarified. "A sack of infection inside him." Knowing that terror was contagious, she forced herself to be calm for Little Red's sake. "From the look of it, it's been there for a long time, perhaps since the injury that caused the scar."

Little wonder the man was thin and pallid. Such a smoldering infection taxed all the body's resources, leaving the patient highly vulnerable to any illness or injury.

Nonna had taught her the symptoms: intermittent debilitating fatigue; unexplained weight loss; focused pain, rigidity, or redness; fevers that come and go with no apparent cause; night sweats.

Claire shook her head. "It was a miracle the abscess didn't burst when he was hit. But it's so large and invasive, I cannot remove it. I'll have to drain it, and quickly. If it ruptures, I'll never be able to cleanse away all the poison."

"What if you leave it?" Little Red deliberately kept his eyes on Claire instead of the oozing cavity in the man's abdomen. "Just close him up. Let nature take its course."

"I don't think we dare." Claire inspected the whitish, pulsing mass again. Perhaps it was only her imagination, but with every heartbeat, the abscess seemed to grow fractionally larger. "It looks as if it's about to explode. If we don't evacuate it, and soon . . ."

She felt a consoling grip on her shoulder.

"You can do it, Dame Claire. I know you can." Little Red's eyes pleaded with her. "Please try."

As long as there was a chance, she must try.

"All right. Look on my workbench over there," she instructed Little Red. "There's a glass object there that looks like a little trumpet. It has a globe sticking out of one side and a reed waxed into the mouthpiece. Dip the wide opening into the boiling water, then bring it to me, along with a clean basin."

When Little Red obliged, she took the instrument and laid it at the ready. "This is used to draw out pus or other poisonous bodily fluids." She made certain the mouthpiece was secure. "Now, I'll need some boiling water to rinse it with."

Little Red hurried to bring a kettle of the boiling water. Meanwhile, Claire soaked two clean cloths in anti-infective solution. She could only hope that if some of the infection should escape, the cloths would provide a barrier to keep it from spreading through the abdomen.

Claire reached inside her patient and arranged the protective cloths as best she could around the pulsing abscess. It never ceased to amaze her how hot the inside of a person felt, particularly one as fevered as this man.

Once that was done, it was time to aspirate the infection.

Holding the glass aspirating instrument at the ready, she made a small incision in the most accessible area of the abscess. As the poison erupted, she placed the instrument over the incision and sucked hard on the mouthpiece, then blocked the reed with her finger.

The resulting suction drew poison out of the abscess at an alarming rate. In no time, the glass reservoir was full.

Claire released the suction and emptied the instrument as quickly as she could, then dipped the glass into boiling water, wiped the rim, and repeated the procedure until the abscess was almost empty but the basin full.

"Red," Claire asked, "I need you to bring me another basin and empty the poison from this one. Can you manage it?"

"Aye," Red squeaked with the voice of a ten-year-old. Then, despite the alarming pallor of his face, his voice deepened in resolve. "You do your part; I'll do mine." He handed her a small, empty basin and took the larger one and its gruesome contents to the back doorway.

He returned with a decidedly greenish cast, took one look at the gaping incision, and slithered to the floor, unconscious.

He'd done far better than she, for a first-timer.

Claire glanced away from her patient only long enough to be sure Red was lying comfortably, then she went back to work. Layer by layer, she closed the incision with tidy silken stitches. Already, the tissues and vessels were losing their angry redness.

Claire was just finishing up when Little Red moaned and sat up. "Oh, Dame Claire." He staggered to his feet. "I'm so sorry—"

"Do not reproach yourself." She smiled with real affection at the boy. "No grown man could have done better, even your father. You held up when I needed you. That's all that mattered." After applying more powder, she covered the wound with clean, dry bandages.

She laid her palm against her patient's neck. His heartbeat pulsed steady and even beneath her touch. And the feel of his skin told her that the fever had gone down, at least a little.

"Things went far better than I anticipated. He came through it well," she said. "Now all we can do is wait."

"Is he out of danger?"

"Only time will tell."

Little Red cast a worried look at the pale, motionless figure. "When will you know?"

"When his fever goes away. Or when he wakes."

Her tension at last released, Claire stood up a bit too quickly and discovered that she was none too steady on her feet, herself.

"Whup!" Little Red caught her elbow in support. "Can't have you fainting, now. Who'd look after the rest of us?"

"Thank you." Claire managed a feeble smile. "I just stood up too fast." She stretched the stiffness from her arms and shoulders. "Don't worry about me. I am weary, but I'll set a pallet next to the bed and get some rest."

Claire patted the boy's upper arms in gratitude. "Your parents are probably frantic with worry. You must not keep them waiting any longer." She urged him toward the door. "Oh, and on your way, please let Father Kendall know I have a seriously ill patient. Perhaps he'll recognize the man."

She opened the door and steered him across the threshold. "I'll look after your cart. Feel free to leave it here as long as you wish."

Little Red left her in the doorway, but when he reached the cart, he turned a look of absolute adoration in her direction. "Dame Claire, I don't know how to thank you." He blushed profusely. "Most respectfully speakin', melady, but you are the most beautiful, the bravest, wisest, most daring lady I have ever known, and I, Roderick, son of Roderick the Pitchman, shall be your devoted servant until I die."

Not wanting to make light of the young man's tender feelings, Claire covered her surprise with a deep curtsy. "I am most humbled, sir, but undeserving of such esteem."

She straightened and watched him, red to the hairline, back a few steps toward the gate, stumble, then turn and lope away.

Claire shut the door behind her and bolted it, praying that no more unexpected developments materialized . . . at least, not before she got some rest.

This day had brought surprises enough: a seriously ill stranger strapped to the surgical bed, and now a boy from the village with a crush on her.

She checked her patient one more time, then spread a pallet on the floor beside him and lay down.

Weary but satisfied, she closed her eyes, only to see Little Red's adoring face. Claire groaned, then let out a chuckle, able to laugh at herself for the first time in years.

Ironic. It had been six years since she had lain beside a man, and she didn't even know this one's name. She was still smiling when she drifted into exhausted slumber.

The next morning, she opened her eyes to find Nonna peering down at her.

Nonna pointed to the sleeping man. "And who, might I ask, is *that*?"

"Nonna!" Claire scrambled to her feet. "You spoke!"

"Of course I spoke," Nonna grumbled, frowning over the stubbled stranger.

Stiff and sore from sleeping on the floor, Claire rose to hug her good-mother. "But I thought you couldn't speak."

"I could speak. I just didn't want to. Too melancholy." Nonna cast an assessing gaze over the patient. She lifted the bandage for a look, then let it drop. "Nice job of stitching."

Amazed, Claire nodded. "Thank you."

"Stab wound?"

"No." Flustered but grateful for this unexpected turn of events, Claire tried to collect herself. "Abdominal abscess. I managed to drain it without spilling any into the surrounding area.''

Nonna's eyebrows lifted. ''Good for you.'' She paused. ''But why didn't you call me? I imagine you could have used some help.''

''Because . . .'' Claire wasn't sure how much she could say without offending. ''You've been sleeping so much, lately. I thought you needed your rest.''

''I've been sleeping because I didn't have anything to *do*.'' Nonna eyed her caustically, then turned her attention to the patient. ''Who is he?''

''I don't know. And neither does the boy who brought him in. You remember Roderick the Pitchman's son . . .''

''Hmph.'' Nonna straightened. ''Can't say that I do.''

''Little Roderick brought him here from Bitterne. Said the man told him he was from Linherst.''

Nonna peered at the stranger again, then straightened, shaking her head. ''Never saw him before.'' She hugged Claire briefly. ''Next time, call me.'' Without further explanation, she returned to her room, closed the door, and bolted it.

''Well, I'll be a cardinal's mistress,'' Claire murmured, thoroughly perplexed.

''A cardinal's mistress?'' a deep, rasping male voice rumbled.

Claire spun around to see that her patient's eyes were open, his face rigid with pain.

''Water,'' he rasped, his blue eyes glazed with fever.

She fetched a cupful of clear, cool water and brought it to the sickbed. When she raised his head and held it to his lips, he gulped greedily. ''Not too much,'' she cautioned softly. ''Take it slow, or you might be sick, and believe me, you don't want to be sick. Not with a six-inch incision in your belly.''

The stranger glared at her over the rim of the cup, but slowed his intake. Then his head lapsed against her arm, his blue eyes closing. Claire eased him back to the bed.

But he hadn't fallen back into unconsciousness, as she had feared. ''Where am I?'' he croaked, struggling ineffectually against his bindings. ''And who are you?''

''You're back in Linherst. Roderick, son of Roderick the Pitchman, brought you here for help. You've been very ill,'' she said soothingly. ''I am Claire Freeman, wife of Palmer Freeman and apprentice to Dame Nonna Freeman, a healer.''

''What!'' The blue eyes shot open so wide she could see the bloodshot whites all the way around. ''You are not!'' Struggling in earnest now, he glanced wildly around the room, then froze, his neck still straining to keep his head erect. ''My God. Oh, my God. I'm home.''

''Aye. You're back at Linherst.'' Claire pressed his shoulders back down onto the bed. ''Please, sir. I pray thee, lie still, lest you rip open my fine stitching.'' She felt his muscles release in ragged increments until he lay quietly on the bed, but his wild blue gaze glared up at her yet.

''Can you tell me your name?'' she asked earnestly. ''So I might send for your kinfolk. Or your religious order—''

''My religious order?'' He barked out a mirthless chuckle, then winced at the resulting pain. ''I'm no monk, woman. What makes you think I am?''

Confused, Claire frowned even as her cheeks warmed with embarrassment. ''A natural assumption, I should say, since you told Little Red you had no name, that he should call you Brother.''

''I did?'' His forehead wrinkled more deeply. ''Can't remember . . .'' His eyes registered confusion, then focused on her, radiating an agony far deeper than his physical suffering. Through clenched teeth, he ground out, ''My name is Palmer Freeman, and I have no wife!''

Feeling as if her bones had just deserted her, Claire sank heavily to the stool. ''What?''

''You heard me.'' The muscles in his neck roped with effort as he again lifted his head to scan the room again. ''Where's my mother?''

Stunned, Claire could scarcely move, much less speak.

''What have you done with her?'' he accused, writhing against his bindings like a wild animal caught in a snare.

He *looked* like a wild animal, the muscles in his lean body standing out in clear relief, his brown hair wild, his bloodshot blue eyes glittering, and the dark stubble on his jaw in stark contrast to his pale skin.

Claire rose to her feet and backed away, as confused as she was frightened. ''You can't be Palmer Freeman,'' she gasped out. ''Nonna just saw you! She would have recognized you . . .''

Or would she?

More confused than ever, Claire tried to sort some sense from this lunacy. ''If you are Palmer, then what about the letter?''

''What letter?'' He shook the iron frame with his efforts to free himself, shocking Claire with the strength he managed to muster so soon after the ordeals of his past two days.

"The letter you sent to Nonna, asking me to marry you!" she blurted out.

"I sent no such letter!" Spots of blood appeared on the bandage over his incision.

"Now look what you've done!" Forgetting all else, Claire hastened to his side and lifted the bandage. "Be still," she ordered crossly. "Or you'll not live to straighten this mess out." Lips set, she glared back at him.

He struggled once more, then collapsed, his limited reserves spent at last.

Surely there had to be some rational explanation for this. Perhaps the man was delusional. Claire wiped her hand across her mouth, trying frantically to come up with a logical explanation for all this. Could he be a friend of Palmer's, someone who knew where Palmer had come from—someone who for some reason had assumed his identity? But why would anyone do such a thing?

Her mind spinning with outlandish possibilities, she rose. "I'll get you something for the pain."

"Oil of poppies," he murmured, "ten drops in a sip of wine. Stir in a spoonful of willow bark and a pinch of chamomile. But no dwale. It causes irregular heartbeat."

He spoke the very words she'd been thinking!

Was he a healer, then? Or a sorcerer?

Claire paused, still holding the oil of poppy she had just picked up. "Are you a healer?"

"I grew up here!" The blue eyes bored into her for only a second before he subsided, exhausted. "With my mother," he said to the ceiling, "it would have been impossible *not* to learn."

A tingle of foreboding crawled the back of Claire's neck.

By all the stars of heaven, what if he were telling the truth?

Her heart twisted within her. Then she realized . . .

Nonna! She *must* solve this mystery, and quickly.

"Wait." Claire backed toward Nonna's room. "Nonna can clear this up."

"No!" He reared up, the panic in his voice stopping Claire short. "For God's sake, woman, don't let her see me like this, tied like an animal." He settled back unwillingly. "It's been four years. Bad enough that I'm weak as a kitten and flat on my back." He turned glazed blue eyes toward Claire. "Please. Don't let her see me like this."

Claire's mind told her she was being foolish, but her heart reacted to the shame on the stranger's rugged face. "Will you give your oath not to struggle or try to rise?"

"You have my word."

"Nonna has not been well," she explained. "I cannot have you upsetting her. Swear it, sir, upon your very soul."

The stranger's eyes seemed to sink even deeper in their sockets, making his prominent cheekbones almost stark. "I swear it, lady, but not upon my soul. I have no soul." She caught a glimpse of depthless suffering in his face. "Not anymore."

"Then you are in good company, sir, for neither have I." She crossed over and loosed the leather straps, then took a few cautionary steps back.

"Thank you." The stranger rubbed the bands of reddened skin on his wrists but remained on the cot. "My clothes," he rasped. "Where are they?"

Claire shook her head. "I'm sorry. I had to cut them off you. But they will be washed and mended in only a few days."

"Hmph." He raised an eyebrow. "Might I have some cover, then, at least?" He waved a long, well-formed hand across his torso. "This way, I look like a body just washed for burial."

Claire felt a blush warm her cheeks. "You had a high fever. We were trying to cool you down."

"We?" One dark brow lifted again. "And who is 'we'?"

"Little Red and I." Something about his face unsettled Claire. "He brought you to us. Said you'd been in a fight in Bitterne . . ."

"Little Red?"

Disconcerted by the spark of intelligence in his eyes, Claire escaped his scrutiny by fetching a clean sheet and pillow. Then, all too conscious of his nakedness, she covered the man decently, lifted his head, and slipped the pillow beneath. "There. That's better." When she smoothed a wrinkle from the sheet, he caught her hand, his fevered grip hot against her skin.

"Thank you." He nodded briefly. "For setting me free."

Claire withdrew her hand. "Remember," she cautioned, "no upsets, for you or Nonna."

She opened Nonna's door and found her sitting in her chair, looking out the window to a fine summer's morn. "Nonna, I need you."

With an all-too-familiar dazed look, Nonna rose, but did not speak.

"Here. First, let me fix your hair." Claire picked up Nonna's comb and tamed the long white locks, then tied them back neatly with a ribbon. "Beautiful.

"Come, dearest." She led Nonna toward the workroom. "There's someone who wants to see you." Nonna moved almost as if in a trance.

Claire led her into the main room and was surprised

to see the stranger's eyes well with tears. "Mother . . ."
He reached out for her.

Nonna ignored both the salutation and the gesture.
She followed Claire to his bedside and sat on the stool.

Claire crouched beside her. "Look closely, Nonna.
This man says he's Palmer, your son."

"Oh, no," Nonna said vaguely, her eyes drifting to
the window. "That couldn't be Palmer. Palmer's
dead."

"What?" Claire and the stranger asked in unison.

Was this some new delusion caused by Nonna's illness? Claire gripped Nonna's arms. "Nonna, darling,
look at me." She willed the dull, distant stare to her
own. "What do you mean, Palmer's dead? Why do you
think that?"

Now it was Nonna's eyes that welled with tears.
"The man said so. He came here and told me." Her
face crumpled. "He said he saw Palmer die in Hungary."

"No," the stranger moaned. "True, I was injured,
stripped of everything, but I was not killed."

"When?" Claire demanded of Nonna. "When did
this man tell you?"

A look of frightened cunning darkened Nonna's features. "That's my business. I don't want to talk about
it." She tried to rise, but when Claire gently restrained
her, she said like a petulant child, "I want to go back
to my chair now."

"What's wrong with her?" the stranger asked.
"Why doesn't she know me?"

This was only making things worse, not better.
Claire waved the stranger to silence behind Nonna's
back. "Think, dearest. Think about Palmer. Tell me
what he looks like."

Nonna brightened. "Ah, he's the sweetest little boy.

So good. He's always bringing me little presents whittled from sticks.''

"That's wonderful, Nonna," Claire went on, "but what about when he was older? Does this man look anything like him?"

Nonna granted the stranger a cursory glance, then looked back to Claire, smiling. "Oh, no. My Palmer was a plump little lad, not a big, hairy man."

Frustrated beyond measure, Claire tried another tack. "What about the letter, Nonna? The letter that asked me to be Palmer's wife?"

Nonna grinned and pulled Claire close. "Yes. Wasn't that perfect? Now you are my daughter, indeed. Two widows. Just like Ruth and Naomi." Abruptly, her smile faded, the pressure of her embrace increasing. "Promise me you'll never leave me, Claire. Promise."

Claire buried her face in Nonna's shoulder, her words muffled. "I promise, dearest. I promise." She felt Nonna ease.

"I'm so glad, daughter." This time when Nonna tried to get up, Claire did nothing to hinder her. "I'm going back to my room now, dear. Call me if you need me." She leaned over for another good look at the stranger. "I am pleased to have met you, young man." She pointed a finger toward him. "You may count yourself fortunate to have my daughter looking after you. She's the finest healer I have ever known." With that, she left them alone.

Claire turned back to see the stranger's forearm across his eyes, his breathing irregular. She thought he might be overcome with anguish, until he removed his arm and glared at her with such hostility, she recoiled.

"What have you done to her?" he demanded, his whole body shaking with rage. "Put a spell on her? Drugged her?" His hands gripped the sides of the cot so tightly the knuckles whitened. "Tell me!" He formed a fist and brought it down, hard, against the iron frame, making a dull, ringing thud that traveled to the stone beneath.

"Stop that!" Claire whispered harshly. "And keep your voice down." She wished in earnest, now, that she had not set him free. The stranger looked dangerous. "I've done nothing to Nonna," she reassured him in a low voice tight with emotion, "save love her and care for her these past few months when she could no longer care for herself."

Her neck throbbing hot with indignation, she glowered down at the lunatic stranger. "She's ill! Can't you see that?" Claire paced back and forth beside him, her voice an angry whisper. "She's losing her memory. And her speech. Some days, she doesn't even know who I am!"

"Oh, God," the stranger moaned. "I should have come home sooner." He stared up at the rafters above him. "She doesn't even know me." His voice faltered. "My own mother doesn't know me."

The agony in his words cut through Claire's anger with chilling impact. Either the man was completely insane—the victim of delusions—or he was telling the truth. Either way, she had big problems. Very big problems.

SIX

Had he died?

Palmer had dreamed he'd wakened to the sights and smells of home.

Or was it just a dream? It had seemed too real to be a dream, but it must have been. He couldn't go home, couldn't face his mother, couldn't look at her without seeing the women and children he'd . . .

Can't think about that, he warned himself.

Try to remember what happened here. It had seemed so real.

He struggled inside the darkness, trying to separate reality from illusion. Pain, then home and joy, then . . .

Something had happened, but he couldn't remember what. Why couldn't he think straight? Remember . . . what?

His mind was all amuddle.

Home. That was it!

Or a dream of home.

No. Not a dream—a nightmare whose images replayed in his brain as stark as a midnight forest under a winter's moon.

He'd seen his mother, but she had denied him, turning for comfort to a stranger—a stranger who claimed to be his wife.

None of it made sense, but the pain of his mother's denial still seemed so real, it almost overpowered the stabbing he felt in his belly each time he moved.

Maybe he *had* died, and this was his own private hell. And a fitting hell it would make, to be trapped forever in agony, denied by his own mother.

Not that he didn't deserve it; he did, but the irony surprised him.

There was more, though. Another memory took shape in the darkness, sharpening into undeniable clarity. He relived it all, now: the woman, with her cool hands and soothing voice and potions that returned him to oblivion, rescuing him only long enough to make him crave the deep, enveloping darkness, then bringing him back to feel the stab of every movement.

Palmer closed his eyes and willed himself back into the darkness.

But the cooling whisper called him back. "Here," the woman murmured, gentle arms lifting his head to drink. "This will ease your suffering and help you rest."

Palmer smelled the bitter scent of herbs and spice even as he felt cool crockery touch his mouth, but in the only gesture of defiance he could manage, he shut his lips against it.

"Drink." Her voice was like a song, soft and sweet, the perfume of her potion promising not death, but temporary nothingness. Against his will, he drank, cursing himself all the while for giving in, because he knew that he would wake again in painful resurrection.

"That's it. Sleep," the whisper sang again. "Each time you wake, the pain will be less."

Slow-spreading numbness melted through him.

If this was, indeed, hell, he would have eternity to come to terms with his penance. If not, he would sort things out later. For now, the darkness beckoned.

"Claire?" Father Kendall rapped the heavy door knocker.

Claire opened the door and found the priest waiting with an anxious frown on his face. His color looked better today.

Claire placed a finger across her lips to quiet him. "Thank you for coming, but please tread lightly," she whispered to the priest. "My patient's had a bad morning, and he's only just fallen asleep."

The priest doffed his hat and stepped inside. "Little Red said he brought an injured man to you ... a man from our own village."

"I was hoping you might recognize him," Claire answered, uncertain how to broach the stranger's claims. "He's over there." She fixed a troubled look on the priest. "You knew Palmer Freeman, didn't you?"

"Knew him?" Father Kendall paused. "Past tense? Has something happened?"

"I'm not sure." Claire was beginning to feel just as she'd felt those last, terrible months at Castle Compton. Frightened. Uncertain. Angry. But as always, she hid her agitation behind a cool mask of detachment. "Take a look at this man, please, Father, and tell me if you think he could be Palmer Freeman."

"Palmer Freeman!" Father Kendall's outburst stirred the patient to a low moan, but did not wake him.

"Shhh!" Claire pointed to the sleeping figure. "Tell me. Is that Palmer Freeman?"

"Palmer, come home?" The priest's eyes widened. "Thanks be to God. Nonna will be so happy." He crossed the room with careful steps, then peered down at the haggard sleeping patient.

Slowly, the seconds ticked away. Claire clasped her hands together tightly, willing the truth to manifest itself. She watched as Father Kendall ran his fingers over his jaw, an uncertain frown on his face.

At last, he sighed and returned to Claire. "I wish I could say for sure, but I can't." He glanced back at the man. "He's tall enough, that's certain. But Palmer was a robust young fellow when last I saw him—solid as an oak." He shook his head. "This one is so thin. And I seem to recall Palmer's hair as being much lighter."

"An impostor?" Claire's mind churned to find a reason, no matter how farfetched, why anyone would do such a thing.

"Let us not be too quick to judge," the priest cautioned. "After all, many a man's hair darkens with age, and it has been five years since I bid Palmer Freeman Godspeed."

"Is there anyone else in the village who knew him well?"

"Only a few," the priest answered, his lips pursing. "But I can't think of any man who's still here. Like Palmer, several of our young men undertook Peter the Hermit's quest. Lately, even more have followed the princes to Normandy. They're all so eager to answer to the Holy Father's appeal for men-at-arms to liberate the Tomb of Christ from the infidels."

He looked to Claire. "But why this mystery? Just ask Nonna. She's bound to recognize her own son."

"Not necessarily." Claire squirmed. At Nonna's request, she had said nothing until now of the memory loss or the lapses, but Claire decided that the time had come to tell Father Kendall the truth. People were bound to find out eventually, anyway. "You see,

Nonna has been forgetting things. Some days she seems almost normal, but more often than not, she comports herself like someone in a dream." Claire folded her lips inward. "Sometimes, she doesn't even remember me, and she sees me every day."

She leveled her gaze with the priest's. "Palmer has been gone for five years. If he is this man, he's been ill for some time. That could account for his loss of weight and strength."

The priest remained uncertain. "But surely when you told him who you were . . ."

"When I told him who I was, Father," Claire interjected, "he said he had no wife." She sank to the workbench. "He claims to know nothing of the letter."

"Oh, dear. Now *there's* a fine kettle of brine." He sat beside her, frowning.

Then he brightened. "But of course . . . the letter. Perhaps that could clear things up." He nodded. "The bishop still has it; I sent it to him with the request for the proxy marriage. But I could write and ask him to return it. Then, it would simply be a matter of comparing handwriting. Palmer's was rather distinctive, as I recall."

"That might work, but only if the handwriting matches." Claire's analytical mind immediately came up with a complication. "If it doesn't, nothing would be proved. Nonna's son might have hired a scribe to write it for him."

"Aye." The priest grew pensive. "Ah, dear heaven . . ."

Claire saw the light of an idea dawn in his eyes, bringing his brows together in alarm. "But surely it couldn't be that . . . No," he said to himself, his anxiety giving way to sheepishness. "The mere thought is unworthy."

"What?" Claire had to find an answer. "Please tell me, Father."

The priest colored. "What if the writing matched someone else's?"

"Someone else's?" She didn't understand what he was getting at. "Whose?"

"Nonna's."

"Why, that's absurd!" Claire was about to dismiss the outrageous notion when a daunting explanation occurred to her. She rose, the priest standing politely as she did, then started pacing. "What reason on earth would Nonna have to do such a thing? It simply doesn't make sense."

Or did it?

Never leave me, Claire. Promise you'll never leave me. Nonna's desperate words echoed through Claire's mind.

"No. It doesn't make sense," Father Kendall responded. "But alas, we mortals are often far from rational."

Palmer's dead, Nonna had said. *The man told me so.*

Chilling in its clarity, the unforgettable image of Nonna weeping in silent agony beside the dead stranger shaped itself in Claire's memory. Nonna had changed after that, grown almost secretive. Until the wedding.

Never leave me, Claire. Swear it. Promise you'll never leave me.

"Oh, dear God . . ." A jolt of alarm shot up Claire's back. "She did it to make me stay."

"What?"

"This morning when I asked Nonna if this man could be Palmer, she said Palmer was dead." Claire looked at the sleeping stranger. "She said a man had told her Palmer was dead." Hugging her arms close across her stomach, she resumed pacing. "You remember. Last autumn," she reminded the priest. "A dying man came here from the Crusade. Nonna cared for him, but when I tried to help her, she almost panicked, ordered me to my room. Later, I peeked in on her and saw her doubled up in grief on the floor." She turned wide eyes to the priest. "That must have been the man."

Even as she said it, Claire knew that it was true. "He told her Palmer was dead," she mused aloud.

"But why would she keep that a secret?"

"I think she was afraid I would leave her." Claire exhaled heavily. "Poor Nonna. With Palmer gone, she was probably terrified that I too would abandon her."

"But this is fantastic. Surely there is another explanation." The priest studied her with a shrewdness that belied his bumbling mannerisms. "Did Nonna have reason to fear you would leave her?"

"Nay." Claire paced to the window. "I vowed to care for her, and care for her I shall, until one of us dies."

"What about him?" Farther Kendall looked to the sleeping stranger. "If he is Palmer Freeman and insists that you are not his wife . . ."

"I quake to think of such a thing." Dear heaven, what would she do then? "Even if I wanted to leave Nonna, which I don't, I'd have nowhere to go." Why did life have to keep getting more and more complicated? Just when everything had begun to settle into a comforting routine . . .

Claire forced down the panic that rose inside her. Only days ago, she had thought her troubles hard enough, what with caring for Nonna and doing all the work of a healer alone. Now, those burdens seemed inconsequential by comparison. However would she make sense of this?

She didn't have to make sense of everything, not right away. One thing at a time, Nonna had taught her. Don't waste your energy worrying about everything. Focus on the *next* thing.

And the next thing she must do was find out whether or not the man lying in their workroom was, in fact, Palmer Freeman.

"I wish I could be of more help to you, my child," the priest said, "but Palmer was always a serious, rather solitary boy. Very devout, mind you—he rarely missed a Sunday in church. But the rest of the week, he stayed in the forest, either helping his mother or roaming the woods alone. He did not mingle with the villagers. I doubt anyone was truly close to him." Father Kendall absently stroked his chin. "But now that I think of it, I seem to recall something about Beta—"

"Oh, no. Not Beta." The one woman in the village who hated her . . . Claire prayed it wouldn't be Beta who held the missing pieces to this puzzle.

"I daresay Beta should recognize him. She ought to," Father Kendall observed dryly. "She threw herself at him often enough."

So *that* was why Beta hated her!

"I think it might only complicate things to introduce Beta to this delicate matter. We'll find some other way to discover who he really is."

"Then you don't want to ask Beta if she thinks he's Palmer?"

"No. She's so hostile to Nonna and me. . . ." Claire had enough problems. "She might lie, just for spite."

"Aye. She might." Father Kendall bowed to Claire.

"I'm off, then. I'll let you know the moment I discover anything useful."

"Thank you, Father." Claire followed him to the door. "You will be discreet, though?"

"Oh, aye. As indirect as a bishop's heart," the priest promised.

"And if he *is* Palmer Freeman . . ." Claire said, her knuckles white as she gripped the edge of the door.

"We'll cross that bridge when we come to it." The priest made the sign of the cross. "God's blessings be upon you, Claire." He smiled. "Trust me. I shall get to the bottom of this." The priest donned his hat. " 'Fear thou not, for I am with thee,' " he quoted from the Holy Writ. " 'I will comfort thee, I will help thee. I will lift thee with the right hand of my great power.' "

Claire's mouth turned down in a worried frown.

"Do not despair, my child," he offered her. "No matter what we discover, I know you are blameless."

"Aye. I'm blameless," she retorted, "but that has never protected me before."

"Pray without ceasing," he told her, "and trust that all will be well, in God's good time."

Claire wanted to believe him, but she couldn't, any more than she could pray.

SEVEN

"Claire, dear . . . ." Nonna's voice carried through the kitchen doorway, across the yard, and into the herb garden.

"I'm in the garden," Claire called back. Would she never be able to complete a single chore without being interrupted?

"Something's wrong with my clothes, dear." Nonna's inflection bore an all-too-familiar note of baffled frustration. "Could you please come help me?"

She sounded for all the world like a winsome but inept child, and that was exactly how Claire had come to think of her good-mother—as a sweet, loving, demanding, sometimes petulant child.

What now? Claire wondered without rancor. She had actually been enjoying the mindless rhythm of weeding, the late summer sun warm on her back. Shaded by the deep brim of her straw gardening hat, she rocked back onto her heels in the loamy earth and massaged the aching muscles at the base of her spine. A quick scan of the gardens confirmed her opinion that this unseasonably wet July had profited both crops and weeds alike. No matter how diligently she tended the tidy plots of vegetables, herbs, and flowers, new weeds seemed to spring up full-grown with every dawn. "I'm just finishing up the weeding, Nonna. I'll come in anon."

"All right, then."

Awkward because of the soft soil and her own long legs, she struggled to her feet. Claire tossed the freshly pulled nettle, already limp, into the basket with the rest of the weeds destined for the muck heap, then pulled off her leather work gloves and laid them on top.

"Here," a low, masculine voice said from behind her, frightening her half to death. "Let me finish that."

She spun around to find the man who claimed to be Nonna's son. His pale complexion looked even whiter in the bright sunlight, but he seemed to be standing steady enough.

"What are you doing out of bed?" Heart pounding from the fright he'd given her, she spoke more sharply than she intended. "I seem to remember telling you to stay in bed."

A ghost of a smile softened the harsh lines of his mouth. "I've been in bed for almost two weeks. If I'd stayed there any longer, I'd have put down roots."

She couldn't help smiling. "So you do have a sense of humor, after all."

"None whatsoever," he said, the twinkle in his eye making a lie of it.

Claire carefully stepped over a patch of rosemary, eased between two thick stands of sage, then straddled a pungent row of mint that bordered the path where he was standing.

He seemed so much larger, standing up. Taller, and far more substantial. Once she was near the stranger— she refused even to think of him as Palmer until presented with proof—she studied him with the practiced eye of a healer.

He held himself straight, his broad shoulders squared and long legs planted firmly on the path, his torso no longer bent to favor the side with the incision. There was even a hint of color in his cheeks, but the skin still clung too tightly to his high cheekbones and strong chin. A few more weeks of good food should remedy that.

Without thinking, she stepped to within a foot of him and peered up to inspect the whites of his eyes.

No longer bloodshot, thank goodness. But what was that musty smell?

Suddenly she realized he was inspecting her just as closely as she had looked at him, his expression one of amused surprise.

She pulled back, flustered. "You do look better," she said, feeling she had to say something but not knowing why. "Perhaps it has done you some good to get up and walk a bit. Still, it's far too soon for you to do something as taxing as weeding."

Catching another musty whiff, she realized the smell was coming from his clothes. "Those aren't the clothes you were wearing when you came here," she blurted out. The garments were a bit too large, but fit him well enough. They were simply yet artfully fashioned from fabrics more appropriately worn by a young nobleman than a mere freeholder. "Where did you get them?"

His eyes narrowed to a brittle glare. "They're mine." Clearly, he resented the accusation in her voice. Then, just as suddenly as his anger had flared, it disappeared behind a bland expression. "I'm surprised my mother kept them."

Claire flinched inwardly at his use of the word "mother."

"She scarcely waited for me to outgrow anything before she gave it away." An affectionate smile eased the harshness from his features. "It's a sin, she said, to keep perfectly good clothes once I'd outgrown them, when so many of those she cared for hadn't a decent tunic to their names."

Claire could almost hear Nonna saying those very words.

He plucked at the fullness in the tunic, fixing Claire with a wry look. "It seems I'm far less than the man I was when I left." His mouth and eyes hardened. "In more ways than one, I fear."

"Claire!" The summons wafted from the house. Judging from Nonna's anxious tone, her already short patience was clearly wearing thin. "Do hurry, dear. I can't find my . . . thingy."

The stranger turned toward the sound of Nonna's voice, his expression wistful, then turned back to Claire. "Go to her."

"Poor darling. She's always losing things," Claire heard herself explaining. "Or hiding them and forgetting where. Either way, both of us spend far too much time rooting about for hairpins, shoes, and clothing."

"You're needed inside, then." Her patient's long, elegant fingers reached out and pulled the basket of weeds from her hands. "Leave this to me. I can work sitting down. If I don't have something useful to do, and soon, I fear I shall go raving mad." He pointed to the gloves. "Those look big enough for me to use. You take care of Nonna. I'll finish the weeding."

A hot tide of embarrassment warmed Claire's neck. It stung to have him notice that her own hands were almost as large as his. But before she could think of a retort, both of them heard, "Claire, dear! Did you hear me?"

"Don't worry," the stranger reassured her. "I'll be fine."

"Claire!"

Torn between protecting her patient and helping Nonna, Claire glanced rapidly from the house to the stranger, and back again. "All right. But promise me you'll stop the moment you begin to tire."

"I promise."

Against her better judgment, she left him to the weeding.

Inside, she found Nonna's door closed. Claire knocked. "I'm here, Nonna."

The door sprang open. Hair askew, Nonna greeted Claire with one sandal in her hand. "Ah. There you are." She was wearing her clothes backward and inside out.

Claire couldn't help laughing. "Ah, poor Nonna. That must be very uncomfortable." She gave her good-mother a hug. "Let me help you get your clothes turned right."

Nonna smiled benignly. "Oh, my clothes are fine, dear, no need to bother with that. But I can't find my other . . ." She scowled, waggling the sandal in front of her. "My . . . button." Her scowl deepened. "Not button. Why can't I recall the word?"

"Your sandal, Mother," Claire prompted.

"No, no. That's not it." Nonna glanced wildly around the room. "I know there's another one. I just had it. Do you think someone might have stolen it?" Her white eyebrows lifted. "That man! The one you've got sleeping in the workroom. He took it, I'll wager."

"No one's stolen your sandal, dear." When Nonna got wound up like this, there was only one thing to do. Ignoring the older woman's rapid, disjointed chatter, Claire hugged her, hard, and did not let go until the agitated monologue subsided and Nonna relaxed.

"That's better." Claire steered Nonna to the bed and sat her down to undress her, then put the clothes back on as they should have been. Happy again, Nonna chattered away about everything and nothing while Claire set her clothes to rights. At last, she combed Nonna's hair, braided it, pinned up the braids, then draped a clean wimple around Nonna's face. "There," she said with satisfaction when she was done. "You look like yourself again."

Nonna waggled her sandal at Claire, lifting her bare feet for emphasis. "There's still the matter of this . . . of this, this . . . hootdoot."

Again, Claire was helpless to suppress a chuckle. Nonna's speech difficulties were always creative, and often entertaining. They laughed together, then both women searched for twenty minutes before Claire gave up and fetched Nonna's soft boots. She had just helped Nonna into the left one when she heard a knock on the front door.

Not an urgent knock—just a polite, sociable one.

"Just a moment." Was it too much to hope that she might complete even this one small task without interruption?

Once Nonna was decently shod, Claire hastened to open the door. She was pleasantly surprised to find Father Kendall waiting outside.

"Father Kendall. What an unexpected pleasure." Claire glanced anxiously back toward the bedroom, but Nonna did not come out. Her voice dropped to a whisper. "Have you heard from the bishop? The letter . . . has he sent it back?"

"Not yet. That's not why I came." The little priest peered up at her in concern. "I was praying for you, as I do every day, and felt a burden on my heart. There was nothing to be done, then, but come and see for myself if all is well with you.''

It might have been the genuine affection in his voice, or perhaps her own weariness and frustration, barely held at bay these past few weeks, but Claire—to her abject horror—promptly burst into tears.

Covering her face with her hands, she felt the priest's arm circle her shoulders.

"Ah, poor child. Such a burden God has vouchsafed to visit upon you." He steered her to the wooden settle by the hearth and sat beside her. "That's it. Cry it out." He patted her shoulder with the awkwardness of an unfamiliar uncle. "God gave us tears for just this reason. They rinse the bitter humors from our blood." More patting. "Why, even our blessed Lord wept, on more than one occasion," he said in a soothing tone. Gently, he pulled away her straw hat, the brim of which was smashed against his neck. "Rejoice with those who rejoice, the Scripture says, and weep with those who weep." He laid the hat on the seat beside him, then fell silent while Claire cried away.

Why now? she wondered even as she wept. Her troubles of late were hardly as grievous as the losses and tragedies of her past. "I'm sorry, Father," she managed between shuddering sobs. "Please forgive me for such a display. I'm just tired, that's all."

"I think 'exhausted' would be more accurate," the priest said briskly. "Why, you've been doing the labor of three people these past few weeks, and both your and Nonna's work for months before that." His patting quickened with the growing vehemence in his voice. "Not to mention the strain of your present circumstances. That, alone, would try the patience of a saint." He was rocking back and forth now, as if he were comforting a fevered child. "Well, never fear. I'll find help for you."

He puffed away a stray lock of her hair that had fallen in his face when he'd removed her hat. "Any number of people in the village would jump at the chance to be of help to Nonna, or to you. I can have someone here first thing in the morning."

As appealing as it sounded, Claire could never allow such a thing. She spoke, her head vibrating with every word owing to her tear-stuffed nose. "I can't brig id outside help, Father." She succumbed to an undignified snuffle. "Noda doesn't want adyone to know how ill she is."

"Ah, dear Claire," the priest said with compassion, "ours is a small village. Such a thing can hardly be kept secret. I can't think of anyone who *doesn't* know of Nonna's difficulties. They all saw the signs. A few remembered how it was with her aunt and her mother. So no one questioned why Nonna sent you to care for them in her place."

He was right. "True," Claire confessed. "No wud ever asked why Nonna stopped working. They simply accepted me in her place."

"Aye, and came to trust your healing skills as they had once trusted hers, without reservation." He shook his head. "You are not alone, Claire. Nor can you continue to do everything here all by yourself. Let me get someone to help with the work. You're weary to your soul, child, and far too thin. It will do Nonna little good for you to fall ill." He gave her shoulder a final pat, then moved away. "I shall send someone over first thing tomorrow morning. For now, though, why don't you retire, take a little nap? I'd be glad to look after Nonna and your visitor until you wake."

"Thang you, Father." Claire took a leveling breath.

As good as his idea sounded, she could not allow it. "But Noda needs reminders—and help—with ..." Her cheeks grew warm. How could she explain this to a priest? "With her most basic bodily functions." She sniffed deeply, clearing her nose. "I daresay she might balk at allowing any man to assist her, even a priest."

"Hrrmph." Father Kendall's color quickly deepened far beyond her own. "Well, when you explain it that way ..." He clasped his hands behind his back. "Then your helper must be a woman. I can think of several who would be glad to work in exchange for your services. Perhaps I can even find a girl who wishes to apprentice."

Her own apprentice? "I hadn't thought of that," Claire admitted, "but the idea has merit."

"It's settled, then."

"Thank you, Father." Claire wiped the last of her drying tears from her cheeks. "I shall welcome the help."

The priest looked askance to make sure neither Nonna nor the stranger was within earshot. "I'll bring the letter here the moment it arrives."

"Thank you." Claire gave the shy little prelate an impulsive hug. "I only hope it doesn't raise more questions than it answers."

"I shall pray that it will bring an answer," the priest responded.

After she had seen him on his way and checked to make sure Nonna was still happily settled in her chair, Claire returned to the herb garden. The weeds had disappeared, but so had the stranger.

Curious, she searched for him in every nook and hedge of the compound before approaching the studio.

Sure enough, she found him sitting inside, the statue of the eagle in his hands.

"What are you doing in here?" she demanded, her heart contracting. How often she had imagined a faceless Palmer in this very place, just as he was sitting. Yet now, seeing the stranger in her own secret refuge, touching things, she felt a protective surge of outrage. "Put that down."

"I shall not," he said quietly, the muscles in his shoulders and arms tightening. He sat with his back to her, his hands caressing the fluid arc of wooden wings as if they knew each curve and cut. "It's mine. *I* found this eagle hidden in a block of wood, and I set him free. No one *but* me has the right to touch this." Slowly and deliberately, he turned a territorial glare on her, his blue eyes dark and threatening as a wolf's. "And no one but me has the right to be here."

Claire recoiled, knowing he was not referring just to the studio. If, indeed, he was Palmer, he had every right to be here, and she had none. These past few days had convinced her that he truly believed himself to be Palmer Freeman. Whether he was or not remained to be seen.

Yet now, sharing this space with him, she felt for the first time like an intruder in the safe haven she had come to think of as home. "I . . . Forgive me. I . . ." she stammered. "All these months of protecting Nonna . . . I cannot stop doing it so easily, even if you are who you claim to be."

"I am Palmer Freeman," he said quietly, almost as if he were announcing his own death. He leveled a searing gaze at her. "What I don't know is, who are you? And why are you here?"

"I've told you already." She looked down, unable to face the wounded suspicion in his gaze. "I was widowed, an outcast. Alone. Nonna took me in as an apprentice, in exchange for my vow that I care for her when she could no longer care for herself."

She lifted her chin in challenge. "As for the marriage, I only went through with it because Nonna wanted it so badly." She faltered. "And because of the carvings."

"My carvings?" He sounded surprised.

Claire grasped the tiny mouse's tail and lifted the carved creature into her palm. "There is so much life and humor in these carvings. I thought, surely the man who made these must be . . . well, he couldn't be cruel or thoughtless."

"He wasn't," Palmer said flatly. "Not then." He closed his eyes with a long sigh. "I don't know what he is, now."

Claire steeled herself to a courage she did not feel. "That doesn't matter, really." She faced him straight-on. "Whoever you are, whatever you are, I mean to stay here with Nonna and care for her, as I promised. My vow was made to her, not you."

"I see." To her surprise, he did not react defensively. On the contrary, he seemed chastened. "Have I asked you to leave?"

"No," she admitted. But the prospect was all too probable. "Would you cast me out, though? Deny our marriage?" She studied him. "I know you must have thought of it."

The stranger said nothing.

If he was Palmer . . . what could he possibly say, denied by his own mother and saddled with a wife he'd never even heard of?

Claire sagged. "Nonna loves me, and I love her. For whatever reason, you are a stranger to her. I cannot leave her with you, no matter who you are. You see that, don't you?"

He exhaled heavily. "Aye. I can see that."

"Then what are we to do?" she asked, miserable.

"For the time being," he said, his voice level, "I suppose we should carry on as we are."

"Then you will not cast me out?" Until she said the words, Claire hadn't realized how terrified she'd been that he would. Assuming, of course, that he was Palmer Freeman.

"No." Brows drawn together, he studied her as if seeing her for the first time. "I would not cast you out. Not as long as Nonna needs you."

"And if she did not?"

He looked at the graceful carving in his hands. "No sense worrying about that now."

So her place here was secure only as long as Nonna needed her. Claire felt as if she had swallowed a boulder. She could scarcely breathe, and her heart ached beneath the strain. To be outcast again . . . "So, for now . . . ?"

He turned unfathomable eyes toward hers. "We go on, just as we are."

She could only nod, all too familiar with the threat of exile that hung over her like a sword, poised to drop without warning. Yet again, her security rested in the hands of one who suffered her presence only because of another.

This time, though, Claire would not give up so easily. This time, she meant to stay, Palmer Freeman or no Palmer Freeman. "I will not abandon Nonna, no matter what you say," she announced.

To her surprise, she saw a gleam of admiration in the stranger's assessment. "I shall not ask you to." He set the eagle on its carved stand. "My mother does not spend her trust, or her love, without cause, and I can see that she has spent both on you. That is enough to secure your place with us, here."

Claire nodded. She would worry later about what would happen to her when Nonna was gone. It was enough to know that she would not be outcast any time soon. "Thank you."

"No. It is I who should thank you," he said without irony. "You care for my mother far better than I ever cared for her, myself." A flicker of anguish sharpened his gaunt features even further. "I never should have left her." He shivered. "But I am grateful that she found you, and that you have loved her, even as I should have."

"I do love her, you know," Claire said with conviction.

He nodded, suddenly looking far older than his years. "I love her, too." She saw the pain of rejection in the deep lines beside his mouth and the silent loneliness in his eyes, and for the first time, her heart went out to him, as well.

As if he sensed her pity, he turned his back to hide his shame. His voice gruff, he said, "Perhaps it would be best if I slept out here from now on."

Claire nodded. "As you wish. There's an extra cot and mattress in the storage house. I'll bring them over straightaway, along with some linens."

"Good." He nodded, but did not turn to face her. "Once I'm settled, I would appreciate it if you did not come here without an invitation. I hope you understand."

Claire understood, all too well. She would miss this quiet refuge, but even if he wasn't Palmer Freeman, the man had a right to some privacy. "As you wish."

She left the stranger to the place she had once thought of as her own.

EIGHT

The next morning, Claire had just gotten out of bed when she heard someone knocking insistently on the front door.

At this hour?

Then she remembered Father Kendall's promise to send a helper.

She hadn't yet dressed, but since he'd promised to send a woman . . . Claire drew her muslin robe together over her nightgown and called through the bolted door. "Who is't?"

" 'Tis I," an excited young female voice answered. "Ardra. Your new apprentice."

Ardra! Father Kendall had sent *Ardra*?

Of all the females in the village, what in blazes had prompted the priest to send her? Surely he knew how Beta felt about Ardra's illicit hopes of becoming a healer.

Claire fumbled with the bolt, then drew the door open.

Sure enough, there in the damp of morning stood Ardra, her belongings bundled in her arms and her face wreathed in smiles.

"But your mother . . ." Claire protested, thoroughly undone. "She was against this, you said. Surely she would not allow you to come here."

"Her." A sullen frown extinguished Ardra's radiance. "Father Kendall took care of her, thank goodness." Brightening, she peered past Claire into the workroom. "Is Nonna awake yet? I'd love to take her breakfast in bed." She started to brush past, but Claire caught hold of her arm.

"Wait just one moment, young lady." She lifted her eyebrows in skepticism. "What do you mean, 'Father Kendall took care of her'?"

Ardra jabbed the toe of her soft leather shoe at the worn stones of the stoop. "This wasn't my idea. Truly. It was Father Kendall's." Her wide hazel eyes implored Claire to understand. "Father knows I don't want to be a midwife; I want to be a healer, like you." Her mouth went flat. "I've confessed it often enough, and done penance aplenty." She shrugged. "Well, last night, Father came to Mum and said Nonna was ill, and you needed someone to help care for her." Her young face wrinkled in concern. "Of course, Mum said no. Said she didn't care if he was a priest, she wasn't about to let me work for a healer, when my own mother needed me to help birthing babies."

Her eyes widened. "But Father Kendall didn't give up. As a matter of fact, he was most kind to Mum, praisin' me sister Corly and tellin' Mum he knew how hard it must be to have a child like me who wasn't willin' to follow in her mother's footsteps. The way he carried on, I feared they were going to pack me off to a dungeon for wayward daughters, straightaway."

"And?" Claire prompted, wondering where all this was leading.

"And," Ardra went on, "then he said that this might

be just the thing to change my mind, working here, doin' thankless drudgery.'' Her smile returned, bringing a deep dimple to her cheek along with it. ''He said I'd have to care for Nonna as if she were a babe, washin' soiled clouts and everything.'' She let out a snort. ''I could see Mum liked the idea of *that*.''

''Well,'' Claire corrected, ''that's not entirely accurate. Nonna does have an accident now and then, but usually, she just needs to be reminded to use her chamber pot.''

Ardra chuckled. ''I saw what Father Kendall was up to, all along. He knew just how to get Mum over to his side. Told her if she kept saying no, it would be forbidden fruit, that I'd never give up the idea. But if she let me come and I saw how hard it was, then I'd probably grow weary of the whole business in only a few months.'' Ardra giggled. ''By the time he finished, you'd have thought I was bein' sent to do three months of penance instead of the very thing I wanted to do.''

She mocked her mother's voice and expression. '' 'It'll serve the headstrong little chit right,' Mum told him. And before you could say 'Jack in the pulpit,' she'd given permission for me to work here. But only for three or four months, to start with.''

Whatever could the priest have been thinking? Claire's life was complicated enough without Beta and Ardra.

It occurred to Claire that Beta might even have allowed her daughter to apprentice so she would have an excuse to visit here and see Palmer again.

Still, Ardra was all aglow with enthusiasm for her new position. And under the circumstances, refusing the girl might make Beta even angrier than taking her in.

''Please let me stay, Dame Claire. Please.'' If Ardra

could have turned herself inside out to convince her, Claire knew she would have. As it was, the girl shifted anxiously from foot to foot, her big hazel eyes pleading.

What choice did Claire have, really?

"Very well. You may stay."

Ardra jumped up and down. "Oh, thank you, thank you, thank you!"

"But only because your mother has given her permission," Claire felt compelled to add. "And only if you promise to go back without complaint if she needs you. For anything."

"Whatever you say, Dame Claire!" Ardra threw her arms around Claire and hugged her so hard they both almost went tumbling. "You'll never regret this, I promise you."

Unaccustomed to such a display of affection, Claire hastily extracted herself from the girl's embrace. She looked up just in time to see Palmer lope around the corner of the house, wrapped in a blanket that covered his thighs and torso but left an indecently large portion of his bare chest, calves, and shoulders exposed.

He stopped abruptly and frowned. "I heard shouts. Is everything all right?"

"Oh, my heavens!" Ardra took one look at him, then modestly hid her face in Claire's shoulder. "Who is *that*?" Obviously, she had not recognized him.

Claire wasn't about to explain the man and his claims to Ardra. Instead, she settled for just enough of the truth to suffice. "He's one of my patients. He . . . lives in the studio, for the time being. I'll introduce the two of you later—" She glared at Palmer, raising her voice to make sure he could hear. "—when he's decently dressed." Sheltering the girl from such an inappropriate sight, Claire made for the threshold.

Palmer called after her. "I was in the bathhouse, just about to get into the pool," he explained, his voice acid, "when I heard a female voice yelping."

That would have been Ardra's cries of gratitude.

"You will forgive me for not stopping to dress. I thought you might be in danger." He lifted one eyebrow and threw the corner of the blanket over his shoulder, revealing even more of his muscular calves. "I humbly beg your pardon."

"Sir! Cover yourself," Claire retorted. "If not for my sake, then for the tender sensibilities of this maiden."

She hustled Ardra into the house. "Pay no attention to him. Come. You can help me prepare to break our fast." As she closed the door behind her, she could have sworn she heard a dry chuckle from Palmer's direction.

She guided Ardra straight for the kitchen.

Now that the girl was part of the household, Claire would have to speak to Palmer about his behavior.

"Are you all right, Dame Claire?" Ardra asked, unable to suppress the smile of mischief on her lips.

"I'm fine." Claire shot a last, poisonous look toward where Palmer had been standing. "You would do well, though, to stay away from that man until I've spoken to him about proper decorum."

"He looked like a very interesting man, to me." Without having to be asked, Ardra picked up a pitcher and filled it from the trough of running water. "Quite handsome, really."

Now that Claire was removed enough from the situation to see the humor in it, she couldn't help smiling. "He looked rather silly to me. Rescue, indeed."

Ardra stepped to the kitchen window and watched Palmer retreat to the bathhouse. "Oooh. He's so tall.

And look how his muscles move when he walks.''

"Ardra! Remember yourself.'' Claire motioned the child away from the opening.

The stricken expression on Ardra's face stopped Claire cold, the air still ringing with the bitter edge of her own scolding voice.

Saints! The child had scarcely been here five minutes, and Claire was acting like an ill-tempered task-mistress.

Was that the woman the hardships of her life had made her?

Claire's heart twisted within her. "Forgive me for speaking so sharply, Ardra.''

She looked into Ardra's young face and saw the girl that she, herself, had once been—carefree, impulsive, ready to take on the grand adventure of life.

Ardra would discover life's hard realities soon enough. Claire did not want to be a part of that disillusionment, any more than she wanted to be the bitter, rigid, scolding woman she'd become.

A few short years ago, she had loved to laugh and joke and tease. Where was that Claire now?

Could she find that Claire again, for Ardra's sake? And Nonna's. And her own.

Claire wasn't certain, but she made a vow, then and there, to try. She had lived in shadow far too long.

Mustering a playfulness she did not feel, she turned to Ardra and teased, "What about Little Red?'' She smiled in earnest at Ardra's answering blush. "Nonna told me you planned to marry *him* someday.''

"Not anymore.'' Ardra did her best to look haughty. "Who wants him, anyway?'' She crossed to the banked ashes of the cookfire and crouched to stir the embers. "Not me, I can tell you.'' She blew the embers to life, then began poking kindling into them, her tone petulant. "He's given his heart to another, the faithless lout." She frowned up at Claire. "He wouldn't tell me who it was, but I'll find out. And when I do . . ." Ardra snapped a twig of kindling. "I'll break her in two, the hussy. Roderick and I are promised, and everyone knows it."

Never mind that she'd just said she didn't want him.

But if Ardra should discover that Claire was the object of Roderick's misplaced affections . . .

Claire resolved to think of some way to discourage the boy without hurting his feelings. It would not do for Ardra to see her as a rival, and Little Red followed Claire around like a calf whenever he came to visit Palmer, which was often.

Ah, well. She'd think of something. For Ardra's sake, she must.

Ardra stole a peek toward the bathhouse on her way to pick up the kettle by the sink, and it was all Claire could do to suppress a chuckle.

At least Ardra seemed well on her way to a distraction of her own. Unless Claire missed her guess, Palmer was about to become the object of the inevitable infatuation with an older man that marked a girl's transition to womanhood.

Unbidden, Claire's mind conjured the long-forgotten memory of the hapless blacksmith who had won and lost her twelve-year-old heart without ever even knowing it.

All that raw male energy, sweat, and muscle.

She shivered, even now, with remembered ecstasy at the heady, overwhelming power of her childish fantasies about the man.

Such joy. Such dreams. Such world-shattering agony when it had ended. She'd seen him kissing two different serving girls in a single day and taken to her bed for almost a week, nursing a broken heart.

"Dame Claire?"

"I'm sorry, Ardra." Claire came back to herself. "I'm afraid I was wool-gathering. Did you have a question for me?"

"Aye." Ardra nodded earnestly as she hung the kettle over the growing flames, then poured it half-full with water "I asked if you had any notion what I should do about Roderick."

"Boys can be awfully silly, sometimes," she said to Ardra, "but Roderick is bound to come to his senses eventually. He'd have to be a fool to spurn a girl as lovely and accomplished as you, and he's no fool. He'll come around."

"That's just what Mum said—that he'd come around," the girl responded, astonished.

Claire couldn't help smiling. She and Beta, agreeing? Now, that was something unexpected. Perhaps this arrangement with Ardra might work out, after all.

As long as Roderick didn't let the fish out of the net.

"You've already started the porridge, I see." Claire nodded toward the kettle. "What say, you finish it while I do the milking and gather the eggs?"

"I make very good porridge," Ardra announced without hubris, "and bread. Shall I start a few loaves, then?"

"Aye." Claire liked the girl's confidence. She would need it as a healer. And she was more than glad that the girl knew her way around a kitchen, doing what was needed without being asked.

Well satisfied, Claire headed to the barn and a few moments of peace. There was little doubt that Ardra would fit into the household. The only question was, how could Claire discourage Little Red before Ardra guessed the truth?

Claire drew up a stool beside the nanny goat and placed the milking bucket beneath the animal's bulging udder. "Any ideas, Nanny?"

"Naaaah!" said the nanny, as always.

"Me, neither," Claire replied, tugging on the warm, elastic teats.

It was in the nethertime between night and daylight that Palmer felt most alive. At the first note of birdsong announcing the end of darkness, he woke alert, his naked skin protected from the morning cool by only a thin muslin sheet. He lay still in his bed, watching the clerestory windows high above him take shape in the gloom and brighten until the dim light transformed the unadorned lime-washed walls of his studio from gray to pristine white.

Rain or shine, the ritual remained the same. It was a simple thing, this daily sacrament of transformation, but the process anchored him, somehow. For a few, brief moments, he was whole, suspended between the relentless torments of his dreams and the inescapable anguish of reality.

Ardra's knock barely penetrated the heavy wooden door.

"Coming."

Palmer rose, splashed water on his face and dried it, drew on his chausses and tunic, then raked a comb through his hair and bound it at the nape.

When he opened the door, Ardra greeted him—as she did every day—with a shy, luminous smile.

"Good morning to ye, sir." She crossed to the small, marble-topped table and sat on one of the two stools beside it. "I pray ye slept well."

"Well enough." The nightmares were his own business, no one else's.

Ardra laid out two thick slabs of buttered bread, a small pot of honey, two bowls of creamed oat cereal, and two mugs with a steaming ceramic pitcher of sweet cider.

He hadn't intended to share his breakfast with her every day, but the girl had seemed so eager to stay and talk with him from the very first, he hadn't the heart to send her away. As a consequence, he'd broken his fast for seven mornings running with Ardra for company.

Not that he minded, particularly. She, alone, had accepted his word that he was Palmer Freeman, even though she'd been too young when he'd left to remember him clearly.

And she was good company. Winsome as a woodsprite, the child had charmed him with her enthusiasm and relentless curiosity. He'd been that young once, and just that meddlesome. She reminded him of a time he'd almost forgotten, when his future had been spread before him, bright with promise.

He didn't even mind her incessant questions, for her curiosity was as ingenuous as the rest of her nature.

When she asked a question he did not wish to answer, he simply smiled at her in silence, and she readily shifted to another topic of conversation. Today, though, she seemed to have lost some of her usual luster.

Palmer settled opposite her at the little table. "You're awfully quiet this morning," he noted. "Is something the matter?"

"Aye." Ardra poured a mug of hot cider for each of them. "Have you ever been in love, sir?"

Palmer hid his smile behind the rim of his mug. The warmth felt good in his hand. "Why do you ask?"

Her eyes downcast, she blew on the hot cider to cool it. "I love someone, but I dare not tell him."

"I see. Quite a grown-up problem, that." Palmer studied the girl as he sipped the sweet, pungent cider. "How old are you, child?"

"I am not a child," she retorted, her cheeks splotching in indignation. "I'm almost thirteen." She sat as tall as her slender spine could make her. "My mother was only fourteen when she married Papa, God rest his soul."

"Ah." Palmer did his best to keep the irony from his voice. "So you're almost a woman, then."

"Aye." She turned soulful eyes to him. "And it isn't easy being a woman, I can tell you." She popped a chunk of bread into her mouth and chewed thoughtfully.

"And you're in love."

"Umm-hmm." A deep sigh accompanied her nod.

"But you cannot tell him."

Woefully, she shook her head.

"And why not?" Beginning to weary of this little game, he took another sip of cider.

Ardra's gaze dropped to her lap. "Because he's married."

Palmer swallowed most of his cider the wrong way and promptly choked. Coughing violently, he felt Ardra pound frantically on his back.

"Oh, no!" she wailed. "Look what's happened, now! I knew I shouldn't have told ye."

"I'm all right!" he managed between coughs. "Stop whacking me!"

Panicked, she continued to strike him with astonishing strength. "You're choking, and it's all my fault. Me and my big mouth. Please don't choke!"

"I'm not choked!" he gasped, stifling the next cough.

"Thanks be to God." Ardra stopped whacking him,

a wan smile on her face. "Please forgive me. I should never have said anything." Her large hazel eyes blinked at him like an owl's.

Why did he suddenly feel uneasy?

Palmer let out a last cough and made up his mind. "Ardra, do you not think such matters are better discussed with . . . well, with your mother?"

"Mum? I can't tell her anything," she sulked. "She just yells at me and says I should be like Corly, the tell-a-tale. I can't talk to Corly, either, even if she is my twin. She couldn't keep a secret if her life depended on it."

Employing a decidedly calculating feminine gesture, Ardra looked up at him through thick lashes. "But you . . . you're different. You listen, treat me like an adult."

"Mmmm." Palmer's sense of unease deepened. Suddenly he was aware of the dangers inherent in the situation. A young girl, confiding things more properly discussed only among women. The two of them, unchaperoned. How could he have been so thick as to allow this in the first place?

"Ah . . ." He put on a casualness he did not feel. "I've been thinking about it, and, since you are such a fine young lady, I would hate to compromise your honor in any way. So perhaps it would be best if we no longer spent time alone, unchaperoned."

Her eyes widened. "But we've only talked. Nothing improper . . ."

"Of course, nothing improper . . ." Palmer rose and crossed to his workbench. He picked up a fine chisel and resumed carving on the crosspiece pattern for the new sword he planned to make. "But I doubt your mother would approve, in any event. What say I break my fast in the kitchen with you and Dame Claire, from now on?"

"But—"

Palmer gave no opening for objections. "We can still talk, but your reputation will be secure."

Instead of being angry, as he had anticipated, she let out a deep sigh, her hands clasped to her chest, and looked at him as if he were a saint. "How noble of you, to concern yourself with my reputation, and me a mere apprentice."

Her gaze still glued to him, she set the mugs and dishes back on the tray, then glided toward the door. When he opened it for her, she breathed a soft "Adieu." Like someone in a dream, she drifted toward the kitchen.

"That's all I need," Palmer groaned, closing the door behind him. Bad enough, that he'd come home to find a wife he'd never even heard of and a mother who did not recognize him. Now he was master of a moon-eyed virgin who confided her secret love for some poor, unsuspecting married man who probably didn't know the girl existed.

Then a disturbing thought occurred to him. What if the married man did know Ardra existed, and had designs on her innocence?

Palmer resolved to keep an eye on things, just in case. Not that he would be here long. He could not stay. But he would not allow himself to be with her alone again.

By mid-July, Claire had begun to enjoy the predictable routine into which the household had settled. With each dawn, Ardra got up, woke her, then made breakfast while Claire saw to her own and Nonna's waking needs. Next, while Claire gathered the eggs and did the milking, Ardra took Nonna's food to her on a tray and made sure she ate well. She then joined Claire and Palmer at the kitchen table for the first meal of the day.

But little conversation transpired there. All three of them seemed ill at ease.

Perhaps, in time, that would change, but for now, Claire concentrated on her morning meal, as did Palmer and Ardra.

She could see, though, that Little Red wasn't the only one who'd gone moon-eyed for someone older. Whenever Ardra thought Palmer wasn't looking, the girl looked to him with such intense longing and adoration that it was all Claire could do to keep from sitting the girl down and reminding her that Palmer was a married man, old enough to be her father.

Not that she had any right to say a word. Though the letter had yet to be delivered to Father Kendall, Palmer claimed emphatically that the proxy marriage should never have taken place.

If that were true, the marriage had been based on fraud and so had never been valid. And if the ceremony was not valid, Claire had as little claim to Palmer as Ardra did.

Still, she couldn't blame the girl for liking Palmer. Claire liked him, too. Despite Nonna's lack of recognition, he visited with her daily, taking his mother for leisurely walks in the garden, or talking quietly with her in her room. Always gentle, always patient, he listened just as intently when Nonna's ramblings made little sense as he did when she could speak plainly. When she was silent, he sat beside her in companionable silence.

He wore his own silence easily, like a man well satisfied with his own company. And he was thoughtful, not just to Nonna, but to Claire and Ardra. They never had to ask him to chop more wood or replenish the supply at the fireplaces.

He worked hard without being asked: weeding, gathering wood in the forest, hoeing, harvesting, mending walls and harnesses, restoring the forge, repairing the house. He'd even started cutting and dressing wood for new gates—an enormous undertaking for a single man, alone.

But underneath his quiet, hardworking demeanor, Claire sensed some secret sorrow. She saw it in the way he stared into space when he thought no one was looking, his shoulders slumped beneath some unspoken burden. And she sensed it in the way he kept his own counsel, almost as if he were afraid to open up for fear of what might escape.

Claire understood that, all too well. So she did not pry. She simply tried to take each day as it came. What with the compound, Nonna, and the needs of Claire's practice, there was work enough to keep all of them from wasting time with worry, about past or future. Each day had its own demands, so none of the souls in Nonna's house wasted time with speculation. Except, perhaps, for Ardra, who mooned after Palmer with a virgin's relentless romanticism.

"Isn't he handsome?" Ardra sighed after him early one midsummer's day. "So brave, and yet so kind. He must be of gentle birth."

"Nay, silly." Claire recognized the stars in Ardra's eyes. "Not if he's Nonna's son."

"He is Nonna's son," Ardra declared defensively. "I know he is. But he could still be a prince." She swept the broom in wide arcs across the floor, as if she were dancing. "What if a king had come here and fallen in love with Nonna? Palmer could be his."

"Ardra, wherever do you get such outrageous ideas?"

"It could be true." Ardra sighed. "I wish it was.

Then Master Palmer would be a prince. A secret prince."

Claire shook her head. "Be careful what you wish for, young lady. You just might get it, and wishes can claim a terrible price."

"Really?" Ardra sobered. "How do you know, Dame Claire? Did you ever get your wish?"

"Aye." Something deep and long-suppressed twisted painfully within Claire. "I got my wish, and I was happy, for a while. But then I paid the price."

"Aye?" Ardra asked her. "What was it, then, the cost for getting your wish?"

"Everything that mattered," Claire said quietly, the emptiness within her growing. "Everything."

NINE

The sun had been up for only an hour, but it was already hot and muggy when Claire rode by the little church in Linherst. Frieda's rolling homeward gait had lulled her half asleep in the saddle, but she was roused by the summons of a familiar voice.

"Dame Claire!" Father Kendall hurried from the front of the church. "The Peterson baby . . . I've been praying that everything . . ."

So weary and discouraged she could not trust herself to speak without crying, Claire merely shook her head.

The priest crossed himself, compassion transforming his kind face to a mask of grief for a loss he would never truly understand. "And Helen?"

Claire let out a hard breath. "We lost her, too."

"I think she expected it. She asked for the last rites yesterday, and I administered them." The priest crossed himself again and murmured a brief prayer, then looked up at her with compassion. "You mustn't take it so personally, my child. Women and children often die in childbirth, no matter what efforts any midwife or healer might make to save them, or how we would all wish it otherwise."

"I know that, but not all of them have to die. Not these." Claire ran a shaking hand over her eyes. "Forgive, me, Father, but the Peterson baby might never have fallen ill, nor would his mother, if only Beta had listened when I begged her to wash her hands and cleanse her instruments between birthings."

The priest frowned. "I do not understand."

Too angry to guard her tongue, Claire spoke the truth without thought of the consequences. "Three days ago, Beta delivered Alice Lovell of a stillborn son. Alice died shortly thereafter, of childbed fever. From there, Beta went straight to the Petersons' to attend Helen's delivery. Ardis Peterson said that Beta's clothing and instruments, even the knife she used to bleed Helen, was still caked with Alice's blood. Beta never even washed her hands. She delivered the baby, then cut the cord with that same filthy knife, then left mother and baby in the appearance of good health." Claire closed her eyes, suppressing a mild wave of nausea. "Neither mother nor child had been ill, but within twelve hours, both had come down with fever."

"An unfortunate coincidence, perhaps," the priest offered, "but only a coincidence."

"No," Claire stated emphatically. "Does not the Holy Writ command those attending the sick to cleanse themselves before touching those who are not unclean? Not to mention those who have come in contact with the dead?" Claire fixed a dark look on the priest. "I am convinced, Father, that disease and infection can be spread by the mingling of blood, even in tiny amounts, and sometimes by contact alone. And I am not alone in this. Many of Nonna's ancestors believed the same thing and recorded it in their journals."

"Their journals?" Father Kendall's eyebrows fairly

lifted off his forehead. "They left journals, and you have read them?"

Blast. She'd said far too much. "Aye. I've read them. There is wisdom there, Father, generations of it that can benefit our village. But not if ignorant, stubborn people like Beta close their minds to the very possibility that such wisdom exists."

Father Kendall frowned. "Take care, good lady. I know Dame Beta well. Like all of us, she has her weaknesses, but she is not evil. Frightened, perhaps, but not evil. She would not willingly harm the women and children she works so hard to save."

"Then why would she not listen to me, at least try what I suggested?" Claire was beyond caring what the priest, or anyone else, for that matter, thought of her. "She acted as if I'd asked her to dip her hands in devil's blood, instead of merely wash them. It makes no sense."

Father Kendall looked anxiously from side to side. "You're tired, my child. Come inside and let me prepare some food and drink for you." He reached for the reins. "We can talk in private."

"I know you mean well, Father, but food and drink can be of no help for this." Straightening, she pulled the reins from his grasp. "And neither can talk. It's gone beyond that. Something must be done."

"I'll speak to Beta," he promised. "Give me a day or so, to catch her at an opportune moment. Perhaps she'll listen to me." He made the sign of the cross at Claire. "Until then, I would ask that you pray for her with all your heart."

At Claire's look of surprise, the priest exhorted, "If, in fact, she has unwittingly endangered the lives of those entrusted to her care, then hers will be a heavy burden to bear. I would expect you, as a woman and a healer, to help her carry that burden. And to pray that the Holy Spirit will convict her of the truth.'' The shy, rumpled little man looked straight through to her soul. ''Pray not in anger, Claire, but in love. And in mourning for the grief she will bear.''

Stricken, Claire nodded. ''For what it's worth, Father, I shall do as you ask.''

''Then God will hear you.''

Unconvinced, Claire turned her mare toward home. It would take a miracle to change Beta's mind, and Claire was hardly one to believe in miracles.

''Oh, Dame Claire,'' the priest called after her, prompting her to rein her mare to a stop. ''I'm expecting the bishop's monthly report any day. I'm certain he'll send along the letter we requested with it.'' He trotted up beside her, his tone dropping. ''It occurred to me that perhaps we should have a sample of Palmer's handwriting. Do you think you could find one?''

''I don't know.'' Claire considered. ''I haven't seen any of Palmer's papers among Nonna's belongings, but perhaps there might be something stored away. Or perhaps some papers in the studio.''

''It was just a thought,'' the priest said.

''And a good one.'' Claire had another idea. ''I could, though, get a sample from him. Assuming he can write.''

''He can write. All the Freemans are literate.'' He nodded. ''I'll come to see you as soon as I've talked to Beta. Or gotten the letter.'' The priest made the sign of the cross. ''May the Lord keep you and lead you to all truth. In the name of the Father and the Son and the Holy Spirit.''

''That's one prayer,'' Claire confessed wearily, ''to which I can say a hearty amen.''

She entered the compound some time later to find Palmer measuring for the new gates. He took one look at her and eased down from the pilaster at the base of the wall. "Are you all right?" Without asking, he reached up and pulled her from the saddle into his arms.

"Stop that," she chided irritably as he set her to her feet. "It's scarcely five weeks since your surgery. You have no business lifting anything heavier than a hammer for at least another week."

"No harm done." He grew unnaturally still, as if sensing some unseen danger. "But you . . . you look as if you've been dragged from Canterbury to Constantinople. What happened?"

He was so close, and so tall. Claire wasn't accustomed to men who were so much taller than she.

She turned her face from his. "I'd rather not talk about it."

"You lost a patient," he said softly. "I'd know that look anywhere. Mother was the same way. She never got used to losing them."

His clear perception sent a chill straight through her. How could he have known, unless . . . ?

"I lost them both," she heard herself say. "Mother and child."

"I'm sorry, Claire." The words were simple but heartfelt, melting through her thin shell of reserve.

No. She would not let him see her cry.

Claire pulled free of him and ran all the way to the house. Only when she was safely in her room with the door locked did she allow herself to fall into bed and shed bitter tears.

Why did he have to be so kind? she wondered as she drifted into exhausted slumber. She could deal with things so much more easily if he wasn't so kind.

*   *   *

Two more days passed before she came up with a reasonable excuse to ask Palmer to write something.

The sun was almost directly overhead when she found him working in the unwalled shed that sheltered the forge. Palmer had repaired the waterwheel that drove the bellows, and with every watery turn, the furnace belched white-hot flame onto the long, thin strip of glowing steel he had folded and now was hammering back into a single unit. A second strip of steel lay across the lip of the forge.

"Why do you fold it like that?" Claire asked, more than a little curious.

"It's a secret technique that originated in the Far East," Palmer explained without missing a hammer stroke. "In Hungary, I healed a yellow-skinned blade-smith from the islands beyond China where weapons have been made this way for centuries. The man had no money to pay me, so he taught me the secrets of his art." He inspected the now-fused strip of glowing steel. "The more folds, the more resilient the blade."

"And how many folds is this?"

"Forty-seven," he panted. "I'll do twice as many again before it's finished."

"Seems like an awful lot of trouble for an ordinary sword," she observed.

Palmer stopped hammering and fixed her with a dark-blue stare, perspiration dripping from his temples. "Nothing I make is ordinary. I should think you would know that by now." He plunged the fused blank into a deep barrel of water, then shifted the second into the flames. "These are no ordinary swords. The better of the two, I mean to barter to the king."

"The king?" Claire was surprised. "And how, pray tell, do you intend to gain access to the king?"

"William Rufus hunts this forest every summer. I'll see him then." Palmer lifted the steaming steel from the barrel and looked it over carefully.

Claire was not convinced. "And what would you ask of His Majesty in exchange for your extraordinary sword?"

"Only what my family has been granted these past six centuries . . . the right to hold our lands in peace."

Claire had heard the townspeople complaining of the king's taxes on the peat they dug and the wood they took and the autumn acorns their pigs ate from the New Forest. Until William the Conqueror, the inhabitants of these parts had paid no tariffs for nature's bounties. Now, His Majesty's verderers wanted money at every turn. At Nonna's instruction, Claire had paid the fees. "What makes you think the king will even grant you an audience, much less agree to your bargain? Everyone knows he's a harsh and unjust man."

"Aye," Palmer responded confidently. " 'Tis said he loves nothing and no one, but I know better. Our king loves an elegant blade. The one I make for him will put his others to shame."

Claire had little doubt it would. The combination of Palmer's artistry and this secret technique should produce the finest weapon in Christendom. But Claire had other matters to attend.

The unnatural flames of the forge illuminated the sweat that glistened on Palmer's bare chest and arms.

By glory, but he had filled out in the past few weeks! She hadn't realized how much until just this moment, seeing him with his tunic peeled to his narrow waist, his broad shoulders rippling, and the muscles in his arms corded with effort as he folded the red-hot steel back onto itself and began to hammer it.

The smell of burning charcoal mingled with a hint

of aging leather and the sharp, erotic scent of a healthy man hard at work. Claire had almost forgotten that smell. She stood watching him for long seconds.

A woman could do worse for a husband, she thought with an unexpected stab of desire.

Then she remembered her purpose for coming here.

"Palmer," she called over his hammering and the splash, creak, and rumble of the waterwheel that drove the bellows. "You look as if you're about to melt." She lifted the tray. "I thought you might need a cool drink."

Palmer nodded and thrust the red-hot blade into a bucket of water. "Good idea!" To her disappointment, he drew a sooty towel from the rafters and swabbed himself dry before pulling his tunic back into place.

Claire made for a nearby rose arbor. Setting the tray on the bench beside her, she watched Palmer fold his long limbs to sit on the opposite bench. He seemed too large for this sheltered space, but the dappled shade offered welcome relief from the heat of the forge.

As if on cue, a cool breeze set loose a shower of tiny rose petals all around them. Claire picked up the pitcher and poured. "Here you are, sir, complete with a garnish of rose petals."

"Thank you," he rasped, his voice harsh from smoke. He drank deeply, then opened his eyes to peer at her from over the mug. After another gulp, he lowered the vessel. "None for you?"

"I had some before I came." Claire prayed she could pull this off. Nervous, she took the mug from his hand and refilled it. "There. And there's plenty more. I kept the pitcher cooling in the spring all night."

"Most considerate. Again, I thank you." He fixed her with a pointed look. "And to what do I owe the honor of these kind attentions?"

Claire did her best to remain casual, but her blasted cheeks gave her away. "In truth, I've come to ask you a favor."

"Ah. A favor." Palmer took another long draught. "And would that favor have anything to do with the ink, quill, and paper on the tray?"

Claire felt herself coloring in earnest. "Actually, yes." He'd seen right through her. How much of the truth should she tell him?

If he knew why she was asking for the sample, though, he might refuse or try to disguise his handwriting.

"Nonna has been struggling to remember names from your family. I thought perhaps . . ." She swallowed heavily. "If you could write down the names and relationships, as best you remember them, perhaps I could help her remember who she wishes to tell me about." That much was true enough. "She gets so frustrated, trying to remember. I hate to see her that way."

"I do, too." Palmer glanced at the pen and paper. "Was there some reason you wanted me to do this now, or might I take some time with it?"

She knew he suspected something. "Take your time, if you wish. No hurry."

He folded the paper, then tucked it, along with the vial of ink and the quill, into the small poke tied to his belt. "Fine, then." Palmer rose. "I'll give it some thought and hand over the list when I'm done."

And how long would *that* be? she wondered.

Ah, well. At least he'd agreed to do it.

He handed her the mug. "Thank you for the drink, Claire."

"Not at all."

Why hadn't she said she needed the list right away? Claire fumed inwardly.

Because he'd suspected something, that's why, her inner self argued back. He might never give her the list. Now she'd probably have to find something written by Palmer before he left for the Crusade, after all.

That meant that changes would have to be made. She couldn't search thoroughly the way things were now. The secret entrance to the underground tunnels and archives was in Nonna's bedchamber. To gain unrestricted access to the tunnels and their secrets, Claire would have to swap rooms with her good-mother.

She carried the tray back into the kitchen, where Ardra had just taken two fresh loaves of bread from the oven on the wooden baking paddle.

"If you can spare a minute, Ardra," she said, "I could use a little help."

"Of course, Dame Claire." Ardra slid the rounded loaves onto the tabletop, then stood the paddle beside the oven. "I'm done in the kitchen, for now."

"Good." Claire took one last look out the back door to make sure Palmer was still at the forge. Then she set her plan into motion. "My room is larger than Nonna's. I'd like to swap chambers with her, so she'll have the morning sun and more space to sit in her chair and look out the window."

Ardra tucked her chin. "Shall we move the beds, too?" Clearly, the prospect daunted her.

"No. The beds are almost identical. We'll move only the smaller furniture, then transfer the bedding and linens. That should be enough."

"Very good." She thought for a moment. "Perhaps it would be better if I took Dame Nonna to a shady spot in the garden until we're done. I'd hate to confuse her."

"Ah, Ardra," Claire said with a smile, "if the rest

of you was as big as your dear, darling heart, this house couldn't hold you.''

Ardra blushed, then hastened to Nonna's room to prepare her for an afternoon in the shade of the garden.

Claire was close behind her, mentally calculating how she could most easily make the transfer of clothing and furniture.

From this night on, Nonna's secrets would be hers to protect. And as soon as everyone else was abed, Claire would go hunting in the archives. Surely she would find something the real Palmer Freeman had written.

The sun had long since set when Claire crept from her bed and listened at the door of what used to be Nonna's room. She lifted the latch with painstaking slowness and crept into the darkened workroom. Ardra, exhausted from the labors of moving, slept quiet and still on the cot near the door to the east bedchamber, her breathing deep and even.

Step by cautious step, Claire tiptoed past her and listened at the bedroom door. Nonna was snoring away in her room, just as Claire had hoped.

Once she had regained the security of the west bedchamber, Claire gingerly slid the bolt into place, then looked for the third time toward the studio. The clerestory windows had been dark for more than an hour. After working all day at the forge, Palmer should be soundly sleeping by now, too. She closed the curtains, then felt along the deep sill for the lamp and flint she had left there.

Three strikes, and the lamp was lit. Despite its diminutive size, the small clay vessel held enough oil to keep burning for almost four hours. That should be time enough to find what she was looking for.

Just to be on the safe side, though, she lit a candle

and set it on the far side of the bed, then stuffed a spare into her pocket.

Claire carried the lamp to the head of the bed. She had found none of Palmer's papers at all in the trunk and dresser she and Ardra had emptied, then moved to the other room. Nor had she come upon anything when she'd searched the workroom and kitchen, claiming to have lost a precious needle.

That left only the secret cubbyhole and the subterranean dark to be explored. Claire prayed she'd find what she was looking for in the secret compartment behind the headboard. For though she had made several trips to the archives before Palmer had arrived, those trips had been in the daytime. She had no desire to go creeping about all alone down there at night.

Unfortunately, the only contents hidden behind the headboard were the same journals that had been there when Nonna first revealed the hiding place. The pages held many references to Palmer and his father, but no mementos had been tucked between the leaves. Claire checked through the journal she had taken over for Nonna, then closed the secret cubby and stuffed the wad of wool back into the leg of the headboard.

Like it or not, she would have to search the archives, and she would have to do it at night. She dared not chance Palmer's noticing something amiss if she closed her curtains and locked herself away during the day.

Claire stood before the fireplace for a long time before she had the courage to press the stones. As she pushed each one, she winced at even the subtle scraping of the trip stones, but when the slab began to rumble open, she would have sworn anyone within a mile could hear it.

She feigned a coughing fit to cover the sound, but when the racket was finally finished, she listened and discovered that the house lay in peaceful silence, undisturbed.

By the wavering light of the clay lamp, she descended the dark, eerie stair.

It's just a stairway, she told herself. And just some tunnels at the bottom. There are no ghosts. No demons. No villains waiting to attack her. No dragons lurking in the shadows to devour her.

Step by step, heartbeat by hammering heartbeat, she made her way down to the tunnel below.

At last, the stairway ended. She should have worn slippers. The floor of the stone corridor felt cold as ice on her bare feet, and she could see her breath.

Claire closed her eyes and reviewed the pattern of the garden paths that were a map of the hidden tunnels.

You can do this, she told herself. Think. Breathe slowly. In. Out. Stay calm. You know the way.

Sure enough, she managed to find the entrance to the archives with only one false turn. Standing in front of the formidable wall, she took a deep breath and pushed the sequence of stones as Nonna had taught her to do.

With a click that sounded loud as a clap of thunder to her sensitive ears, the enormous stone panel swung open. Claire drew it almost closed behind her, then set about exploring for something, anything, that could be identified as Palmer Freeman's handwriting.

Shelf after shelf, scroll after scroll, book after book, she searched in vain.

At least she was finding out just what the archives did contain, and where things were. But she found no sign of school papers, poems, childish drawings, or keepsakes. It seemed this archive was meant to house only the working library of the household and the chronicles of Nonna's people.

Claire had inspected the contents of all the shelves but one when the lamp began to flicker. She looked into the reservoir and saw, to her horror, that no oil remained.

"Don't you dare go out," she murmured in desperation, fumbling in her pocket for the candle. "Stay," she commanded, careful not to breathe on the fragile flame.

Her fingers closed on the candle. Just one more second. The candlewick was only inches from the flame when the light quavered, then went out. "No!" she cried, far louder than she intended.

She made a frantic effort to revive the glowing red ember, but succeeded only in putting it out for good.

Standing there, she felt the darkness, black as the breath of hell, close in all around her.

She wanted to scream, run, but part of her said she must stay calm.

You are safe here, she told herself, but she didn't believe it. Take your time. Move slowly. You can feel your way back. You don't have to have the light.

Claire forced her rapid breathing to slow. With shaking hands, she felt her way to the massive door.

She had made it that far. At last, she was outside.

Slowly, deliberately, she leaned against the door until it clicked loudly shut, causing her to jump.

Just peel one turnip at a time, her mother's voice reminded her.

"You are safer here than upstairs," Nonna had told her.

Claire slid her hand across the rough stone until she felt the side wall.

Follow that until the corner, then turn left.

Sure enough, she made the first turn.

Good. Good.

Now follow that until—

Far away, she heard an ominous scrape of stone.

Every hair on Claire's body rose.

Terrified, she pressed herself against the wall. It couldn't be Nonna. The door to the bedchamber was securely bolted.

A cold current of air sent a chill straight to Claire's bones.

Dear God! Who was down here in the dark? Or what?

Was that a footstep, or had she imagined it?

Again, she forced her breathing to a calmer pace.

Should she run for it? Hope she could find her way and make it up the stairs before whoever, or whatever, it was caught her?

She could go back into the archives and lock the door, but how long would it take to find the trip-stones without a light? Even if she did manage to get inside and lock the door behind her, then what? She'd be trapped, and no one would know where to look for her.

Claire slid into a tight ball, her back to the stone, and wished with all her might that she had never left her bed.

Then she heard it: a footstep, not a light one, and close.

She held her breath, her heart hammering against her ribs.

She could feel it coming in the darkness, something big. Something stealthy.

And then it bumped right into her—something huge!

With a bone-rattling scream, she leapt for her life.

"What the—!" a rasping growl exploded, even as two powerful arms struggled for a hold on her.

Claire kicked, bit, and flailed away with all her

might, but the grunting monster held her fast around her middle.

"Stop, you rabid little vixen, before you kill us both!"

She managed to land several more blows before she realized she'd heard that voice before.

"Palmer?" Claire went limp.

"Yes, it's Palmer," he snapped. "Who did you think it was?"

"A monster!" she blurted out. Relief, swift and sudden, drained all the fight from her. To her horror, she began to laugh and couldn't stop.

It wasn't funny. Palmer had frightened her almost to death, and she had doubtless done him harm. But she couldn't stop laughing.

Instead of chiding her, he scooped her, now boneless and bordering on hysteria, into his arms. "Shh, shh, shh," he soothed. "It's all right. No one's going to hurt you."

Just as inexplicably as it had come, Claire's laughter turned to tears. She curled against his hard chest and wept with relief and anger.

"You frightened me half to death," she gasped between sobs, landing an ineffectual blow to his shoulder. "I could kill you, you beast, sneaking up on me in the dark like that."

"I frightened *you*?" A deep chuckle rumbled through his chest. "More the other way round, I should think." He reached the stair and began to climb, his pace slowing perceptibly. "I thought you were a midnight marauder, someone who'd stumbled into the tunnels and was creeping about with larceny in mind."

She felt him tuck his chin, his breath warm on her hair.

"Why in blazes didn't you have a light?"

"I did." Her tears had stopped, but now her breath was catching in her throat. "But I was . . . so interested in what I was . . . reading in the archives . . . that I forgot about the time . . . and it went out."

"The archives?" Palmer stopped, his head level with the hearth. His voice hardened. "How did you know about the archives?"

Suddenly, Claire felt so weary she couldn't keep her eyes open. "Nonna showed me, when she handed the chronicles over to me."

"She trusted you with the chronicles?"

"With all her secrets." Claire was half-asleep already when he hitched her up in his arms to shift the burden of her weight. Instantly, she realized he had just carried her up a full flight of stairs. "Put me down," she grumbled. "I thought I told you not to carry anything heavy."

"I think that belly punch you landed did far more damage than carrying you. Still . . ." He lowered her feet to the step beside him, his wry smile barely visible in the frail light of the candle she'd left burning on the far side of the room.

Owing to the cramped stairway, she found herself all but smashed against him. She gave him a nudge. "Move along, then. You're in my way."

Again, he did as she demanded, but the amused smile on his face said he did it only because he wished to, not because she'd wanted him to.

Claire struggled from the opening onto the bedroom floor, still unsteady on her feet.

"Careful," Palmer murmured, sweeping her into his arms again. "You've had enough excitement for tonight. Can't have you falling, can we?"

He pulled the covers back and set her on the bed.

Gently, he drew them back over her thin night rail and leaned close to tuck her in.

For a moment, she thought he might kiss her. And for a moment, she wanted him to.

Instead, he murmured softly, "I see you've taken over Mother's room, as well. And how does she feel about that, I wonder?"

"Why, you . . . !" Humiliated, Claire reached back to slap the smile from his face, but Palmer caught her wrist in time to stop her. "Temper, temper," he mocked. And then, with a grin, he turned and disappeared back into the depths.

Claire glared after him, fuming, for several moments before she realized what had just happened.

He knew! The tunnels. The archive. He knew it all, every secret.

"Each building has access to the tunnels," Nonna had said.

Palmer must have heard her down there and come to investigate . . .

Claire sat bolt upright in bed, in the grip of a cold sweat.

No one would know about the tunnels . . . no one but the real Palmer Freeman.

TEN

Palmer closed the panel leading from the tunnels to the studio, then crossed to his bed. As he lay down, the muscles to the right of his navel sent out a dull reminder of Claire's belly punch.

He couldn't help but laugh.

The woman had cut him open, rummaged around in his guts with those large, capable hands of hers to rid him of three years' agony. She'd saved his life—no doubt about it—then sewed him back up as neat as a lady's sampler, only to turn around five weeks later and attack him like a wildcat in the dark.

Not that he could blame her. Palmer was as comfortable in the tunnels without light as with it; he'd grown up playing there, dreaming of dragons and kings. But to Claire, suddenly left without light in the unfamiliar maze . . . little wonder she'd been terrified.

He shouldn't laugh. It wasn't funny, really. But when he thought about the sound she'd made when he'd stumbled upon her in the passageway . . .

Both of them had jumped a mile, but she had come down fighting. Teeth, nails, flailing feet . . . What a scrapper! Palmer started with a rumbling chuckle, then let it roll into a belly laugh that ached where Claire had hit him, but was well worth the pain.

By glory, he couldn't even remember the last time he'd "tumped over his tickle box," as Nonna used to call it.

When at last the laugh subsided, he let out a deep breath and shook his head.

Interesting woman, Claire. There was something about her . . .

Palmer flashed on the seductive mixture of fresh herbs and stale fear her skin had radiated when he'd held her close and carried her. She had struck him even as she'd clung to him, still shaking from her desperate efforts to save herself.

A man could do worse than a woman like Claire. With those big bones of hers, she could probably spit out a dozen children without so much as a fare-thee-well. And she was devoted to Nonna. Intelligent. Useful. Strong. And very much a woman, if he was any judge.

A stab of desire knifed through him just as sharply as it had in her bedchamber. By all the sin in Christendom, how he'd wanted to devour her there in her bed, with her face all flushed and framed by a corona of curls. Instead of covering her up, he'd wanted to rip off her thin rail and taste the hidden places underneath, then bury himself inside her until neither of them could make a fist.

Just the thought was enough to swell Palmer's manhood to painful proportions.

Blessed Saint Jude, but it had been a long time since he'd even thought of bedding a woman, much less had one.

But if he consummated their fraudulent marriage, the union would become binding. That wouldn't be fair to

Claire, tying her to a man who could not stay. He could not—*would* not—drag her and his mother into the shame of what he'd done.

He felt a shifting, huge and silent, as the hourglass of his life turned over yet again. From this moment, his every heartbeat marked a falling grain of sand, and when the sand had emptied, he would have to go.

Palmer tried to content himself with the fact that he could, at least, insure Nonna's rights to their holdings before he left. But he would have to work faster, for grain by grain, the sand was falling.

The next morning, Claire did something she had never done before in her adult life. When Ardra came to wake her, she did not rise to unlock the bolt. Instead, she announced through the door that she wasn't getting up today. Then she pulled her pillow over her head and slept for three more hours. When she woke to the mid-morning chorus of insects from the surrounding gardens and trees, she felt so logy she could barely speak.

But reality would not be slept away. Lying there, her covers thrown back and her nightclothes damp and clinging from the day's heat, she stretched, yawned hugely, then opened tear-swollen eyes to stare at the ceiling.

He really was Palmer Freeman. There could be no other explanation.

And if he was telling the truth about his identity, he might well be telling the truth about the marriage.

He had said he wouldn't cast her out, but . . .

Don't think about that now, she told herself. What will be, will be. Worrying won't change a thing.

Claire moaned and rolled onto her side, but the day had grown too warm to go back to sleep. So she sighed and sat up, her bare feet dangling over the polished floor.

Dirty feet, she observed upon looking at them.

One turnip at a time.

First, a good scrubbing. Then she would sort things out.

Stiff as an old woman, she slid down off the bed and unbolted the door and opened it. "Ardra," she called.

It was Nonna who answered. She had been sitting in her room, but at the sound of Claire's voice, she came out immediately. "Hello, there," she greeted Claire impartially. "And how might we help you today, my dear?"

A flicker of rejection stung Claire, but she managed a smile. "It's me, Nonna. It's Claire." She gave Nonna a nice, long hug.

"And what a sweet girl you are, to give an old lady such a nice hug." Still, there was no hint of recognition in Nonna's bright blue eyes.

Ah, well. Not one of the good days, but not as bad as it might be. At least she was talking.

Claire decided that perhaps the Saint-John's-wort might be helping. In the month since she'd put Nonna on a substantial dose, there had been far fewer episodes of silence or outbursts of fear or disorientation. "I'm going to take a bath," she told Nonna. "Would you like to join me?"

"No." Nonna looked back to her chair. "I have my chair here, and it's such a lovely day. I think I'll just sit for a while."

"Fine." Claire hugged her again, wondering even as she did how long it would be before Nonna stopped recognizing her altogether.

She had put on a robe, gathered her cleansing balms,

and was on her way to the bathhouse by way of the kitchen when Ardra came muttering in from outside, her basket laden with cabbage. ". . . think I've nothing better to do than stand around and watch him watch Master Palmer work, he's got another think coming, I can—" Seeing Claire, she stopped in her tracks and colored. "Forgive me, Dame Claire. I didn't know you were up."

Claire cocked her head at the usually placid apprentice. "And what has you so upset this morning?"

"Hmmph." Ardra set the basket down, hard, on the ledge behind the trough of running water. "It's that redheaded lummox, Roderick, come to see Master Palmer." Her young voice thickened with anger as she plopped the cabbage into the running water, tossed in a bunch of carrots from underneath, and attacked the hapless roots with a wood-bristled brush. "Us promised all these years, and everybody in the village knows it. Yet all of a sudden, he treats me like a pest, a little girl who might as well be his baby sister."

She scrubbed even harder. "Well, I'll show him. Why settle for a boy, when there are real men in the world? Mum's had plenty of offers for me and Corly, that she has. She'd have no trouble findin' me a husband who's twice the man as Little Red."

Ardra wagged the dripping brush in Claire's direction. "Let him have his hussy, whoever she is." She attacked what was left of the carrots. "If that's the way things are, no decent woman will give him a second look, least of all, me."

Claire looked into the water and saw that Ardra had rubbed away a good bit of flesh along with the dirt. "I think those are clean, now."

Ardra glanced down and laughed aloud at what she found. "Oh, would ye look at that—cleaned down to nothin'.'' She shot Claire a wry smile. "Sorry."

Ardra fixed her with a narrow look of assessment. "Are ye feelin' all right, then, Dame Claire?" Her gaze paused only briefly at Claire's puffy eyelids and bruised wrists.

Claire recognized that look: She used it herself when evaluating a patient. Already, Ardra had a healer's eye.

"I'm quite well, thank you. Just needed to catch up on my sleep." She pulled her sleeves down to cover the dark marks that had bloomed on her wrists overnight.

Ardra fished the dripping carrots—what was left of them—from the water and laid them on the channeled lip of the trough to drain. "You'll be havin' a bath, then, eh? Shall I come along and help ye?"

"No. I'd rather you stay with Nonna. She seems a little confused today." Claire nodded to the squash and beans still in the basket. "Anyway, it looks as if you have cooking to do. I'll be fine on my own."

"As you wish, Dame Claire." Ardra paused. "But when you've done with yer bath, might we work on my letters a bit?"

"Of course." The request prompted more than a little guilt from Claire. "I'm sorry I haven't had time for lessons, lately. I'll do my best to make it up to you."

"Oh, I understand," Ardra reassured her, dumping the rest of the vegetables into the running water. "But I don't mind, really, because Dame Nonna's been helpin' me, whenever you were too busy."

"Really?" Claire hadn't even considered that Nonna might still be able to teach. "Doesn't she have trouble with her memory?"

"Not with the letters and sounds." Ardra began to wash the vegetables with her bare hands. "Only with the words, sometimes."

Now, why hadn't *she* thought of that? "You know, Ardra, I think it might be very good for Dame Nonna to help you. Why don't you set aside at least an hour every morning to work with her?"

"She does seem to like it." Ardra smiled. "You can manage without me, then?"

"Aye. For an hour or so, we'll manage somehow."

Ardra glanced away, then looked to Claire with widened eyes. "What about Master Palmer, then?"

The mere mention of his name was enough to draw Claire's eyes to the forge. She could barely make out his back in the shade and smoke of the shed. Roderick was perched on the edge of the woodbox, deep in conversation. "What about him?"

"Well." Ardra went coy. "What if Dame Nonna isn't feeling fit for a lesson?" She turned a hopeful face to Claire. "Might I ask Master Palmer, then?"

"I think not." Claire knew all too well the trouble that could come from *that.* "Master Palmer already does so much for us, what with bringing us wood for the fires and helping in the gardens. I would hate to take up more of his time. He stays very busy."

She shook her head, sympathizing with Ardra's crestfallen expression. "Until things are more settled, perhaps we shouldn't impose any further upon Master Palmer's time."

Ardra did her best to conceal her disappointment. "As ye wish, Dame Claire." She placed the freshly washed vegetables into a strainer, then removed her apron. "I'll just go and work with Dame Nonna, then."

"You do that."

Loath to put herself on display for Roderick or Palmer in her houserobe, Claire took the long way to the bathhouse, skirting the gardens. Once she was safely inside, she stripped off her robe and gratefully waded into the cool, clear water wearing only her shift.

Palmer had done a good job of patching the pool. She felt no rough spots where he had sealed the large marble tiles. Claire leaned back on the wide step that served as a seat and let the whispering water flow gently over her.

There was something so peaceful about running water.

She always felt safe and at peace here. Just beneath the deep eaves, a row of narrow windows preserved her privacy while admitting the warm, fertile afternoon breeze.

Claire closed her eyes and did her best to think of nothing, but Palmer Freeman's face kept forming in her mind. Try as she might, she couldn't erase the erotic tang of man-sweat and wood smoke his skin gave off when he'd bent so close to her face in the darkness.

For the first time in years, she felt a deep contraction of desire. But she could not allow herself to dwell on it.

If Palmer were, indeed, her husband . . . the thought caused her skin to pebble.

But Palmer said he was not her husband. If that was so, she was only tormenting herself to imagine the two of them, together. To wonder what it would feel like to be filled, again, by a man who wanted her, as her first husband had wanted her.

A kind man, her late husband had told her daily of his love and pampered her as if she were a queen, but never having loved a man since her first girlish infatuation, Claire had always wondered if her husband merely lusted for her. Not that she could fault him. Lust and kindness would have been enough, if only he had lived.

Claire shivered as the long-buried memory of heat

and need bloomed afresh with disturbing urgency. The messiness, the recklessness, the brainless animal compulsion to mate. Her husband's desire had been strong enough to ignite her own; she had often found release in his arms. But she had always felt as if part of her held back, untouched and watching.

What would it feel like to mate with a man she loved? Claire wondered.

For that matter, what would it feel like to love a man? Not a childish infatuation, but the kind of love her parents had shared, a rare and indestructible bond that survived trouble and disappointments with equal vigor.

Claire remembered well the look her parents shared, a silent bridge that said far more than mere words. Its silence spoke of absolute trust, unquestioning devotion, and a strength that transcended any and all the world could bring against it.

Would she ever feel that, in this life?

Could she feel that?

Perhaps, a deep inner voice whispered, with a man like Palmer.

Again, a contraction of desire closed deep within her, but the sound of the door opening abruptly snuffed it out.

She heard a rustle of clothing, then Palmer emerged from the vestibule stark naked.

Gloriously naked, his sooty chest and arms a stark contrast to the fine, fair skin and dark curls at his loins.

"You might have said something," he commented. "Made your presence known." He returned her frank stare with one of his own, causing his manhood to leap, then swell.

Claire knew she should turn away, but she was fascinated. How quickly his member came erect! He was bigger than her husband, his body leaner and harder.

Just as she had imagined he would be.

Her hands tingled, closing into fists as she wondered what it would feel like to caress those hard planes of muscle, then move lower . . .

To her horror, Claire heard a long, low breath escape her.

Palmer heard it, too, and smiled—a slow, hungry smile, like a starving predator who had cornered his next meal. But he did not come closer; only his eyes moved, roaming her body with silent intensity. The smile faded, and only the hunger remained.

She could stop this. A single word was all it would have taken. But Claire didn't want to stop it. For once in her life, she wanted to do what she wanted, not what she should.

Slowly, she rose, knowing her shift was completely transparent and enjoying the effect that was having on Palmer.

As she exited the pool, she picked up the leather bucket of water and the bowl of plant extracts she used to cleanse her hair and skin. "You look as if you could use a bath," she said, her voice husky.

Palmer's pupils widened, but he said nothing, made no other move, as if his stillness granted all the choices, now, to her.

Slowly, deliberately, every sensation sharpened by the invisible attraction that pulsed between them, she circled him. Then she scooped some of the soothing extract from the bowl and smeared it across the ribs on his back, then his arms and shoulders.

His flesh quivered at her touch.

She rinsed him, but the tepid water from the bucket did nothing to quench his desire.

Next, she washed his hair, marveling at its rich,

warm brown softness in her hands, and as her fingers moved against his scalp, he met the pressure with his own, rolling his head in silent pleasure toward her touch.

"Lean back," she whispered, and when he did, she rinsed his hair into a sleek, dark curtain that molded to his skull and the muscular cording of his neck.

He was beautiful, she realized with a growing sense of heat. Everything about him—his artist's hands, the fine, strong bones of his face, the shape of his skull, the economical curve of his taut buttocks, the lean power of bone and flesh that moved his body with liquid smoothness, the crisp, clean curls on his chest and arms and legs. All of that, the vessel for a keen mind with a kind heart.

And there he stood, his raw desire held in check by sheer power of will. Strength under control; it gave her perfect freedom to act on her desires, but only because he allowed it. Claire had never even imagined anything so provocative.

She was melting inside. Never, even at the best moments of her marriage, had she felt like this.

Until proven otherwise, their marriage was valid. Why shouldn't she let him be a husband, indeed?

He wanted it; his body had betrayed that with a look. Now she wanted him, as she had never wanted anything like this before. And she meant to have him, even if lust was all that he could give.

It had been enough, before.

Claire moved closer to reach around him, her abdomen pressing against his buttocks, and he let out a gasp of pleasure that sent an answering throb straight through her. She moved closer still, her breasts against his back.

Again, he moaned.

She could feel his heart beating at a pace as frantic as her own.

Slowly, methodically, she began to smooth the unguent onto the laddered plates of his stomach, easing away the grime and soot of the forge. Her fingers slick with unguent, she explored the tidy hollow of his navel, then the faint ridge of scar that had healed to a narrow line. Her hands moved upward, next, to massage the crisp curls on his chest and brush against the tight peaks of his nipples.

"Lower," Palmer rasped.

The word was a command, one Claire had wanted to act upon, but feared he would think too bold. At his request, though, she gladly did as both of them wanted, spreading the slick unguent into the base of his member, then moving up along its length.

It was more than any man could stand.

With a feral groan, Palmer turned abruptly and drew her roughly to him. He kissed her, hard, his lips as hot as her own, his tongue probing, urgent as the growing warmth of their desire heated the damp fabric of her shift.

Suddenly, that single, fragile garment seemed too constricting to be borne. As if he had read her mind, Palmer tore his mouth from hers and watched with burning eyes as his hands bared her shoulders, then peeled her wet skin bare.

Claire stepped out of her shift, and Palmer grasped her bare buttocks, drawing her hard up against him for a savage kiss. Instinctively, she wrapped her legs around his hips to draw him closer. Heat met heat, and a shudder rippled through them both.

Palmer staggered backward to the sturdy table where Claire had left her robe, combs, and drying cloth. Kissing, tasting, testing with his teeth as he moved, he sat her atop the table, then raked the objects to the floor and laid her down before him. He ran his hands up and down her ribs, then cupped the heavy fullness of her breasts, kissing and biting gently at the tender flesh.

Claire thought that she would die from pleasure.

Then his hand moved lower, delving into the heat and wetness, making her even hungrier for what was yet to come. And then he found a hidden pearl of desire her husband had never touched. While his lips and teeth brought her breasts to exquisite torture, Palmer rolled the pearl of her desire between his fingertips and released an earth-rending jolt of ecstasy that lifted Claire's back from the table. Oblivious to all else, she called his name and cried out.

Her hand found his manhood and drew it to the emptiness that wept to be filled. "Do it," she ground out, panting. "Take me."

Palmer raised up over her like some towering god of vengeance, his blue eyes almost black, and thrust into her, hot and hard. Claire arched against him, her hands grasping the edge of the table so she could meet him, thrust for thrust.

Lost in the desperate spiral of need, she felt her pulse throbbing in her neck and heard her own breath as ragged and urgent as his own.

Harder and harder, he lunged inside her, until Claire was crying out with each thrust, lifted to the brink of release, and then tumbled over into boneless, panting satisfaction.

Palmer let loose with a final groan of fulfillment, then went still, his feet planted wide and his back arched away from the intimate joining that united them yet.

Claire closed her eyes. Was it real? Had it truly happened?

Then reason reared its ugly head.

What had she done? And what would happen now? Had she lost her mind?

At the very best, Palmer would think her a wanton. At the worst, he would probably think she had deliberately seduced him in order to force the marriage on him.

Claire felt him withdraw, and her heart sank.

What a fool she was. Such pleasure was just another of life's dangerous gifts, one she would undoubtedly pay for, and dearly.

Whatever could she have been thinking? Better never to have tasted such pleasure, than to lose it and forever mourn the loss.

"Oh, God, Claire," Palmer said, his voice shaky. He laid a hand on her side. "I never should have let that happen."

Claire pressed her lips together, tight, and rolled away from him. "Not that, Palmer. Anything but that." Naked and vulnerable, she curled into a ball as shame washed over her. But she would not cry.

"Don't do that. Don't turn away from me." Palmer moved close beside her and drew her, still curled protectively, to his chest. "God knows, I enjoyed what just happened. And I wanted it. I can't pretend I didn't want it." He rocked her gently in his arms, smoothing her hair. "What am I saying? It was transcendent, spiritual . . . amazing. But you deserve more than I can give you. So much more."

"Oh, spare me," Claire said bitterly, scalded by the false nobility he hid behind. "I had thought you better than that, Palmer. At least more honest."

She wanted to be in her own bed, decently clothed and covered. With the door locked.

Claire could feel the tension in Palmer's arms.

"You deserve a husband who can give you his whole heart, his whole life." Palmer's voice thickened. "I haven't a whole heart to offer, Claire."

"And you think I *do*?" She shook her head. "You know nothing about me, Palmer. Nothing." She sat up, oblivious now to the fact that both of them were naked. "You have no idea of the trials that life has dealt me, nor the losses that have torn *my* heart away, piece by piece."

"No. I don't know." Palmer ran his fingers through his hair. "But I do know that I cannot stay here." There was agony in his eyes, and pain hardened his mouth, deepening the lines that bracketed it. "I cannot stay." His features softened. "You and Nonna managed well enough without me. You shall again."

"How can you say that?" she demanded.

"I can say it because it's true." He let out an impatient breath. "Claire, I never meant to come back here. If Little Red hadn't brought me—"

"If Little Red hadn't brought you," she said through anger-locked teeth, "you'd be dead right now, as Nonna thought you were. Then I would be a proper widow."

Palmer pulled back. "Mother thought that I was dead?"

Claire couldn't look at him. She was too angry—angry at herself, at Nonna, and at Palmer. She lunged free of him and grabbed her robe. Only when she was covered did she have the courage to face him. "Yes, she thought you were dead."

God, he was handsome, standing there with the marks of her skin still ruddy on his own.

She sank to the bench, her head in her hands. "A dying man came to us one night who said he'd fought with you in Hungary. Nonna wouldn't let me anywhere near him, but I looked through the crack that night and saw her in an agony of grief. The next morning, the man was dead, and Nonna presented me with a letter that she said he had brought her . . . a letter from you.''

''I know about the letter. After you mentioned it, I asked Father Kendall. He told me everything.''

Claire looked up in shock. True, she had mentioned it, but why would the priest tell Palmer the rest? Claire had thought she could trust Father Kendall, but obviously, he'd broken her confidence—and Nonna's.

''So you know all about the proxy marriage.'' Suddenly she was tired. She felt old, used up, weary of words. But words were the only weapons left to her. ''At first, I fought the idea. But Nonna seemed so determined to have me accept, that at last she wore me down.''

''And why do you think she was so insistent?'' Palmer asked, his face haggard.

''Probably because she thought you were dead,'' Claire surmised. ''Without a marriage, she had no way to assure that I would stay and care for her as I had promised.''

''Would you have left her?'' His question was cold.

''No!'' Claire leapt to her feet and began pacing, her bare feet smacking the marble tiles. ''I never would have left her.'' She turned on him in challenge. ''And I have no intention of leaving her, now or ever. What passes between you and me is irrelevant. I will honor my promise to Nonna, regardless.''

''Good.'' Palmer nodded, his features softening. ''So you have said.''

''And what about us?''

He picked up her drying towel and wrapped it around him. ''I do not know.''

''What happened between us happened, Palmer.''

No longer angry, she faced him now, head-on. "Don't pretend that it didn't." Palmer opened his mouth to speak, but she cut him off with, "And don't insult me with that 'you deserve better' offal."

She stepped to within a yard of him, her arms crossed. "Something happened between us, here. Something huge. Something special. Face it. I'm willing to."

He glared back at her, his blue eyes guarded. "And?"

"And"—she frowned, at the limit of her patience— "what do you plan to do about it?"

"How should I know?" he exploded. "What do you want me to do?"

"Make an honest woman out of me!" she shouted back without even thinking. "Or are you afraid to marry me?"

"Blast, woman," he roared, his tanned face darkening with rage. "Haven't you heard a thing I've said? Would you tie yourself to a man who will only leave you?" He grasped her upper arms as if to shake her. "I said you deserve more, and I meant it!"

Claire wanted him to shake her. It would give her an excuse to poke him in the eye, which she desperately wanted to do. "And what do you want to do?" she railed back at him. "Run away, as you did the last time? Leave Nonna and me to fend for ourselves? There's nothing noble about that, Palmer."

He let go of her and stepped back. Claire saw the look of betrayal in his eyes and realized, too late, that she had struck at him where he was most vulnerable. She could sense him withdrawing, turning inward.

"I'm sorry, Palmer. That was unfair. I never should have said it."

Palmer looked at her with what she could only describe as loathing. "All right, then," he said quietly. "I'll marry you for good and all, if that's what you want."

How could things have gone so wrong, so quickly? She'd wanted him to ask her, but only if he wanted her. Not like this.

Claire hadn't wanted to hurt him so deeply . . . or had she? Perhaps she had, she admitted to herself, to punish him for what he'd said.

"Did you hear me?" he asked, his expression cruel.

"Yes." Her answer was scarcely above a whisper. "Palmer . . ." She reached out to him, but he recoiled.

"I'd like for Father Kendall to solemnize the marriage as soon as possible. Since we're already technically wed, there should be no reason for delay."

"Why are you doing this?" Claire could endure anything but the cold, distant way he was looking at her.

"I'm doing it for my mother," he said without emotion. "And, strange as it may seem, for you."

Claire should have been grateful, but she wasn't. Somehow, everything was ruined. "So this will be the price for my moment's pleasure," she said to him.

"What?" He seemed genuinely surprised.

"I shall have a husband after all, but one who doesn't want me. One who will leave me one day."

Palmer closed his eyes, his face pained. "Perhaps you would prefer to be a proper widow, as you put it."

"No, Palmer." What was the use? Talk would solve nothing. He did not want her, yet he would marry her for Nonna's sake. Claire picked up the bowl of unguent. "I would not wish you dead. I would wish only that you find contentment here with us . . . or peace, within yourself."

"That won't be possible for me in this life," he said

bitterly. He bent and scooped up his discarded clothes. "But at least Nonna will be happy with this marriage. That will have to be enough for both of us." He left her to gather her scattered belongings along with her shattered hopes.

ELEVEN

Father Kendall's timing was as bad as it could possibly be. Claire had scarcely finished combing, plaiting, and binding her braids with Ardra's help when Ardra had to leave her to answer the door.

"It's Father Kendall, Dame Claire," her apprentice returned to announce. "He says he has a letter you wanted to see."

Perfect. In light of what had just happened between her and Palmer, marriage was the last thing Claire wanted to talk about. But she could not simply ask the priest to come again another day. Nothing he had discovered about the letter would change anything, for she was now certain that Palmer was who he claimed to be.

Claire neatly tied off the colorful binding at the tip of her braid. "Help me with my dress, then ask him in." She peered through the tiny diamond-shaped panes that gave onto the gardens. "Have you seen anything of Master Palmer?"

"Aye." Ardra picked up Claire's plain white kirtle and gathered it so as to slip it over Claire's head. "Master Palmer came into the kitchen, his expression black as a thundercloud, and got the axe. Said he was going to fell a tree for the gates—a big one.''

Good. He'd gone to work off his anger. That might prove convenient.

As soon as Claire was properly dressed, she turned to Ardra. "On second thought, why don't you take Father Kendall in to visit with Nonna? I need to get something from the studio before I speak with him."

"Aye, Dame Claire. As you wish." Ardra's curiosity was patent on her face, but she had the good manners not to ask what was going on.

Claire was out the kitchen door before Ardra invited the priest inside. Grateful she wouldn't have to worry about bumping into Palmer, she hurried to the studio.

Please, she prayed to no one in particular, let Palmer have already written down at least some of the names I asked for. And let me find what he's written in the studio.

When she reached the closed doors of Palmer's domain, she paused to collect herself, then knocked. "Palmer? Are you there?"

Silence.

Claire tried the mechanism and was relieved to find it unlocked.

Feeling like a thief, she slipped inside and started searching for the paper she had given Palmer. It took only minutes to inspect every logical, visible place he might have left it. Whatever he'd done with the list, he hadn't left it lying out anywhere.

Not that there were many other places he might have left it. There was no desk in the studio. No closed cabinets. No trunks. No boxes. No drawers. Palmer's spare clothing hung on hooks, but she found nothing in the pockets.

Nothing under the mattress, the pillow, or the bed linens.

The large worktable was cluttered with saws, carving implements, shavings, and sawdust, but no paper. There were, though, two substantial, irregularly shaped objects and one rounded object covered with dusty drapes on the worktable. Claire pulled one of the drapes away from the middle-sized object and was captivated by what had been hidden underneath.

It was a statue—a beautifully executed rendition of two female forms dressed in flowing fabric—one holding the other, just as the Blessed Virgin held her crucified son in the pietà at the cathedral. The woman who was being held had Nonna's face, her head curled against the other woman's shoulder. But the other figure's face had yet to be carved.

Until this moment, Claire's mind had been convinced that Palmer Freeman was, indeed, who he claimed to be. But this . . . this struck straight to her heart. Claire knew little about art, but seeing the emotion conveyed by the two figures, she was stunned by the impact of Palmer's ability and technique. He had taken a block of wood and transformed it into a representation of devotion that captured all the tenderness she and Nonna shared. And there was absolutely no doubt that the same hands that had made this statue had fashioned the eagle, the owl, and the rest of the statues she had found here those first few weeks.

Now it was her heart that told her he really *was* Nonna's son.

How horrible it must have been for Palmer to come home, suffering as he had, only to find himself a stranger to his own mother. For the first time, Claire began to understand with her emotions how much that homecoming must have hurt Palmer.

He should have been jealous of Claire. She'd have been jealous of him, if the tables had been turned. But there was no jealousy in the statue he had made. It was all compassion and tender care.

Claire looked closer and saw that the woman holding the other had large hands. She looked at her own hands and recognized that they were the model for those hands, but Palmer's rendition made them look strong, not masculine. And the sandaled feet that mercifully only peeked from the hem of the flowing carved gown were hers, too, right down to the crescent-shaped nails and the odd crook in her second toe.

Her fingers still tingling from the shock of unveiling the first statue, she pulled the cover off the figure next to it, and her heart skipped a beat.

The life-sized face on the carved head was familiar, yet not. Claire had seen herself in a looking glass often enough to recognize the strong features and resolute chin Palmer had carved, but she marveled at his romantic interpretation. She had long ago reconciled herself to the fact that she was no beauty, but the wooden face before her was beautiful, and so lifelike she almost expected it to blink. There was energy and humor in the lines of the ample, smiling mouth, and the eyes were almost alight, somehow.

How had he done that, with mere wood?

Looking at Palmer's work was like looking into his unguarded heart.

Claire sank heavily into the only chair, staring from one statue to the other.

Was this how Palmer saw her? Devoted? Tender? Kind?

Beautiful?

It made her want to weep with joy and anguish, all at once, because she knew that whatever tender feelings

Palmer might have had for her, she had extinguished this very day.

One more carving, the largest, remained covered.

This might be her last chance to see what lay hidden underneath the drape—a last look into Palmer's soul. Claire rose and drew the cloth away.

She gasped aloud.

There was no tenderness here. The wood was dark, the figures twisted in pain and rage in a jumbled scene of savage debauchery and destruction. Women, their faces contorted in terror, mouths wide open in silent screams, lifted their crucifixes as they tried in vain to shield their babies from the swords of brutal attackers— attackers who wore tunics emblazoned with the cross of the Crusader. Other women were being raped by soldiers of the Cross, their naked bodies violated even as their throats were cut. Amid pillage and burning, the elderly were trampled underfoot. It was a hideous, writhing scene straight from the bowels of hell, every detail of which burned itself into Claire's memory.

"Oh, Palmer," she breathed, tears welling in her eyes and overflowing. No wonder he claimed to have no soul, if this was the horror from which he had returned.

Nonna had said that Palmer had followed Peter the Hermit as a true pilgrim, his faith a shining, yet untried, well of idealism. To have seen this . . . Soldiers of Christ, raping, robbing, killing their own brethren . . .

Had Palmer been one of them?

Claire was soul-sick, just thinking about it.

If he had been, that would explain the depth of his anguish and guilt.

Whatever sins he might have committed, though, she was certain he'd repented. What a terrible burden to bear. Was that what drove him, what kept him from staying here with her and Nonna?

With shaking hands, she covered the living nightmare.

Claire stroked the line of Nonna's figure before covering the others.

If only she had seen this before—

"What are you doing here?" Palmer's voice, tight with anger, came from the doorway behind her.

Claire dashed the tears from her cheeks and took a shaky breath before she turned around. "I thought you were in the forest cutting trees."

"I was, but the blasted axe handle broke." He glared at her. "You still haven't answered my question. What are you doing poking about in my room?"

"I was looking for you," she said smoothly. Nothing would be served by Palmer's knowing what she'd uncovered. The last carving . . . seeing that was a violation he would likely hate her for.

Claire did her best to appear calm and collected. "Father Kendall has arrived. He brought the letter."

"Mmm." Palmer looked pointedly to the covered statues, his expression skeptical. "A simple knock would have told you I wasn't here. Why did you come in anyway?"

Claire decided that at least a little of the truth was needed. "You've seen through me. I wasn't looking for you. I was looking for a sample of your handwriting."

He regarded her through narrowed eyes. "I wondered why you asked me to write those names." Palmer frowned. "Why didn't you simply tell me the truth and ask for a sample of my writing?"

The truth had worked so far, so Claire spoke frankly.

"I wanted a natural sample, not one you made knowing I was going to look at it."

"Here, then." Palmer pulled the list of names from his pouch.

Claire did not have the courage to look at it. She read Palmer's face, instead.

He was flushed from exertion, but she saw no anger there. Only a guarded expression.

"Will you come with me," she asked, "to see what Father Kendall has discovered?"

"If that's what you want."

"Aye, it is." Claire walked past him to the door. "Even though I already know what the letter will tell us."

"You know?" He followed her into the hazy sunlight.

"The handwriting will be Nonna's," she said flatly, their footsteps crunching on the graveled pathway. "I'm convinced she cooked up the whole scheme when she thought you had been killed."

"Are you angry with her for that?" Palmer asked with more than a touch of defensiveness on his mother's behalf.

"No." Claire's pace slowed as she got closer to the house and the reckoning that waited inside. "How could I blame her for anything? She was losing her mind, and she knew it. She did what she thought she had to do."

Palmer said nothing until they reached the kitchen door. He hesitated there on the threshold. "Claire, this thing between us—"

"We don't have to sort that out today." She searched his face for some sign of forgiveness, but found none. "There will be time enough, later, to work things out."

She placed her hand on his forearm. "If, after all is said and done, freedom is what you want, I'll give you your freedom. You may leave at any time, no explanations needed. But for Nonna's sake, I would ask you to try, at least, to make our marriage work." She peered into his blue eyes. "Can you do that much, at least?"

Palmer exhaled heavily, his expression pained. "Making you my legal wife is one matter. I have no reservations about that. But promising to live here as your husband . . . that's another matter, entirely." Inner struggle darkened his eyes and deepened the creases bracketing his frown. "Claire, I never intended to come back here. I've stayed only to make certain the king doesn't steal the land out from under my mother. But once Nonna's security is assured—"

"I know," Claire interrupted softly. "I'm not asking for forever, Palmer. If the time comes when you must leave, then so be it. All I'm asking for is your best effort . . . that you'll give our marriage a decent chance, nothing more."

Something indecipherable intensified his gaze, giving Claire the impression he really did want things to work out between them.

But perhaps that was only wishful thinking on her part.

"You have my promise, then," he vowed. "I'll do my best."

"That's all anyone can ask," she answered, wondering even as she said it how hard *she* was willing to try, herself.

It was a start, at least.

"Are you ready, then?" Her question had implications far beyond the letter.

"Aye." Palmer grasped his wrists behind him, his

fingers circling the bones like manacles. "Perhaps it's just as well the priest came when he did," he said grimly. "He can marry us straightaway."

"Today?" Claire swallowed hard. She hadn't thought he'd be willing to validate the fraudulent marriage so soon.

"Today." Palmer's hard blue stare would brook no dispute.

With great misgivings, Claire entered the kitchen. She found Nonna chatting amiably with a still-flushed Father Kendall.

"Forgive me for keeping you waiting, Father," Claire said.

Ardra rose from her corner seat the moment they walked in. "Dame Claire! Father Kendall brought word from my mum. He's convinced her to let me stay here and work for another three months!"

"That's good news, Ardra," Claire answered half-heartedly. Her mind was definitely preoccupied. She watched as Palmer crossed to the empty fireplace and leaned against the mantel, obviously anxious to move on to more important matters.

If Ardra noticed the tension that had entered with them, she gave no sign. "I'm so glad that Mum's letting me stay," the girl said with conviction. "But she wants me to come home for a few days to visit." She tugged the ends of her apron strings. "May I?"

"Of course." Claire nodded toward Father Kendall. "I'm sure Father Kendall will be happy to accompany you back to the village." Noticing that the priest seemed ill at ease, she saw that Nonna was holding his hand tightly in both of her own.

He'd tried to get up when Claire came in, but Nonna wouldn't let him. She maintained a death grip on the priest's hand, compulsively rubbing over his knuckles.

As usual, Nonna ignored Palmer and greeted only Claire. "Ah, there you are, Claire, just in time for the big announcement."

"Announcement?" Claire glanced to Palmer, who seemed as puzzled as she.

Father Kendall loudly cleared his throat and tried, unsuccessfully, to reclaim his hand.

"I must confess," Nonna said, "these past few months have been most trying for me. Most trying." She shook her head. "So many nights, I've lain awake, asking God how I could go on. First, losing my husband, and now, my only son." She sighed. "Ah, how many nights I've wept." She brightened. "But then, today, as I was praying, God told me he was going to give me another child."

Nonna beamed, rubbing Father Kendall's knuckles even faster. "Well, you can imagine how confused I was. After all, I'm a widow-woman, with no husband. How could God give me a child?" She looked with adoration to Father Kendall. "Then dear Thomas arrived, and I realized that was the answer."

Thomas?

Father Kendall blanched as all eyes turned to him.

"All of a sudden, everything came clear." Nonna granted the priest a beatific smile. "God has chosen you to be the father of my baby, Thomas. Isn't that exciting?"

Father Kendall let out a strangled "Awk!" and fought vainly to get his hand away from her, his eyes bulging to such an extreme that Claire was convinced they'd pop out and plop into his lap any second.

Ardra stifled a shocked chuckle behind her hand.

Claire bit her lips to keep from laughing out loud. Served the priest right, for breaking her confidence and Nonna's!

She knew she should rescue Father Kendall, but Claire preferred to watch him squirm a little, first.

"Mother!" Palmer barked in embarrassed disbelief. He started forward to intervene, but Nonna stopped him with a glare and an emphatic pointed finger.

"Not another step, young man!" She glowered up at him. "I would remind you, sir, that you are a guest in my house." After granting Claire a brief, indulgent nod, she rounded on Palmer with a vengeance. "Up to this moment, I've tolerated your presence—not to mention your disturbing delusion that you're my dead son— but only because my daughter-in-law seems to want you here." She straightened where she sat, but would not let go of the priest despite his efforts to pry himself free of her grip. "There are limits, though, to even my hospitality. So I will caution you, young man, not to interfere in this matter. It is none of your concern."

With that, she stood up, bringing the priest to his feet with her. "Come along, Thomas. We have work to do. Babies don't just happen all by themselves."

"Dame Nonna, please!" the shocked little man implored. He turned to Claire. "Do something! She won't let go of me . . ." He looked to Palmer. "Don't just stand there, man. She's your mother. Stop her!"

Claire knew perfectly well that Nonna's proposal only *sounded* shocking; surely she wouldn't act on it. But no sooner had Claire formed the thought, than Nonna started dragging her unwilling captive toward her bedchamber.

Father Kendall did his best to stay where he was, planting his sandaled feet firmly on the rug, but Nonna easily dealt with that by stepping onto the bare floor and dragging him, rug and all, toward her lair.

"Goodness," Claire commented to everyone and no one. "I had no idea she was still so strong."

"Claire," Palmer growled, "do something!"

She hated to put an end to the fun, but Palmer seemed genuinely stymied, and Father Kendall's face reflected real panic. If someone didn't rescue the priest, and soon, he was liable to burst a blood vessel and expire on the spot.

"Oh, for heaven's sake, Thomas," Nonna scolded. "I told you it was the Lord's will, yet here you are, acting as standoffish as Palmer's father on our wedding night." Her lined face rosy with effort, she stopped tugging for a few seconds without relenting her hold. "You might cooperate at least a little, you know. It would make things much easier for both of us."

"Mother, for God's sake . . ." Flushing red as a summer rose at Nonna's tactless confession about his father, Palmer started again for his mother, but this time, it was Claire who waved him back.

"Strong-arm tactics will do no good," she said quietly. "Leave this to me."

Moving close, she addressed her good-mother. "Nonna, darling," she said calmly, "you're a little confused." She grasped Nonna's forearm and began to pry loose the fingers of one of her hands.

"I'm not confused," Nonna countered. "Why, Sarai was well past ninety when she conceived Isaac." She looked at Claire through whitened lashes. "I may be old, dear, but I haven't forgotten how to make a baby."

"I'm sure you haven't," Claire answered, at last managing to pry loose the other hand so that the shaken priest could escape to take refuge behind Palmer. "But I'm afraid your business with Father Kendall will have to wait a bit."

Claire motioned Ardra forward, giving her a surreptitious wink. "Right now, though, Ardra has a little sore throat, and Palmer and I have urgent matters to discuss with Father Kendall.''

"Urgent matters?'' Nonna asked, her confidence faltering.

"Quite urgent.'' Claire looked to Palmer and the priest, who nodded vigorously in confirmation.

"Urgent,'' Palmer echoed seriously.

"Extremely urgent,'' the disheveled priest panted from behind him.

"I think a little slippery-elm tea would be just the thing for Ardra's throat,'' Claire lied. It was the only excuse sure to distract Nonna—telling her she was needed to help someone. "I'd let Ardra do it herself, but she's still learning. She could use some supervision, don't you think?''

"Hmm.'' Nonna considered. "Aye. She's still green, yet.''

Always quick on the uptake, Ardra added her own appeal to Claire's. "Please, Dame Nonna. I know the slippery elm is in the kitchen, but I've quite forgotten where.''

"Dear me.'' A cloud crossed Nonna's face. "I'm not certain I remember, either.''

Palmer rolled his eyes heavenward, but Ardra kept her wits about her. She took Nonna's arm and drew her gently toward the kitchen, talking as they went. "We can find it together, I'm sure. And after that, I need to fetch some comfrey from the herb beds. Could you help me with that? I'm always gettin' it mixed up with the valerian.''

"Oh, but the two are so different, dear.'' Nonna patted her hand. "Don't worry. I'll show you how to tell them apart.''

Ardra shot Claire a look that said she'd keep Nonna occupied, and Claire nodded back in gratitude.

She waited until the kitchen door was firmly shut before she addressed the two men standing before her. "Shall we sit, then, sirs?" She subsided onto a bench, while Palmer and the priest claimed the only two chairs.

Father Kendall still wore a slightly stunned look, but Palmer seemed determined to move past the embarrassing incident they'd all just endured. He went straight to the point. "Claire said you have the letter."

"Aye." Father Kendall rummaged behind his scapular, then presented the rumpled epistle.

Instead of reaching for it, Claire handed him the list Palmer had written. "Here is a sample of Palmer's handwriting, but I know already that it will not match the hand that wrote that letter."

The priest frowned, but spread both papers side by side across his knees. He looked up at Claire in surprise. "You're right. They do not match. They're not even a little alike." His brows drew together. "How did you know?"

Claire decided to let Nonna's journals speak for themselves. "Please wait here." Both men stood politely when she rose, then watched, puzzled, as she went to the room that had been Nonna's for so many years. She closed the door and crossed to her desk to flip through the pages of the journal. When she found a page of innocuous medical notes in Nonna's writing, she took the open book back into the workroom. "This is Nonna's medical journal. I think you'll find the handwriting similar to that of the letter. Perhaps identical." She laid the large book on the worktable and stepped back.

Both Palmer and the priest crowded close to the book, comparing the letter and the journal entries.

"I can't believe it." Palmer sat down heavily. "It is my mother's writing."

The priest put his hands to either side of his head and moaned. "How could she do this to me? The bishop . . ." He looked to Palmer with alarm. "The proxy marriage I performed . . . if you didn't write the letter, that means—"

"The marriage was predicated on fraud, so it was never binding," Claire finished for him. "But surely Nonna cannot be held accountable, either legally or spiritually. She was ill, even then, and desperate. All three of us were the victims of that desperation, but I forgive her."

Palmer said nothing. He only looked at Claire, his face unreadable.

Father Kendall was still too upset to speak of forgiveness. "When the bishop finds out . . ." He sank back into the chair. "And I was the one who assured him everything was in order." He closed his eyes. "May God have mercy upon me, but at just this moment, I'd like to wring Dame Nonna's neck. When His Grace discovers the proxy wedding was fraudulent—"

"His Grace need never find out," Palmer interrupted. "There's a simple solution, one that can save us all a great deal of trouble."

"And what, pray tell," the priest demanded crossly, "might that be?"

Palmer's gaze pinned Claire's. "Marry us, today." There was no emotion in his words. "I can ride for Roderick the Pitchman and bring him back to act as witness within the hour."

"That *would* clear things up rather nicely." Father Kendall looked to Claire. "What think you of Palmer's proposal, Dame Claire?"

Claire leveled a piercing gaze on the man who was

about to become her husband, indeed. "My wants have no bearing in this matter. I shall marry Palmer today for the same reason I went through with the proxy ceremony . . . because Nonna wants it."

"By all the saints," Father Kendall muttered, looking seasick. "Dame Nonna's subterfuge has dropped us all into the chamber pot, up to our necks!" The priest rubbed his temples in an effort to calm himself. "But you're right: if we validate the wedding, then no one has to be the wiser . . ." He glanced from Claire to Palmer and back again. "As your spiritual shepherd, though, I must ask you both, have you come to this decision of your own free wills?"

"Aye," the two of them said in unison.

"Very well, then," the priest said, shaking his head no even as he agreed to do as they asked. "I'll marry you."

TWELVE

August 1, 1099, had gotten off to a spectacular start in the bathhouse, but the afternoon was a gloomy disappointment for Claire.

By any standard, her third marriage ceremony was pitiful, indeed—even more pitiful than the hasty proxy wedding. Considering the lack of enthusiasm on both her and Palmer's part, Claire fully expected a vengeful God to part the heavens and smite both bride and groom with a bolt of lightning for profaning the sacrament.

Palmer was grim, but resolute.

Nonna was hospitable, but politely confused.

Big Roderick reeked of pine sap and perspiration.

Ardra alternately gazed in pained adoration at Palmer and glared at Little Red, who had come uninvited with his father.

And Little Red watched in sullen resignation as Claire married the man whose life he'd saved.

After Father Kendall had written the necessary documents, obtained the signatures or marks of the necessary parties, then sworn all present to secrecy on peril of their very souls, he raced through the ceremony as quickly as he could manage.

The nuptial Mass was celebrated with the last of the previous year's elderberry wine and a hastily baked paten of unleavened bread.

No sooner was the ceremony complete, than Father Kendall hurried everyone but Claire, Palmer, and Nonna out of the house.

Claire followed and beckoned the priest away from the others. "Father," she ventured, glancing aside to make certain no one overheard. "I have a boon to ask of you, one which involves a most delicate matter of the strictest confidence."

Fortunately, Little Red and Ardra were waiting a dozen paces down the road, absorbed in a less-than-amicable discussion. Big Roderick stood just beyond them, doing his best to ignore his son's woman problems. Claire knew she could speak without being overheard. "I hate to impose on you, especially after that wretched business about the proxy wedding, but I have nowhere else to turn."

"Your confidence is safe with me." The priest met Claire's worried expression with one of compassion. "Whatever I can do to help . . . it's yours for the asking."

Claire knew he meant it, and she was grateful beyond measure. "This involves . . . a relative in Suffolk, a child. His name is William—" Just saying her son's name caused her throat to constrict after so many months of secret sadness and endless longing. "—William DePeche, only son and heir of the late Lord of Compton. He would be seven years old now." Seven years, two months, and a day.

She took a leveling breath. "If only I could know how he fares, if he's well and safe." Fear added an edge of urgency to her voice. "But no one must know the source of the inquiry. I worry already for his safety, but if his grandmother or his uncle should find out someone has been asking questions . . ." She faltered, the memory of Sir Robert's threat too terrible to contemplate. "I tremble to think what might happen. His very life . . ."

"Oh, my dear, dear child." Father Kendall patted her arm. "Rest easy. By God's Providence I have a cousin near there in Milford whose son is in service at Castle Compton."

A twinge of hope lit Claire's despair.

"It will be a simple matter for my cousin to ask his son about the goings-on at the manor."

Claire went weak with relief.

"My cousin is a man of honor and discretion, quite subtle. His son need not even know the reason behind his questions." He nodded in reassurance. "It will take some time, but we'll find out about the lad, and no one will be the wiser."

"Thank you, Father. God bless you." Claire wanted to hug him, but feared that might arouse suspicion should anyone see her do it, so she settled for a heartfelt, "And may He bless this endeavor." The hope that a merciful God might do so was enough to make her want to believe He existed.

"God will bless this endeavor. I firmly believe it." The priest granted her a wry smile. "As I believe He shall bless your marriage." He looked pointedly to the open doorway where Palmer had just appeared. "Your husband awaits you."

"Aye," Claire said without enthusiasm. Her back to the house, she watched Father Kendall and the others pair off and exit the compound, Ardra and the priest toward town and Roderick and Little Red toward the darkening forest. Only then did she turn to see that Palmer was no longer waiting in the doorway.

Once inside, she closed the door and, ready or not, went to face the man who was truly her husband before God and the world. She found him talking quietly with his mother in the kitchen.

"Well, there you are," Nonna said. "I was beginning to worry about you." She turned back to Palmer and embraced him briefly. "Welcome to the family, young man. If my daughter-in-law loves you, then I shall love you, too." Her eyes bright and lucid, she fixed him with a look of candid assessment as she said to Claire, "It will be good to have a man in the house again, won't it, daughter?"

It warmed Claire's heart to see Nonna so rational and cheerful. "Aye," she answered. "It will be good to have a man in the house again." Remembering the heat of her coupling with Palmer this very day, Claire wondered if her husband had any idea just how good she thought that would be.

But another question made her wonder even more: Would Palmer share her bed on this, their wedding night, or retreat to his studio?

Her first husband had been prone to leave her and sulk alone for days when things didn't go just his way, but he inevitably returned to exercise his husbandly prerogatives, quite often sooner than she would have wished. Claire had enjoyed her solitude, though she hadn't really minded her husband's quick and awkward couplings—she'd known no other way.

But with Palmer, things were so different. This morning, what they had shared . . . just thinking of it sent a jolt of desire straight through her.

To be honest, she did not want him to sleep in his studio. She wanted him in her bed, tonight and every night, God willing. For however short a time Palmer would be with her, she wanted to feel his warmth beside her. She wanted to be able to touch him the way she had this morning and take pleasure in his response.

But what if he did not want to share her bed? What if he preferred his privacy?

There had been a time when that possibility, alone, would have kept Claire from asking, but that time was long past. She had lost too much and suffered alone too long to forfeit any comfort for lack of asking, even a comfort solely of the flesh.

She reached out to Palmer. "It's our wedding night, husband." Her eyes asked for peace between them. "Let us retire together, as husband and wife should."

Before Palmer had a chance to respond, his mother grumbled good-naturedly, "And I had thought t'would be I who lay with a man this day." Nonna let out a disgruntled sigh. "Ah, well. There will be other days."

She shot the newlyweds a knowing smile and herded them toward their conjugal bed. "Consummate, my dears. Consummate." Pausing on the threshold once they were inside, Nonna added dryly, "It's cold comfort, of course, but I'm glad *somebody* in this house will be well-bedded tonight."

Palmer let out a strangled chortle at his mother's frankness, but Claire laughed aloud.

"Make all the noise you want," Nonna added without looking back as she headed for her own room. "These walls are almost two feet thick. I won't hear a thing."

Senile though she might be, Nonna definitely had her moments.

Claire chuckled as she closed the door and bolted it. But when she turned to find Palmer glowering at her, her happiness faded as abruptly as her smile. "You are upset about something," she said equably, unfastening the girdle at her hips.

Palmer's scowl was replaced by consternation when he saw her remove the heavily embossed and gilded girdle. "What are you doing?"

"You know perfectly well what I'm doing." This might just prove to be entertaining, after all. "You're a man of the world; I have no doubt you've seen your share of women undressing."

Palmer made straight for the fireplace and pushed the trip-stones to the secret exit.

"Hold, sir," Claire said firmly. "I would remind you of your promise. Leaving now would not honor that promise."

Palmer placed his hands on the mantel and leaned toward the fireplace in tense silence.

Was he feeling trapped? Did he regret, already, what he had done?

"My mother believed that husband and wife should never sleep apart, even when they are in disagreement." Claire sat on the bench at the foot of the bed. "She said that when it comes to marriage, the body has a wisdom of its own."

As she did every night, she lifted her skirt and loosed her knitted garters, then rolled down her stockings and took them off. Then she carefully unrolled the stockings and laid them neatly beside her girdle and garters on the bench. "That makes sense to me. What do you think?"

Palmer turned to her, his blue eyes dark with something troubling and indefinable. "Very well. I shall sleep here, if you wish."

"Good. But do not worry," she hastened to reassure him. "I shall never force myself on you." She removed her kirtle, folded it on the bench, then unlaced the front of her soft white woolen gown. "I do, though, hope that we might occasionally enjoy such bodily pleasures as God permits husbands and wives. When you are agreeable, of course.''

Pulling the shoulders wide, she stood and let her gown fall to the floor, leaving only the thin fabric of her sleeveless linen shift between her and the man who was now her husband. She picked up the garment and laid it neatly beside her kirtle so that she could dress quickly, should her healing skills be needed in the night.

Doing her best to pretend disinterest, Claire unbound her hair, then crossed to the dressing table and sat to comb through the long, curling locks until they hung in shining waves all around her. While one hand was busy combing, the other discreetly loosened the ribbons that laced the front of her shift.

When she rose to face Palmer, Claire saw that he was watching her every move, just as she had hoped.

''Would you prefer that I sleep naked?'' she asked, all innocence. ''My late husband used to say that he liked to see me wearing only my hair.'' She crossed her arms to remove the straps of her shift and let it too fall to the floor. ''What do you think? With or without?''

''Without,'' he said raggedly, undone at last.

Stepping out of his shoes, he untied the waist of his chausses with a pull of the cord, then stepped free of them. Off came his belt, then with one motion, he shucked off his shirt, and they were standing there, naked, only yards apart, his desire for her evident.

Claire prayed he would come to her, and come to her, he did.

He kissed her, hard and hungry, then he buried his face in her hair as his hands stroked the rise and swell of her body, the pulsing heat of his erection pressed hard into the nest of curls at her loins.

He might not love her, but he wanted her, and that was enough for now.

Claire wanted him, too. She wanted to feel him, hot and hard inside her, wanted to dig her fingers into the taut flesh of his buttocks and draw him even deeper, wanted to feel the friction of his stubbled chin against the smoothness of her breasts, her neck, her belly. She wanted to taste the sharp, metallic saltiness of his man's skin and breathe in, deep, the mingled odors of his man's desire.

Emboldened by desire, she whispered archly in his ear, "Consummate, my dear. Consummate."

Palmer let out a harsh chuckle, then kissed her to silence.

Claire urged him on, her own heart beating wild with his, her breath shallow, rapid, her hands grasping, stroking. She wasn't certain how they ended up in bed. Suddenly, they were there, and he was ravaging her, plundering, exploring every hidden contour with his fingers and his tongue.

He moved without thought or nuance, driven now by need, not pleasure. There was nothing calculated, nothing deliberate about the way he took her, but she was ready for him.

So many nights she'd slept alone, and now, for the second time in a single day, her own aching emptiness went hot and slick, melting into an eager receptacle for the satisfaction Palmer could give her.

His skin hot against her own, he forced her legs apart and drove inside her, plunging to the hilt in savage rhythm, each thrust punctuated with a primal utterance that sounded halfway between a groan and a cry of conquest.

Claire rode the desperate wave of desire to her own fulfillment, letting out a hoarse, guttural shout of release. Hearing it, Palmer made one last, monumental thrust of release, then collapsed, panting, atop her.

She lay there, anchored by the relaxed, satisfying warmth of his body, listening to the reassuring rhythm of his breathing.

It was almost dark, now. The house was quiet, serene in the peaceful dying of the day.

Claire wished she could lie there forever, sated and boneless beneath Palmer's weight, but as the minutes passed, he grew heavier and heavier. Only when his breathing lapsed into the deep, sonorous rhythm of sleep did she ease herself from underneath him and curl, smiling, with her bare bottom pressed to his thigh. She was so grateful for this fragile moment of contentment—grateful to Palmer, to Nonna, to life or fate or God or whatever had given her the gift—that she could not keep it silently inside. ''Thank you,'' she whispered softly.

''Thank *you*,'' came Palmer's deep, ragged reply.

''You . . .'' Claire turned to face him. Unable to muster even a semblance of proper outrage, she laughed instead. ''I thought you were asleep.''

Palmer chuckled, loose and easy. ''I thought *you* were wonderful.''

She tucked herself into the crook of his shoulder, her cheek to his chest, and his arm curled around her, drawing her even closer. They fit well together.

''Any regrets?'' she asked, wishing even as she did that she had let things lie.

''Hundreds,'' he said without rancor, his deep voice resonating beneath her ear. ''Thousands.'' The pause that followed loomed huge and awful. ''But not about today.''

She could breathe again. ''Nor have I. But I do have a wedding gift for you.''

He yawned, then asked drowsily, "Hmmm? And what would that be?"

"The truth," Claire said softly, "about me. My past."

She felt him tense. "Claire, that's not necessary, really. You don't have to—"

She laid her finger to his lips, silencing him. "But I want to, for both our sakes."

"But—"

"Please, Palmer."

He let out a sigh of resignation. "I'm listening, then."

"My grandfather came to this country from Normandy with the Conqueror. He was a common foot soldier, but he acquitted himself bravely. After the war was over, his valor was rewarded with a position of service under one of the Norman barons who'd been granted vast lands in Suffolk. My father was bailiff to that lord's son. He met my mother there—she was maid to the lady of the manor—and they were granted permission to marry."

Sweet memories of her parents warmed Claire's heart. "They were very happy, my parents, devoted to each other. My childhood was a happy one; I entered service when I was six and knew no want or fear. Then, when I was twelve, a traveling minstrel brought pestilence to the household. Within a week, both my parents were dead, along with the lord of the manor and many others."

Claire fought back the tears that threatened to escape whenever she spoke of her parents' deaths. "My mother had taught me the skills of a lady's maid, and the master's widow looked with favor upon me, so I was given my mother's place."

She sighed. "At first, I was grateful. The work was

easy enough, and I was given my lady's cast-off dresses to wear. And even though the hours were long, I was allowed to attend my mistress at great feasts and entertainments.

"I did not know what a dangerous gift my position was until I turned sixteen and came into the fullness of my womanhood. That was when my lady's eldest son, the new master, took note of me and began to pursue me."

Claire looked up to Palmer's face in the dim light. "He could have had anyone. Why he wanted me, I shall never know, but the more I tried to avoid him, the more determined he was to have me, one way or another." She shook her head, remembering. "I had seen what happened to the serving girls who were used by men like him, then cast aside. Not me, I vowed. So I made certain he never caught me alone."

Palmer stroked her hair, but said nothing.

"When my lady found out he'd been pursuing me, things went from bad to worse. She was furious, not with her son, but with me for 'enticing him.' She wanted to banish me—so did his brother, Sir Robert—but my master would not let them. The harder they fought him, the more determined he became to have me." She glanced up to Palmer's face, but it had grown too dark to see anything but his silhouette.

"The three of them quarreled about it like bears in a pit. In the end, I think he did what he did more to spite his mother and his brother than for love of me."

"What did he do?" Palmer asked her, his arm tightening protectively around her.

Claire sighed in earnest. "He married me."

"He *what*?" Palmer sat bolt upright, bringing her with him.

"He married me." Claire pushed him back down onto the pillows.

"My God." Palmer exhaled as if he'd been punched in the belly. "So you were—"

"Mistress of the castle," she finished for him. "Aye."

Claire settled back into the protective circle of his arm. "Not that I wanted to be, mind you, but I had no choice in the matter. I had no family to speak for me, no other suitors. My lord and master willed it, so I became his bride."

"Never, in a million years, would I have imagined—"

"Well, it's true," she said, more than a little defensive. "I was wife of a lord. A very good wife, I might add."

"Oh, of course," he was quick to say. "I'm sure you were."

She could sense that he was grinning, but she wasn't sure whether it was from amusement or amazement.

He stroked the hair from her temple. "Mistress of the castle."

"I rather enjoyed it, at first," she confessed, "except for the open hatred shown by my good-mother and brother-by-law whenever my husband's back was turned. In his presence, they were all kindness, but whenever he left me alone with them . . ." She shivered. "They tormented me with words but dared not harm me. We went on that way for six years, during which I conceived and delivered two sons and a daughter." Her throat tightened with remembered grief. "None of them lived more than a month." She lay silent in the darkness, glad for the warm security of his embrace. "I've often wondered if their deaths were punishment for such an unsuitable marriage."

"Nay," Palmer soothed, still stroking her hair. "You said yourself, you had no choice in the matter."

"Not punishment for me," she said softly. "For him."

She shifted back to her story. "Then, when I was twenty and two, I gave birth to a healthy son." Strange, but it did not hurt her quite so much to speak of him to Palmer. "He was so beautiful, and so strong. We named him William. My good-mother did her best to take him from me, but as long as my husband was there, I was able to keep my baby with me.

"Then my husband told me of the vow he'd made." The old pain loomed larger. "During my confinement, my lord husband asked God for a healthy son. He vowed that if his prayer was granted, on the child's first birthday, he would answer the Holy Father's call to go to the Holy Land and liberate our Lord's tomb from the infidel."

Claire fought the growing pressure in her chest. "I begged my husband not to leave us, but he was convinced our son would die if he did not keep his vow. So, the day after William's first birthday, my lord husband set out for the Holy Land with all his soldiers."

"Leaving you at the mercy of his family." Palmer's voice grew bitter. "What a fool."

"It wasn't easy, but I managed well enough. William was the heir, and I was his mother. That kept my husband's brother and my good-mother at bay."

Get it over with, she told herself. Palmer is your husband now. He deserves to know. Just say it, and never again will you have to mention it.

"My son was three when we received word that my husband had been killed." Claire took a leveling breath. "Sir Robert wasted no time. I had scarcely gotten the news, ere he took my William from me and cast me out, alone except for my maid Marissa.''

''Surely he couldn't do such a thing!'' Palmer protested.

''He did.'' She turned her forehead against Palmer's resilient warmth. ''He tore my son from my arms and gave him to my good-mother. I can still hear William's terrified screams, as if it were only yesterday. Sir Robert then swore that he would kill William if I refused to leave or went to the law or even tried to come back to claim my child.''

''Oh, Claire.'' Palmer tightened his arms around her. ''My God.''

''Your God, perhaps, but not mine,'' she said bitterly. ''That was when I stopped believing in Him, when my child was taken from me and I was cast into the world with only my mare, my clothes, a purse full of coins, and Marissa.'' The old ache swelled in her heart to crushing proportions. ''William was the only thing standing between Sir Robert and the title. I knew his threat was not an idle one.'' She would have cried, but all her tears for her son had long ago turned to dust. ''The dowager's love for him is William's only protection now. As much as she hated me, Lady DePeche adores my son. She would not let anyone harm him, not even Sir Robert. But she was more than happy to cast me out.''

Wearily, she finished her story. ''Marissa and I wandered for almost two years, searching for somewhere, anywhere, we could settle. But the world had no place for us. Then, winter before last, she fell ill and died. I went on alone until I came to Linherst, where Father Kendall directed me to seek shelter here.''

For the first time since she had begun her story, she smiled. ''Your mother was waiting for me with open arms. She said she had asked God to send her an apprentice, and there I was.''

Claire stroked the fine hairs on Palmer's chest. "I was truly alone in the world, with nowhere else to go, so I stayed. In exchange for training me as a healer, Nonna asked only that I make a solemn promise to care for her when she could no longer care for herself.''

Claire stilled. "She knew she was losing her memory, even then." Suddenly, she felt so weary she could scarcely speak. "You know the rest.''

Several long, pregnant moments passed before Palmer spoke. "I'm glad you told me.''

Claire nodded, her eyes closing at last. "Never again,'' she said as she drifted into the blessed oblivion of sleep, leaving Palmer to lie awake and wonder what her final words had meant.

Never again . . . what?

Never again would she love as she had loved the child she lost?

Or had she meant that she would never speak of that loss again?

How blind he had been, so obsessed with his own torment that he hadn't even guessed at the brutal losses Claire had borne alone in silence.

Palmer could scarcely take in the depth of her grief. He couldn't help thinking it would have been easier for her had the child died. That way, she could have mourned, then gotten on with her life. But to have her son taken away by those who hated her . . .

How could she bear it? he wondered. To live in constant suspense and worry, never knowing whether the child was well or ill, strong or frail, loved or abused . . . How could she stand to wake each morning to such relentless uncertainty?

Yet she'd cared for him and all who needed her

without complaint. He marveled at the quiet dignity of her resignation, a new admiration welling up from deep within his closely guarded emotions.

Palmer had known many women in his life—more than a few of them in the biblical sense—but never had he met anyone even remotely like his bride.

Not for Claire, the guile and calculation of womanly deception. She spoke her mind, and plainly. A rare—and dangerous—gift, such levelheaded frankness in a woman.

And courage . . . She had borne her tragic secrets with a lack of self-pity that put most *men* to shame.

No wonder Nonna loved her so. If he wasn't careful, he might just end up feeling the same way about her.

Yet he couldn't fathom how could she go on living, caring for others, when she had lost her child, her home, her husband, her place in the world, even her last friend.

The bravery of war required only momentary sacrifice, but Claire's quiet courage manifested itself every single day. It made his own futile efforts to atone for his sins seem transient and facile.

It made him ashamed of his own self-obsessive guilt.

And it made him want to put his arms around his wife and hold her safe from all that might threaten her.

If only he could do something, anything, to set things right.

But Palmer knew he could no more mend Claire's broken heart than he could mend his own. Their pasts were an indelible part of them both; what had been done could never be undone. The dead would still be dead. That which had been stolen would still be lost. The faith that had been shattered by evil could never again be made whole.

And he could not remain here with her. Sooner or

later, the demons within him would drive him from her, no matter how much he might want to stay.

But they had each other for now. He drew her naked body gently closer, marveling at how good her warm smoothness felt against him.

At least in sleep, she seemed at peace.

Palmer wished he could say the same. But it was when he slept that the torments from his past came to life—the smell of carnage, the sound of every scream, the details of every atrocity as real and horrifying as the day they had happened in Hungary.

He shut the thought away and concentrated on being where he was, stroking the long arc of Claire's hip and taking comfort from the peaceful reassurance of her presence, giving her the comfort of his own.

He could give her that much for a while, even if he could not share with her the sins he had long since repented.

Even if he could not stay with her forever.

THIRTEEN

Claire wasn't certain how it happened. Perhaps the incessant rhythm of survival kept her and Palmer so busy that neither of them had the time, the strength, or the inclination to address the invisible barrier that yet held them apart. Perhaps they were both afraid to risk shattering the fragile refuge of habit into which they had so smoothly settled.

Regardless of the reason, husband and wife lived together as wholly separate people—courteous, kind, but distant people.

Day in and day out, they rose from the same bed, broke their fast together at the same table, expressed the same polite concern for each other's health and comfort, shared the same devotion to Nonna, met their respective obligations with the same selfless vigor, supped at that same table while exchanging insignificant conversation, and retired to the same bed to share the warmth and wants of their bodies.

Even Nonna stayed the same, showing no further signs of deterioration. At least they both had her to love. That was one of the few areas in which the circles of their lives intersected.

So quickly in so much sameness the time had slipped away, almost as in a dream.

Claire should have been content.

So smoothly the days rolled into weeks, the weeks into months.

The changing of the year took them to a new century, yet nothing really changed. Despite the usual dire predictions from seers, old women, and the clergy, there was no sign of Armageddon, so life went on just as before.

So easily, Claire let the busy, lonely days slide by. So silently, she passed the lonely nights in Palmer's arms, touching, yet untouched.

And still, no word of William.

The only jarring note was Palmer's nightmares. They had started in the fall, infrequent at first, then more and more often.

At first, he only tossed and moaned within his sleep. But as the demons gathered strength and frequency, he battled them in earnest, sitting up and fighting them off while he gasped for air, covered in an instant sweat that bore the acrid stink of terror.

Every time it happened, Claire remembered the image of torment he had fashioned with his own hands. She held him tight and willed his demons to leave him alone. Then she soothed him back from the brink of hell with soft strokes and gentle words.

Sometimes he wakened, drained, and clung to her until his breathing evened. Other times, he never truly wakened, just gradually subsided into troubled sleep, never knowing she had stood against the demons with him.

But they never spoke of what had caused the nightmares.

They never spoke of anything that hid within their hearts.

Winter was hard upon them when frantic knocking intruded into Claire's warm cocoon of slumber.

"Help! Dame Claire! Come quickly!"

Still half-asleep, she sat up and struck a flint to the wick of the small oil lamp beside the bed, then slid from the warmth of her bed to the icy reality of this cold January night.

Usually a sound sleeper, Palmer sat up beside her. "Sounds like Little Red." He rolled out of bed as quickly as she did.

"You needn't get up," Claire offered, already seated on the bench at the foot of the bed and pulling on her heavy stockings. "I can see to it." She didn't like the panic she heard in Little Red's voice.

Perhaps responding to that same note of panic, Palmer seemed unsettled. "Nay. I'm going with you." He donned his clothes with the same swift efficiency as she, then pulled on his winter boots and heavy sheepskin coat. "The snow is at least a foot deep. You shouldn't go out alone."

Claire didn't argue. After almost a week of snow, the wind had been blowing for days at gale force. "I'll answer the door, then, and you can fetch Frieda and the wagon."

As she headed for the front entrance, Palmer made for the back. Little Red was still pounding away when Claire slid open the bolt and pulled the door wide to a howling wind so cold it fairly sucked the breath from her lungs. She drew the lad inside and shouldered the heavy door closed. "What's happened?"

"That big oak by the house," he panted, his face chapped with cold and streaked by dirt and tears.

"Wind blew it over, right atop us." Fresh tears welled in his reddened eyes. "Brought the house down on us in our beds, roof and walls and all, branches stickin' everywhere." He struggled to speak the unspeakable. "The baby wasn't breathin' when we dug her out, and Jane and Pascoe are trapped under the rubble and branches. All we could see of Pascoe is his legs, and the bone's stickin' out of one of 'em. And a big branch pierced Janie's belly. We managed to break the branch loose from the tree, but it's still pokin' out of her. . . ."

A pulse of alarm shot straight to Claire's toes. "Dear God." Not little Janie! Why, just last week, Claire had joggled the giggling toddler on her knee after stitching up a nasty cut on Big Red's leg. And sweet, shy little Pascoe . . . a dried apple had won Claire a heart-melting smile and a bone-crunching hug from the frail six-year-old.

No. She couldn't think that way, not and be of any use to anyone.

She had to think and act like the healer she was. And a good healer brought calm and order in the midst of disaster. "It was good that you didn't pull the branch out of her," she managed. "You did well."

"I told Pa we shouldn't, that we should wait for you to get there." Little Red's voice faltered, his eyes pleading for a miracle Claire feared she could not provide. "Pascoe and Janie . . . they were both alive when I left." His bloodied hands closed on Claire's arm with desperate strength as he pulled her toward the door. "Please hurry, Dame Claire. You've got to help them."

"I will," she said firmly, prying his fingers from her arm, "but you must release me so I can gather my supplies."

He let go immediately.

Claire snatched up her heavy cloak and fastened it

at her neck. "Ardra! Wake up and get dressed as quickly as you can!"

Quite capable of sleeping through the Second Coming, Ardra responded to the alarm in her mistress's voice by stumbling from her bed without hesitation. She pulled her heavy woolen dress over her winter shift with a loud yawn, then took one look at Little Red and came instantly alert. "Roderick! Dear heaven, what's happened?"

Claire answered for him. "A tree fell on their house, trapping two of the children. They're gravely injured." Even as she spoke, she raced to collect her splints, medicines, and instruments. "We need you, Ardra. Dress warmly, as fast as you can. Then gather some food and wine and meet me out front." She turned to Little Red. "Grab as many blankets and pillows as you can bundle up and carry." She shot a worried glance at Nonna's bedchamber door. "We'll have to risk leaving Nonna alone. With any luck, we'll be back before she wakes."

Laden as instructed, Ardra and Little Red met Claire at the front door just as Palmer opened it. "Good. You're ready." He motioned them outside, nodding to Claire. "On my way out, I heard what happened, so I brought the bow saw and crosscut."

Claire thanked a cold and distant God for Palmer's foresight. She never would have thought of bringing the saws. Leave it to a man to realize they'd need such implements. She hastened to the wagon and saw that Palmer had even thought to bring the nanny goat whose udder bulged with warm milk for the children.

They made a good team, she and her husband. But for how long?

"Hurry along," Palmer urged as Little Red helped Ardra through the foot-deep snow. "There's no time to waste." When they reached the wagon, Palmer heaved the apprentice, basket and all, into the back of the wagon as Little Red climbed the wheel and jumped in with her.

Palmer launched himself into the driver's seat and whipped Frieda on her way, but the going was slow. A single horse could only pull such a heavy load through the snow at a labored pace.

Claire peered up at the lowering clouds and wondered what time it was. Though the clouds obscured the moon, there was just enough indirect light to make out the snow-covered road as it wended through the forest, but not enough to tell the hour.

The wind whistled through the bare forest, whipping snow from the trees and slicing through even Claire's heavy cloak.

It was so cold, and those poor children, badly hurt and trapped in the cold and the dark . . . Claire tried not to think about it, but her mind kept conjuring gruesome scenes of injury and destruction.

Must it take so long for them to get there?

It was all she could do to keep from jumping from the wagon and running ahead on foot, as ridiculous as that would be.

After what seemed like ages but was probably less than an hour, they finally arrived at what had once been Roderick's house.

Everyone in the wagon stared in silence at the huge uprooted oak that all but obscured the rubble of what had once been a tidy thatched daub-and-wattle cottage. Among the tangle of branches and debris, a single flame flickered where Big Red was frantically heaving away beams and chunks of wall in an effort to free his children.

Close by the smashed house in a bare patch of snow,

Claire could just make out a bloodied little bundle lying on the ground, and her heart lurched.

The baby.

Too late. She had gotten here to late to save her.

"They're here!" Little Red's mother appeared from the far side of the rubble and raced toward them, a deep cut above her eyebrow streaming blood. Oblivious to the injury and her bloodied hands and filthy, sodden nightgown, Dame Bridget fairly dragged Claire from the wagon. "Please hurry. They're hurt so bad, and we can't get Pascoe free."

Little Red abandoned his bundle of blankets, grabbed both saws, and vaulted from the wagon, hitting the ground at a dead run toward his father.

While Claire pulled out her basket of supplies, Palmer drew out a heavy blanket and jumped down beside Little Red's mother. He wrapped up the shivering, distraught woman and encircled her in a reassuring embrace. "We'll get them out, Dame Bridget," he soothed. "We'll get them out."

Claire wasted no time finding Big and Little Red. As she struggled through the maze of branches toward the light of the flickering firebrand that marked Big Red's rescue effort, the wind carried the sound of Palmer's voice from behind her. "Ardra! Take Dame Bridget to the barn, out of this wind. Then find the rest of the children and check them for injuries. If anyone is seriously hurt, let us know. If not, wrap them in blankets and take them to their mother, along with the food and the nanny. Make sure everyone's warm and fed before you come help us. Do you understand?"

"Aye, master," she heard Ardra respond.

Claire was more than grateful for Palmer's practical logic and common sense.

When at last she reached the injured child, she

looked down and saw that rubble covered all of six-year-old Pascoe but his pale little legs, one of which lay at right angles to its proper position, the unnatural angle marked by an alarming amount of blood and an obscene eruption of a jagged bone through the skin.

One thing at a time. Decide what must be done next, and do it.

Claire looked closely at the beam that pinned the boy. By a stroke of luck, it was resting on a pile of rubble that kept the weight of destruction from crushing Pascoe's torso. They could afford to stop digging while she attended to more urgent matters.

"Move aside," she ordered Roderick and Little ·Red. She turned to the child's father. "Hold the brand where I can see the break. I must determine if any vessels have been severed."

His chest heaving from exertion and his hands cut and bleeding, Big Roderick looked at her with desperate question in his eyes. "Stop diggin'? But—"

Claire looked without wavering into his eyes. "It's all right," she reassured the distraught father, even though she understood his agony all too well. She pointed to the beam. "Look there. That beam is protecting him from the weight of the rubble. He's safe as he lies for the moment, but I must splint his leg and control the bleeding. And we must get him warmed up. Then we can worry about getting him out."

"My little girl . . ." Big Red raked a bloodied fist across his cheek. "What about her? Bridget said she was . . ." His raspy voice faltered.

"She's not alone. Palmer is with her. He'll sing out if he needs me." She laid a calming hand on Big Red's shoulder. "For now, I need you to hold the torch so I can help Pascoe."

Two fat tears squeezed from his bloodshot eyes as

the big man picked up the torch with a shaking hand, but he inhaled deeply and steadied. "Whatever ye need, I'll do it." His raspy voice faltered. "Just save me children."

"I'll do my best."

Claire felt of the child's legs. Both of them were far too cold, probably from exposure, but she did detect a faint pulse behind the knee of the broken one. "The cold has slowed his bleeding, but I fear he might freeze to death if we don't get him warmed up as soon as I can control the bleeding and reduce the break. We'll need a fire."

"Done." Little Red started breaking off branches with his bare hands for firewood.

"Wait," Claire instructed. "Bring me the blankets, first."

"Aye. Blankets." Little Red crashed through the branches in the direction of the wagon.

As Claire searched her basket for a tourniquet, Big Red started piling up broken branches with his free hand.

Despite the pulse that thundered in her ears, she did her best to show confidence and calm. She slipped the tourniquet under Pascoe's leg and tightened it above the break.

Little Red crashed back with the blankets in amazing time. "Good job," Claire told him. She took half the blankets, then folded one and slid it under Pascoe's legs. "Take the rest to Palmer for your sister. Then come back and get the fire going."

"Aye." Breathless, the young man snatched the rest of the blankets and the bow saw, then clambered away toward his injured sister.

Claire turned her attention to her patient.

One thing at a time . . .

She worked quickly but cautiously to clean the exposed bone and torn flesh, then restore it to its proper position with as little further damage as possible. In a matter of minutes, the sound of sawing and cracking branches told her Little Red was back and working at a feverish pace to cut wood for a fire.

She directed all her concentration to the gruesome wound before her. Only when it was cleaned, stitched, and the leg splinted, bathed in an anti-infective solution, and bandaged, did she notice the warmth of two small fires burning close on either side of her.

Claire had no idea how long it had taken her to set the broken leg. She'd lost all sense of time as well as all sense of fatigue or cold. As always when faced with a dire emergency, she functioned beyond the physical. Only after everything was settled would her body feel the toll. But she wasn't finished yet.

Her fingers closed on the limp little foot beneath the blanket. "I can feel a pulse in his foot," she told the boy's anxious father. "And it's beginning to warm up a bit." Claire managed a weary smile. "You can start digging again, but be sure to keep the fires going. I'll tend to Jane now."

Big Red grasped her upper arm as she rose. "I don't know how to thank ye. I'm—"

"You needn't thank me." All too aware that Pascoe was far from out of danger, Claire pulled free of Big Red's grateful grasp and covered her concern by gathering her supplies. "I must hurry and tend to Jane."

She picked her way through the tangle of bare branches and scaled the massive trunk. "Palmer? Where are you?"

"Here." His voice sounded oddly subdued.

She topped the bole of the tree and spotted the glow of a small fire through the dark jumble of branches. As she drew closer, she heard Palmer's voice in a soothing, almost sing-song cadence.

"That's very interesting," he said softly but with exaggerated animation. "And what did your dolly do when she danced with the stars?"

"She sang a song," came little Jane's strained, breathy reply.

"Can you sing me the song?" Palmer asked. "I'd really like to hear you sing."

Claire scrambled over the trunk and slid down the far side. When she reached them, she found a sight that made her forget her many months of learning to cope with gruesome injuries. Bile rose in her throat.

Wrapped in two of the blankets himself, Palmer sat rigid and tenderly cradled the little girl bundled in a bloody blanket. Jane gazed up at him wide-eyed with suffering, enthralled by the sound of his voice. Yet Claire hardly noticed anything but the jagged branch that protruded from the child's abdomen. With every labored breath, it rose and fell.

Wavering, Claire closed her eyes and struggled to regain her self-control.

Get hold of yourself! Nonna's voice chided her within. She needs you. *One thing at a time. Decide what must be done next and do it!*

Her mother's quiet admonition joined Nonna's: one turnip at a time, dear. One turnip at a time.

"I don't want to sing." Jane's childish voice was weak and thready. "My tummy hurts."

Palmer looked up at Claire with infinite pain, but his tone never wavered. "I know, sweeting. That's why Dame Claire is here to help you. Now I want you to close your eyes and listen to the sound of my voice. Nothing else. There's no cold, and no pain, only the sound of my voice, and you're floating, floating, floating on a warm summer sea, in a boat made of sunshine and clouds.''

Claire knelt beside her husband and searched her basket for the syrup of poppies, marveling even as she did at the gentleness and compelling peace of Palmer's voice. With that alone, he had managed to soothe Jane's fears and ease her panic, if not her pain.

Now it was up to Claire to save her life.

She mixed the syrup of poppies with honey and mint on a narrow wooden spatula, then handed it to Palmer.

Without pausing in his spellbinding narrative, Palmer took the spatula and held it to Jane's lips. ''Don't open your eyes, but I have a sweet for you. It's made with honey and mint, and it will help the hurt go away.''

Jane opened her mouth and licked at the mixture.

''That's it. Take it all. Sweet, so sweet, and then you'll sleep. Sleep on a summer sea, rocking in your sunshine boat. All blue sky and soft breezes, rocking you to sleep.''

Almost immediately, the child's breathing eased into a deeper rhythm.

Claire looked around her at the dim web of branches and rubble that surrounded them. It was so dark, but they dared not move the child.

If only she had some decent light . . . but even a dozen torches wouldn't provide enough, not in this wind. ''Palmer, it's so dark,'' she whispered. ''No healer would dare to attempt an abdominal repair under these conditions.''

His eyes were the color of ice. ''You know what will happen if we don't try,'' he whispered back. ''I can feel the life ebbing out of her, even now. We have to try.''

Claire was nothing if not honest about her limitations, and she knew this was beyond her. "It's not that I'm unwilling to try, Palmer," she confessed. "It's just that I know I can't do it. Not here, this way. It's beyond me."

He peered into her face and saw the truth of it. "All right. I'll do it, then."

"You?" Claire recoiled.

"Yes, me." He carefully shrugged off the two blankets that sheltered both him and Jane, leaving their patient protected by only the one in which she was wrapped. "Take these blankets and fold a pallet on the ground. Then gather some snow to melt over the fire in a kettle. When that's done, I'll prepare the instruments while you make some more torches. Roderick has plenty of pitch in the barn."

Claire folded the blankets as thickly as she could and smoothed them. "Palmer, are you sure? If we lose her . . ."

"If we lose her," he said, his blue eyes darkening, "she'll be one more child who died at my hand."

Claire's blood ran cold as the howling night wind at the bitterness in his voice. "Palmer, I—"

"Fetch the snow," he said harshly, once again the tortured stranger who had wakened in her care.

Stung, Claire drew the kettle from her basket and set out into the darkness.

She returned to find Jane lying unconscious on the blankets, as still as a corpse, her little body bundled completely in the bloody blanket except for her face and a small patch of skin surrounding the hideous stake.

Palmer had already cleansed the blood from her pale skin. His chiseled features gaunt in the flickering light, he took the kettle and set it on the fire. Then, exhibiting the same confidence and efficiency Nonna had once shown, he selected the proper instruments, dropped them into the kettle, then swabbed Jane's wound with walnut-hull extract to slow the bleeding. "I'll need as many torches as you can make," he said bleakly. "As quickly as you can."

Claire did as she was bid, but she couldn't help wondering why Palmer had never told her he was a skilled surgeon.

Once she'd bound up more than a dozen torches with Little Red's help, she had to do some tall talking to convince him he was more needed in the barn with Ardra and the rest of the family than with her and Palmer, but at last Claire managed to return to Palmer's side and set up a circle of illumination.

After cleaning her hands with scalding water from the kettle, she settled opposite her husband, ready with two clean cloths to staunch the bleeding when he cut. Both of them knew that for Janie, time had run out, but when she looked at the little girl's sweet, pale features, Claire still could not bring herself to face the dreadful choice that must be made. "Palmer, one last time, couldn't we wait—"

Without answering, he shot Claire a look as tortured as her own, then put an abrupt end to their fearful doubts by picking up the scalpel and cutting a precise ribbon of scarlet into Janie's abdomen beside the stake.

The fateful decision had been made. With a courage and confidence Claire could not summon, Palmer had done what must be done. Janie's life was in his hands, now. All Claire could do was try her best to help him.

FOURTEEN

Faint wisps of vapor rose from the heat of Janie's open abdomen, but as quickly as each frail breath of warmth met the freezing wind, it was blown away.

Within the ring of flickering torchlight, Claire watched in awe as Palmer's fingers worked with swift precision to repair the damage done by the jagged branch.

Scowling, he closed his eyes and carefully probed the wound with his fingers, guided by touch alone. His eyes once again trained on the wound, he relaxed the grim set of his face. "Good. It did not go so deep as the kidneys, and her liver feels intact. We can be thankful for that much, at least." Palmer picked up a scalpel and widened the wound by careful degrees for better access to the damaged tissues and organs.

Working so fast that Claire would have thought him reckless had she not seen for herself the competence and precision of his every move, he located and repaired the larger bleeding veins and arteries, then turned his attention to the smaller vessels.

He functioned with a speed and surety Claire could only envy. Palmer tied off the larger vessels just as she would have done, but with the smaller ones, he used a technique she had never even heard of, much less seen. Using a delicate surgical hook, he deftly snared the severed end of each tiny vessel, then twisted just above the hook and waited until the blood within had clotted, neatly and securely sealing the smaller bleeders.

Claire's cold-numbed fingers tingled back to life in anticipation of trying such an elegantly simple procedure herself. "The hook and twist," she asked him, "where did you learn to do that?"

Palmer's eyes never shifted from what he was doing. "A Moorish physician taught me. In Poland."

"Fascinating." Careful not to interfere with the surgery's progress, Claire swabbed the fresh blood still oozing from the incision. "But I thought you were a soldier . . ."

"I was. Until I was injured." He shot her a brief, bitter glance before looking back into the incision. "Then I became just one more wounded, disillusioned foreigner a thousand miles from home. I had no food, no strength, no money, no weapons, no tools, no destination." He spoke so quietly she had to strain to hear over the whistling wind. "But wherever I wandered, I came upon the sick and wounded. I couldn't turn my back on them, not after all the harm I'd—" He silenced abruptly.

Claire wished devoutly that he'd finish the thought, but he did not. Instead, he renewed his concentration on the task before him, the burden of his own unspoken pain all too evident in his grim expression.

Why did it take a crisis for him to speak of things that really mattered? she wondered. And what was it about this dark, desperate situation that had inspired Palmer's rare and unguarded honesty?

Ever since she had told him the truth about her own

past, Claire had longed to share the burdens of her husband's heart. Yet Palmer had doggedly kept his secret horrors to himself, just as he'd hidden away the sculpture that spoke so eloquently of the atrocities that haunted him still.

Afraid that he had said all he could bear to say, Claire busied herself with moving the rest of the surgical instruments closer to his reach. She watched him lift a shining pink loop of torn intestine into the light, then suture a small tear with tiny stitches.

To her surprise, he resumed the conversation without prompting. "I never meant to become a healer," he said. "It just happened. Perhaps it was Fate balancing the scale against my sins." Fatigue sharpened the shadows on his face and deepened the lines of his frown. "I did my best to help those I could, using what I'd learned from my mother. But there was so much I didn't know." He gently replaced the sutured intestine, then bent closer to look for further damage. "I learned whatever I could wherever I went. New cures, new procedures . . . anything that had proven effective."

Claire felt betrayed and made no effort to conceal it. All this time, and he'd never given the slightest indication he was such a proficient surgeon! "Palmer, how could you keep such knowledge to yourself? You could have been teaching me, sharing what you learned to the benefit of those who come to us for help."

"I have no magic secrets, Claire." He hooked another vein and twisted. "I've seen you work. You're an excellent healer and an even better surgeon. There's very little I could teach you."

"Nonsense." A flush of exasperation stung her cold cheeks. "That trick with the hook, for one . . . I could have used it a dozen times in the last six months."

Palmer arched a tawny brow. "Your methods worked just as well."

"Teach me what you've learned, Palmer," she repeated, "if not for my sake, then for the sake of my patients."

Palmer removed his bloodied hands from the incision and frowned up at her. "Very well." Then, as if he could not face her and say what came next, he lowered his gaze and resumed suturing. "In whatever time is left, I will teach you."

In whatever time is left . . .

Unbidden, Claire remembered what he'd said last summer. *I cannot promise forever, only that I will try my best to make our marriage work.*

He had tried. They both had, but she couldn't pretend things were as they should be any more than she could pretend she did not care for him deeply, in spite of the quiet desperation that kept him from her.

The thought of life without him . . .

In the flickering light, she stared at Palmer's bowed head and knew that every crease and every plane of his face had somehow been graven forever upon her. For all their differences, he had become a part of her life she could not imagine living without.

And his abilities as a surgeon . . . She watched with renewed admiration the skill and precision with which he retrieved the remaining surgical hooks.

Together, they could do so much more than either of them apart.

Claire managed an unconvincing smile. "I'll hold you to that promise." She faltered. "To teach me." She eyed him closely to measure his response, but before he could react, Ardra swept into the circle of now almost-spent torches.

"I came as soon as I could." With a practiced eye,

the apprentice took in what was happening and clearly
understood that one more pair of hands would only get
in the way. She knelt beside Claire, her voice subdued.
"Everyone's been fed. I gathered up all the hay in the
barn and used it to cover the children, then I made a
fire from broken branches," she said, organized as
usual. "When Master Roderick and Red brought Pascoe inside, I sent Red for water and heated it, then
cleaned Pascoe up and washed out everyone's cuts. So
far, there's no sign of infection in his leg. I bundled
the lad well, and Dame Bridget's holding him. He's
restless from the pain, but there's no fever and his pulse
and breathing are strong." The wind eased, tempering
the cold and making it easier to hear. "All the others
are asleep, except for Master Roderick. I tried to get
him to rest, but he's too anxious. Wants to know if
there isn't something he can do to help."

"Aye," Claire said. "Have him search the rubble
for a board long enough and wide enough to use as a
litter to carry Janie. If he can't find one, several narrow
planks will do, but he must bind them together firmly
so she won't be jostled any more than necessary when
we move her out of the cold."

"I'll help him." Ardra rose. "Can you spare us one
of the torches?"

Claire looked to Palmer, who glanced eastward toward the first faint hint of light in the cloudy sky.

"We can manage without a couple of the torches,"
he said. "Take two from behind Dame Claire." His
own dark-circled eyes lowered to Janie. "If we're not
finished by the time you've made the litter, go back to
the barn and wait. We'll summon you."

"Aye, master." Ardra plucked up two of the short-
ened torches and made for the barn.

Palmer peered down into the incision. "I think that's

it for this side.'' Ever so carefully, he began to remove the retractors. "I'll shift to the other side of the stake and suture the damage there. Then we'll cross our fingers and remove the stake. With luck, there won't be any unpleasant surprises.'' He arched the stiffness from his shoulders. "Then I'll stitch her up and hope for the best.''

"She has the best," Claire said quietly, meaning it with all her heart.

"You could have done it," Palmer countered. "And you would have, if I hadn't been here.''

"No," she said honestly. "I couldn't have done it, not under these conditions, and not as quickly or as well as you. She would have died.'' She willed him to look at her. "But I might learn to be as swift and sure a surgeon as you are, if you will teach me.''

He shrugged. "You're already as good a surgeon as I, but I will teach you what I can.'' Palmer removed the remaining hooks and retractors, then gently pushed the tissues back into place. "I need to stretch a bit.'' He tried to stand, only to sink to his knees. "Blast. My legs have gone to sleep.''

"Mine, too," Claire realized. Suddenly all too aware of the cold and her own weariness, she kneaded the stiffness in her own neck and shoulders. "The wind's died down, but if we don't hurry, we'll both have frozen toes.''

Palmer nodded without expression, picking up fresh instruments to repair the remaining damage. By the time he was ready to remove the stake, the sun had risen behind the clouds.

"I'm down to my last two swabs," Claire told him, worried that they would run out of supplies before Palmer finished.

"Two will be enough.'' He took a closer look at the

thick, jagged branch that impaled the little girl. Careful not to move it, he gripped the bloodied shank. "Hold the swabs at the ready. This branch might be sealing off a severed vein or artery. If she starts to bleed when I pull it free, apply pressure until I can find the source and stitch it." Without hesitation, he pulled out the bloodied stake and hurled it beyond the circle of torches.

Sure enough, an arc of bright red blood spurted onto his shirt in deadly repetition. Palmer snatched up several clamps and a retractor while Claire pressed down at the site of the bleeding. "I think it's deep," he said tensely.

She moved out of the way so he could pull the edges of the incision wider and probe frantically for the severed artery deep inside the wound.

Spurt by spurt, Janie's heartbeat measured out the endless seconds it took to find the break.

"Got it." At last, he got hold of the artery and clamped off the bleeding. That done, he placed a second clamp above the first, located the corresponding end of the severed artery, then repaired it with minuscule sutures. Then he carefully dipped the damaged vessel into the blood collected in Janie's abdomen, lifted it free and waited, dipped it again, lifted it free and waited again, then dipped it a last time and held the now heavily coated sutures in the cold air until the blood had clotted, neatly reinforcing the repair.

"A blood patch," Claire murmured with more than a hint of admiration. "Another Moorish miracle?"

"No," Palmer replied without looking up. "I learned that one from an English friar in a Carpathian monastery." He released the clamps, restoring the flow of blood to the artery, but very little seeped through the sutures.

Both of them let out a long sigh of relief.

"I think it will hold," he announced, his voice slurred by fatigue.

Claire looked up to see that Palmer's face was gaunt with exhaustion. "I can finish, if you wish it," she offered.

"Nay, but thank you for offering. You're as weary as I am. I'll manage." He closed his eyes, then blinked them to clear his vision. "I'm almost finished, anyway." Despite his fatigue, his fingers never faltered. He stitched everything up in half the time it would have taken Claire. Once he'd finished closing Jane's pale skin, he sat back on his haunches, his bloodied hands braced on his thighs. "That's it, and none too soon. I'm done in."

"Little wonder," Claire observed. Now that the worst was over, she could scarcely keep her own eyes open. She felt beneath the blanket for the pulse at Janie's neck. It was weak, but regular. Miraculously, the chid's skin was cool, not cold, to the touch. "Her heartbeat's settled to a steady rate, and I don't think she's deeply chilled. With luck, she won't start to bleed again when we warm her up."

Palmer was too weary to do anything but nod as Claire dressed the incision and began to bandage it.

As she finished, he forced himself to his feet with a mighty groan. "I'll fetch Roderick. None of us needs to be out in this cold any longer than we must."

"Aye." Claire closed the blanket over the bandage as she watched Palmer trudge to the barn. When he disappeared inside, she at long last allowed herself the luxury of lying down beside Janie and placing her arm across the unconscious child. Only dimly aware that she'd stopped shivering, Claire closed her eyes and tumbled into a black abyss of empty exhaustion.

* * *

She woke in Palmer's arms to the gray light of morning, her body tossed roughly and her ears assailed by the clatter and creak of the wagon's progress.

Palmer looked down at her with patent relief. "Thank God," he breathed, his arms tightening around her. "I was beginning to think I'd let you freeze."

"I'm not frozen," she said thickly, not entirely certain she wasn't. She still couldn't feel her feet. "Really," she murmured, "I'm fine."

Why was the smell of smoke so strong? Her thoughts formed the question, but for some reason, her mind seemed to have gone all foggy. But Palmer's arms felt so good around her, she didn't care. And the genuine concern in his voice was so comforting . . .

There was something she needed to ask, something important, but she couldn't seem to find the question in the fog that blurred her mind. "Janie." That was it. "Is she—"

"All warmed up and safely in the barn, doing well so far," Palmer answered.

Claire heard a buzz of subdued whispers and lifted her head to see all of the pitchman's sizable brood but the injured children wedged into the wagon bed along with her and Palmer. Up front, Little Red was driving, one of his scratched and swollen hands holding the reins and the other protectively around Ardra's waist as she slumped against him.

Palmer said haltingly, "The children will be staying with us . . . until we can convert one of our outbuildings into a proper house."

"They are?" Claire struggled to think where they could put everyone, but her mind was still too muddled.

Completely misinterpreting her confused frown, Palmer said defensively, "I didn't think you'd object.

They couldn't very well live in their barn, and—"

"I'm glad you brought them. So glad," she murmured, snuggling deeper into the warmth of his body and the intoxicating security of his embrace. "You're such a good man, Palmer. It's one of the things I love most about you."

As she drifted back into the seductive blackness, she barely noticed that his arms had gone rigid at the word "love."

Palmer hadn't meant to fall asleep alongside Claire in their bed. He'd only intended to lie down for a moment and close his eyes once he'd finally gotten her safe under the covers. But when he woke underneath those same covers still in his clothes with his sleeping wife curled against him, her head on his chest, he could hardly move for the stiffness in his arms and legs.

A fire was burning in the fireplace, and beyond the closed door of their chamber, he heard random bumps, thumps, footsteps, and exaggerated whispers.

What time was it? The curtains were closed, but the bedhangings were open, so he could see well enough to know it wasn't dark outside.

Palmer yawned hugely, annoyed into wakefulness by the tingling that told him the arm circling his wife's shoulders was only now regaining any feeling. He tried to ease free of her, but she muttered something unintelligible and wiggled even closer.

It took stealth and patience, but at last he managed to transfer her head from his chest to a pillow. Strangely weak, he sat on the side of the bed and massaged the tingling in his arm until the unpleasant sensation went away.

He yawned again, swiping his palms down his cheeks. The prickly stubble of his beard told him what his own sense of time had not: He must have been asleep for at least two days, maybe even three.

He barely heard the timid knock at their door.

"Aye," he answered. "Who is't?"

A child's voice mumbled something, but Palmer couldn't make it out. He was about to get up and go to the door when Claire stirred, then stretched, letting out a long, satisfied groan.

"Mmmm." She smiled up at him. "I feel as if I've been asleep for a hundred years." She looked more than fetching, her hair spread out on the pillow and her cheeks still ruddy from sleep.

The knocking came again, stronger this time.

"We have company," Palmer informed her, suddenly wishing that they were alone.

Claire seemed just as disappointed as he by the intrusion on their privacy. "I suppose we should let them in."

"I suppose we should." He rose and padded to the unlocked door. He opened it to find a little boy holding a tray of hot rolls and butter, his hair combed back and his freckled skin scrubbed so clean it shone. "Well, hello there," Palmer addressed him gravely.

"Dame Nonna says you've slept long enough," the boy informed him. Holding the tray with great care, he walked past Palmer and placed it on the bed.

A bittersweet expression shadowed Claire's face as she nodded to the little boy. "Thank you. Which of Little Red's brothers are you?"

"My name is William," he declared with pride. "And I'm seven years old."

Claire paled. Mute, she tenderly caressed his dark curls and gazed with longing into the little boy's deep brown eyes.

Palmer saw the depth of her longing in the simple

gesture and understood its source. If only he could do something to solve the cause of her pain. But how could he heal her suffering when he couldn't even heal his own?

And in the end, he would only bring more pain to her already broken heart. He hadn't meant to stay this long, as it was. The longer he stayed, the more he would hurt her when he left. But until he'd struck a bargain with the king to protect the home that was as much Claire's now as it was Nonna's, he must remain.

He gently ushered the little boy named William back through the door. "Tell Ardra we are not to be disturbed," he instructed. Then he closed the door and bolted it.

Palmer turned in silent understanding to his wife. He had no way to ease the sorrow in her soul, so he offered her comfort the only way he knew how—by holding her close and filling the emptiness with his body, uniting their wounded hearts in flesh, if not in spirit.

And Claire welcomed that comfort, even through her tears.

FIFTEEN

By spring, the pitchman's family was happily settled in the largest outbuilding, their presence making the lively company of children a permanent addition to the once-quiet compound. In many ways, the children were a joy. But every time Claire saw little William, her heart ached with questions about her long-lost son.

Was her William as quick and mischievous as this one? Was he as tall? Did he smile as readily and laugh as easily?

Dark memories of Castle Compton told her he did not, but she did her best not to torture herself with conjecture. She could scarcely avoid it, though, seeing the little boy so like her own day in and day out.

To make matters worse, Father Kendall's cousin had been able to discover very little about her son's circumstances: William lived under the rigid control of his uncle at Castle Compton, yet no one but his grandmother and a few most-trusted, tight-lipped servants ever saw the child.

Thankful to learn her son was alive, Claire nevertheless found the secrecy surrounding his existence deeply troubling. She had sought Father Kendall's help because her heart—a mother's heart—had told her William was in danger, and the news from Suffolk had done little to ease her fears.

She was certain Sir Robert was up to no good, but she dared not go back to see for herself. She could not even risk sending someone else. If Sir Robert found out . . . She could not let herself think of what would happen.

Frustrated and desperate, she turned to the God she had so long denied, pleading day and night for mercy for her son, even though she wasn't certain God was there to hear. She could only hope He was.

Beyond that, all she could do to hold on to her sanity was throw herself into her work. She rose before dawn and was the last one to bed, but she never shared her fears with Palmer, for she sensed him growing more restless with every passing month.

Their time together was running out; she knew it as surely as she knew that deep down, beneath the protective defenses he had built around his feelings, he had come to care for her as much as she now cared for him.

If only that caring could be enough to make him stay . . .

But it wasn't. The sins of his past would drive him from her. The only question was when.

If only she could make him see that the peace he sought could not be found in a place, but within himself. But Palmer would have to discover that for himself. And if he could not, the best she could do for him was let him go, no matter how deeply she loved him and wanted him to stay.

She knew better than to blame him. After seeing the carving and witnessing the torment of his nightmares, she knew that whatever he'd done in the war must have been terrible, indeed, to rob him so completely of any mercy for himself.

So she prayed for her husband, too—that he might one day forgive himself.

Yet by the time winter had turned to spring, and spring to summer, Claire had almost convinced herself that their lives might go on this way indefinitely, the two of them healing the sick and caring for Nonna side by side.

It was almost noon on the first day of August when Palmer sent Ardra to fetch Claire from her apothecary.

"Master Palmer said he would like to see you in the studio, Dame Claire."

"Mmmm." Claire focused on the glass measuring vial and tapped in powdered sulphur a few grains at a time until the yellow substance was even with the etched marking. "There. One dram sulphur." She scanned the crowded table. "Blast. Now where did I put that willow-bark extract? I just had it in my hand . . ."

"I think it might be important," Ardra prompted with more than a hint of criticism. Now that her chest was no longer flat, the girl had adopted a decidedly disapproving attitude whenever Claire failed to jump at Palmer's summons. Claire had no idea what the connection was, unless Ardra's ideas of wifely devotion were inflating in direct correlation to her bosom.

"Just a moment. As soon as I finish this decoction." Claire rather enjoyed pricking the air out of those inflated notions.

"Right away, he said," Ardra added softly, determined as always to have the last word.

Claire squelched a shadow of misgiving, turning a baleful glare on her apprentice. "Have you translated those pages of Homer yet?"

Ardra's self-importance evaporated with a grimace.
"Not yet. It takes forever."

"I gave you until the second to finish it."

"But today's only the first," she protested.

August first . . .

"Then I suggest you get to work, young lady." As
long as there was Greek, Claire would need no rods to
discipline Ardra.

August first . . . something about that date . . .

August first! The anniversary of their marriage . . .
and their physical union.

Claire raised her eyebrows. Could Palmer possibly
remember? she wondered.

No. She chided herself for having such an unrealistic
expectation. Already, she had allowed too many of
those to take root. More would only bring more disappointment.

Still . . .

Claire left her apothecary with a smile. On her way
through the kitchen, she selected a certain pitcher, mug,
and tray, then filled the pitcher with cool water before
carrying it into the hot sunshine.

My, but it was a fine day, the warmest they'd had
this year.

When she reached the studio, she balanced the tray
against her tummy and knocked on the weathered door.
"Palmer?"

"Come in."

Suddenly feeling as skittish as a virgin, she pushed
into the welcome coolness of the studio.

Palmer was waiting for her, a guarded expression on
his handsome face.

She lifted the tray. "I thought you might like something cool to drink."

"Ah . . . just like that day in the rose arbor." Palmer

made an effort to smile, but the result was uneasy.

Claire smiled back in earnest. "Allow me to compliment your memory, my lord husband."

"I remember more than that." He nodded but made no move to come closer, looking down at his shoe to scrape aside a stray shaving. "One year ago today, we were married by Father Kendall." His gaze was uneasy when it rose to meet hers.

She should have been happy that he'd remembered, but something in his manner raised a warning within her. "Aye." Her heart pounded in fear. Was this the day he would leave her?

He picked up a familiar draped object from the worktable. "I want you to have this. It's an anniversary gift."

Relief flooded through Claire. She'd been afraid he'd say . . .

As she so often had of late, she forced her thoughts from fears for the future to the comfort of the present. "But I haven't anything for you."

He smiled in earnest, now. "Mother always said a wedding anniversary was when a husband should give his wife a gift for putting up with him for another year. A good wife is gift enough for any husband, she used to say." He said it awkwardly, as if it was difficult, even painful, to speak of his mother as if she were already dead.

He'd called her a good wife, even if only by inference. Warmed by even so indirect a compliment, Claire nodded. "I can imagine Nonna saying it just that way."

She shifted her attention to the draped statue in her arms. "Thank you, then." Hoping she could make a convincing show of surprise and delight, she reverently removed the dusty covering.

There she was, holding Nonna, every tiny feature on

her face now carved in exquisite precision. "Palmer, it's beautiful." The tears that welled up were real. "It's the most eloquent statement of devotion I've ever seen. I love it." She inspected her own miniature features and was touched to see that he had duplicated the romantic rendition of the life-sized model. This Claire was beautiful, even if she was not. "Thank you. I shall cherish it."

Suddenly awkward, he cleared his throat. "Oh, and I finished the swords." He'd been working on them for months and months, not letting anyone see them, not even Little Red. "I thought you might like to be the first to see them."

Claire placed the statue carefully on the table. "I would be honored." She didn't tell him how many times in the past few months she'd been tempted to search for the swords when Palmer was away so she could steal a look.

"Close your eyes."

She did as he asked, grateful for the pride and excitement she heard in his voice.

"Now hold out your hands, palms flat. Steady, now, it's rather heavy."

Claire extended her palms and felt something cold and smooth contact her left palm even as something warmer and heavier filled her right.

He'd been right to warn her. She had never held a sword before, but this one was heavier than she would have guessed.

"You can open now."

She opened her eyes and gasped.

Before her lay a gleaming creation of lethal beauty and balance, the most elegant battle implement she had ever seen. "I knew you were making a sword, but I expected something . . . useful." She inspected the gleaming armament in awe. "This . . . it's a work of art."

Palmer held the grip of an identical weapon.

Claire inspected the one he'd given her. The handle was fashioned of gilded oak, secured to the steel grip-shank with inset cords of gold. For the pommel, Palmer had cast a heavy golden disk decorated on both sides with the lifelike figure of a writhing dragon. The generous crossguard was deeply sculpted with intricate filigree and overlaid with gold, as well.

But it was the blade that gave the weapon its lethal beauty. Every bit of four feet long, the steel surface was polished to a flawless finish brighter than silver, its only adornment a precisely etched Celtic motif of three intricate plaits that joined in a chevron echoing the blade's V-shaped transition from the thickened plate near the handle to the tapering sides. Below that, on either side of a narrow central groove, the edges of the blade tapered to razor-sharp perfection.

In her life as lady of Castle Compton, Claire had seen knights and swords aplenty, but never had she seen any so fine as these.

Her fingers closed around the perfectly balanced handle. "You're not afraid for me to touch it?"

"Don't be silly." Palmer nodded to his handiwork. "Give it a swing to test its balance."

"My first husband wouldn't let me so much as touch any of his weapons." She tested the grip, finding it surprisingly comfortable, and made a few careful arcs with the blade. "He was superstitious. Said it would bring bad luck for a woman to touch a weapon." The balance was superb, even in her inexperienced hands.

"Superstitions have power only if one believes in them," Palmer said. "Even then, it is the belief that causes things to happen, not the superstition."

How casually he'd granted her another rare glimpse into his thinking. Claire tucked his words away to savor when he was no longer with her, for she knew the time of leaving was hard upon them. The swords were finished. Now the demons of his past would drive him from her, and she was helpless to prevent it.

Claire didn't want to think about that. She concentrated on the elegant sword, instead, swinging the blade with more conviction. "Why, I think even I could use this. It's so perfectly balanced, it almost swings itself."

She handed it back to him. "It's exquisite, Palmer. I've never seen more elegant simplicity of design. Or such perfection in the adornments. Truly, it's worthy of a king." The one he'd been holding looked identical. "How did you choose which sword to give to the king?"

"I didn't," he said simply. "I found no flaw in either of them. Even I can't tell them apart."

Palmer laid each sword onto a cloth he'd spread out on his bed, then he bundled each of his creations up as carefully as he would a newborn baby. "Little Red brought word this morning. King William Rufus is nearby, on his way to the forest for a hunt. I mean to offer him this sword by way of a bribe."

"A bribe?"

"Aye." Palmer carefully deposited the bundled swords into a heavy wooden trunk and locked it. "Bribery is a long-standing Freeman tradition that makes it possible for us to hold our land against all invaders." He tucked the key into his pouch. "Celt, Angle, Saxon, Viking, Jute—every invader has his price. My father haggled with the Conqueror. It cost us eighty pieces of Roman gold to retain our holdings. But you won't find this freehold listed in the Norman's Domesday Book."

"Why not?"

"That was part of the bargain. It's always safer not to be counted in any king's inventory." Palmer cocked a half-smile. "I should get off easier with this king than my father did with the Conqueror. Our sovereign William Rufus might be a black-hearted scoundrel, but I have it on good authority that nothing makes his little black heart beat faster than a fine weapon."

Claire had never seen Palmer so relaxed and candid.

"And now," he said, "for the final surprise." He produced a huge wicker basket covered with a folded quilt. "We're going to the forest, just the two of us. No sick calls. No Nonna. No Ardra. No Little Red." Hooking the basket's large handle over his left shoulder, he reached his right hand toward her. "We're running away from home." He shot her a mischievous wink. "Just for the afternoon."

Running away was a sensitive topic. Claire still smarted from the way she'd hurt Palmer a year ago by throwing that up into his face.

Perhaps his lighthearted comment was his way of letting her know he forgave her.

She smiled. "I don't know which is more wonderful, the fact that you planned this, or the fact that I didn't."

Chuckling, he led her out into the sunshine. "When was the last time you did something spontaneous, just for yourself?"

"I can't even remember."

"Then it's high time. And don't worry. I've arranged for Ardra and Dame Bridget to look after things while we're gone."

Holding hands like two adolescents, they crossed the compound to the walking gate, then exited through the short, narrow tunnel that led through the wall, its armored door opening to the forest.

"I've never run away from anything in my entire life," she confessed, feeling as if a weight had lifted from her shoulders as she left the responsibilities of the compound behind.

Palmer pulled her toward a narrow dog path that led into one of the larger stands of oak.

Claire had explored the copses, meadows, bogs, and streams of the king's forest more times than she could count, but today, with Palmer, she noticed so much more.

High above their heads, the canopy of leaves seemed somehow loftier, the blue sky above them even bluer. Beneath their feet, the pungent, loamy cushion of oak leaves gave them easy passage.

Deeper and deeper into the forest they went, past the old pottery kilns to a rippling brook that ran through a perfect little clearing circled with lime trees.

Palmer spread the quilt on a sun-dappled patch of moss, then began bringing bread, jam, cheese, and apples out of the basket.

They ate in silence, enjoying the sounds of the forest despite the awkwardness both of them seemed to feel in this secluded, unfamiliar setting.

After they had eaten, Palmer leaned back and tucked his forearm behind his head. "Time for a nap." He patted his belly. "I'll be your pillow. Lay your head on me."

Without saying a word for fear it might shatter the fragile sense of intimacy they had found here, Claire rolled into the crook of his arm and laid her cheek to his chest. Lulled by the sound of Palmer's heartbeat and the wind in the trees, she closed her eyes and drifted off to sleep.

Palmer closed his eyes and reveled in the quiet isolation of this place. Why had he waited so long to take

Claire away from all the things that stood between them? He should have done this long ago.

She looked so peaceful there, her head upon his chest. They fit well this way.

They fit well in many ways.

He stroked the silky curls that always escaped around her face, marveling afresh at their softness.

Claire was a strong woman, and sturdy, but she was soft where a man needed a woman to be soft. It would not be easy to leave her, but he must.

The shade dancing on his face, he closed his eyes and gave himself to sleep, knowing somehow that the nightmares would not find him here.

Some time later, he opened his eyes to find Claire watching him, an apple in her hand. "I was waiting for you to wake up. Here's one for you." She handed one to him, then took a big bite from hers. Apple juice ran down her chin.

Palmer took a bite of his own. "Mmmm. Sweet," he said around the crunchy morsel.

Free of their usual audience, they both munched away like two contented cattle. When they were done, he hurled the cores far out of sight. "For the birds."

He saw that Claire still had a streak of apple juice on her chin. Feeling more than a little playful, he rolled both of them over so that he was propped above her. "You missed some." He bent down and licked the juice from her skin. "Mmmm. Sweet," he repeated.

Her deep brown eyes met his in unspoken consent. For all they didn't know about each other, they knew each other's bodies well.

But Palmer was in no hurry. Taking his time, he kissed her gently on the lips. Then the eyelids. Then on her temples. Then on the sensitive skin behind her ear.

She shivered.

Palmer sat back on his calves and untied his chausses.

"What are you doing?"

"That's pretty obvious, I should think," he said without rancor. "You ought to try it. It won't be nearly as interesting if I'm the only one with no clothes on."

He could see her considering, weighing, wondering.

Had her past been so perilous, he wondered, that she couldn't allow herself even this unguarded impulse?

Palmer took off his shoes, hose, and chausses, then stood and stripped off his shirt.

It was all the encouragement Claire needed. She took one look up at him standing above her, his need plain to be seen, and smiled a woman's smile as old as Eve.

Off came her kerchief, her shoes, her hose, her kirtle, and then her shift.

She lay back down on the quilt, her skin like polished alabaster in the dappled sun and shade, the nipples dark as wine on her ample breasts. She patted the quilt beside her. "Come lie beside me, husband," she said, her mouth firm with anticipation.

Palmer's blood pumped harder. What was she up to?

He lay beside her.

In one graceful move, she straddled him, her own heat and wetness pressed around the length of his erection. Her gaze met his as she began to undo her hair. Every subtle shift of position sent new waves of desire through him. He watched her fingers unwind the ribbons from her braids, then slowly begin to separate the silken strands even as the coarser curls at the apex of her legs mingled with his in gentle abrasion.

As unselfconscious as a forest spirit, she spread her unbound hair in a silky curtain all around her. Then she picked up the end of a shining length and stroked his skin with silken fire.

Palmer endured all he could before he rose up and drew her to him, suckling at her breasts.

Claire closed her eyes and arched into the hunger of his mouth.

She tasted so good, felt so smooth and firm in his hands, so hot and wet and hungry on his manhood.

He could not wait any longer. He raised her up and impaled her, then held her close and buried his face into the sweet softness of her neck.

Seconds ticked away into minutes. He savored the heat and pressure as her body held him tight inside her. She contracted even tighter, sending a shiver of pleasure through them both.

Neither of them spoke or moved.

High above them, the wind rustled in the trees. Distant birds sang back and forth from the wood. The brook trickled peacefully on its way.

They were one, for that perfect, timeless moment.

Then Claire shifted against him, catching the tip of his erection on some hidden part of her deep inside, and Palmer thought he would come straight up off the quilt. The unexpected friction sent a bolt of pure, molten lust from his groin to the top of his head.

And then she did it again.

"Holy Mother of God," he gasped. "What are you doing?"

She turned his own words back at him with a playfulness that surprised him. "That should be obvious, I would think." She said it lazily, seductively.

Then she did it again, setting loose another spasm of ecstasy.

"Don't stop." He'd made love to his share of women, but none of them had done this . . .

"Lie back," Claire instructed, her eyes half-lidded with desire, her pupils almost black.

His manhood still firm inside her, Palmer lay back.

She smoothed her hands across the planes of his chest, riffling the taut nubs of his nipples, then she spread her fingers wide over his rib cage on either side.

Slowly at first, she began to move back and forth, catching him deep within her every time and sending paroxysms of pleasure through him with every movement.

Faster and faster, she rode him. He saw her eyes close in mindless abandon. Her hair slipped around them both, shining like a fairy web in the dappled sunlight.

Still watching her, Palmer gripped her buttocks and added his own force to her movement, taking her faster still, harder against him.

"Ah! Ah! Ah! Ah!" With every motion now, her cries escaped, until at last, she arched her back and let out a long, low wail of fulfillment.

The sound of that, alone, was enough to bring his seed full-force.

Claire collapsed atop him, panting.

They lay there, heart to heart beating strong and hard, until she rolled off him onto the quilt.

"Ahhhh." Still breathless, she smoothed her hands down her own body in a gesture of primal satisfaction that was so uninhibited, Palmer would have spilled his seed again if that had been possible.

"Whew!" Claire yawned and covered her eyes with her forearm. "Hot. Very hot."

Palmer lay limp and boneless beside her. "I won't ask you where you learned to do that," he said rather breathlessly himself.

Claire lifted her arm from her eyes and raised her

head only long enough to glare at him briefly. "Good."

"Where *did* you learn to do that?"

By way of response, she fixed him with the exact same look he, himself, had used so often to silence Ardra's tactless questions.

"I don't know who that was who just asked you that question," he hastily recanted. " 'Twasn't I. Nay."

Claire smiled, wondering if Palmer had any idea why she was so happy.

He buried his face in her abdomen and inhaled the scent of her. "Mmmm. Lovely flesh."

No. He had no idea why she was so happy.

It wasn't because of their lovemaking, although that had been spectacular, she had to admit. She was happy because they were being themselves, without artifice or agenda.

They were talking, really talking, and it made her think there might be hope for the two of them, yet.

Palmer yawned, stretching his long, lean body as unselfconsciously as a wild creature, then lay back in the waning sunlight. "Are you ready to start for home?"

"Mmmph," she groaned. Now it was Claire's turn to bury her face in his belly. The scar was just a thin white line. "Must we?"

"Aye," he said with more than a hint of regret. But instead of getting up, he drew her close to his side and stroked the hair from her forehead. "Just when I think I've begun to figure you out," he said softly. He shook his head, chuckling. "Any more tricks up your . . . sleeve?"

"Not that I mean to tell you about, sir." Claire was so happy she almost wished they'd never come here. It had been so wonderful, so different from the strained politeness they wore at home. She dreaded going back.

"I saw that dark cloud drift across your face," he said quietly. "What's wrong, Claire? I'm your husband. You can tell me."

Not if it was about him, she couldn't.

She looked up into his tanned face. He was strong now, free of the illness that had stolen his health. If only she could heal his soul, as well. Then she would not have to live in anticipation of his leaving.

"Promise me something, Palmer."

"Anything." He smiled. "As long as you keep doing whatever it was you were doing to me just then. Mph, I liked that."

"This is serious."

"Mmmm." She saw the old suspicion steal the candor from his eyes. "What would you have of me, fair lady?"

She could not look at him and say it, so she tucked her head against his chest, taking courage from the solid warmth beneath her skin. "If you ever feel the need to leave here, please don't tell me before you go."

She felt him stiffen.

"I couldn't bear it, any more than I could bear to think that I had kept you here against your will." When he started to protest, she looked up and covered his lips with her fingers. "You never wanted this marriage. I know that, just as I know how very hard you've tried to make it work. But I care for you too much to keep you here if you need to leave."

She snuggled back against him, her fingers memorizing the feel of his skin and the soft, springy curls across his chest. "If you must go, let our last day be an ordinary day." Her throat tightened with emotion. "Leave me when I am sleeping. I do not think I could say good-bye without asking you to stay, and I don't want to do that, not if you need to leave."

His silence frightened her more than anything he might have said, but she pushed on. She owed him this, for all he'd done for her and Nonna.

"Nonna and I will be fine, especially now that Ardra's finally convinced Beta to let her become a healer."

More silence.

"I've seen the carving, Palmer."

He went hard as stone beneath her. "Which carving?"

"The one that shows your nightmares." She paused, letting it sink in. "A year ago, when I was looking for a sample of your handwriting."

"A natural mistake, then. Of course one might mistake that particular piece for a piece of paper." There was no levity in his sarcasm.

"I was curious. I had seen the carvings you had left with Nonna. I could not resist looking at those."

"And?"

"And I knew instantly that the same hand had made all those statues: the owl, the eagle, Nonna's bust . . . and the nightmare." She looked into his blue eyes, darkened now with anger and suspicion. "Where did it happen, Palmer? I'm your wife. You can tell me."

Palmer sat up and laid his arms atop his knees, hands limp, and bent his head. "You don't want to know."

"Yes I do."

He glared at her, haunted. "It was in Hungary. I was assigned to the stragglers, riding herd on the Germans at the rear of our army." He shook his head, his eyes losing focus. "If you could call it an army. They were peasants, mostly, with scarcely a weapon among them. Poor people. Hungry. Ignorant. Desperate. Little wonder the towns we came to locked their gates. Food was scarce enough for their own people."

His lids lowered slightly. "But when we reached Semlin, we found the weapons and bloody clothes of our advance party hanging from the walls like grisly trophies. At last, we had reached the enemy. Or so we thought. Wild to avenge the attack, we did not wait to find out that a small party of townspeople, frightened by our numbers and unable to speak our language, had seized an unlucky few of our advance forces and merely beaten them, then stripped them of their clothes and weapons and sent them on their way."

He looked down at his hands as if he could still see the blood on them. "I was just as eager as the rest of them to send some infidels to hell." He stared unseeing into the distance. "At first, we were fighting man to man. I don't know when our troops went out of control, or why, but suddenly, our own people were slaughtering women and children, looting, burning. It wasn't a battle, it was a massacre. I tried to stop it, but things had gone too far." Stricken by the memory of that abomination, he aged before her eyes.

"It would have been horror enough, the atrocities our own people committed. But then I saw the crucifixes in the hands of those we'd slaughtered." His eyes were lifeless when they turned to hers. "Semlin was no nest of infidels. They were Christians. The army of God had become the instrument of Satan, killing babies, raping women in front of their dying husbands . . . committing the very horrors of hell against our own brethren."

He turned his face toward heaven. "I tried to save a woman and her child from one of my own men, but when I lifted my sword to protect her, he snatched the infant from her arms and shoved it onto my blade, then stabbed me in the gut."

Claire closed her eyes with a moan. "Dear God . . ."

"He killed the mother as I fell. The last thing I saw was the child dying on my sword.

"My own army took my sword, stripped me of everything, and left me for dead." He looked into her eyes. "Would to God that I *had* died, but only my soul died that day."

"Palmer, you did nothing wrong." She gripped his arm. "There is guilt there, terrible guilt, but none of it should be yours. As soon as you saw what was happening, you tried to stop it. You were almost killed—"

"I made war without cause against my own kind. I slew men who were only defending their homes, their families. And I killed an innocent child."

"That, at least, was not your fault," Claire insisted, but she understood all too well why he had lived in torment all these years. "Oh, Palmer." What could she say? In the face of such horrors, words were useless.

More than ever, she knew what she had to do. "I meant what I said before we married, Palmer. If you must leave, I will give you your freedom. But I pray, still, that you may find the peace you seek here with us."

"I thought you didn't believe in prayer," he said bitterly.

"A figure of speech." No. She would not lie to him. "That's not true. Sometimes, I think of things Nonna told me about faith, and I wish I could believe. I wish there was a loving God out there. So I pray anyway, even though I can only wish that He will hear me."

"Be careful what you wish for, Claire," he said. "You might just get it."

Palmer arched his back, then retrieved his discarded shirt and put it on. He sat beside her and drew on his chausses.

Knowing this might be her last chance to speak so freely, Claire made bold to ask, "What do you wish for, Palmer Freeman?"

He bent his head. "For the pain to end. That's all. Simply for the pain to end."

"It never does." Claire held her shift over her body to cover her nakedness. Her gaze fixed on nothing, she made an offering of pain in honor of his own. "Every day of the world, I wonder where my William is. If he's warm and well, getting enough to eat. If anyone hugs him and holds him the way I would. If anyone loves him." She drew her knees to her chest and circled them with her arms. "Every day of the world it gets bigger, the hole inside my heart, and there's nothing I can do about it."

A melancholy silence stretched between them until the weight of it could no longer be borne.

Palmer spoke first. "All we can do," he said numbly, "is go on."

"Aye." Claire pressed the back of his hand hard to her cheek. "We go on."

SIXTEEN

By dawn the next day, Palmer was off to seek an audience with the king, his sword carefully wrapped and a purse of Roman gold hidden beneath his shirt.

Claire did her best to fill the morning with work, but still, the hours seemed to drag by. There was plenty to be done, but no matter what she set her hand to, she could not seem to stay the task.

Now that the children had recovered, Dame Bridget took all her brood but Little Red back to their demolished home whenever the weather was fair, to salvage what they could and rebuild. The compound was far too quiet without them.

Claire was worried about Palmer. All of England knew the king's infamy. What if Palmer had met some misadventure at the king's hand?

The morning ticked away.

At least Nonna and Ardra were well occupied. Ardra was spinning beside Nonna's chair, while Little Red sat between the two women, holding the yarn that Nonna was happily winding into a ball.

A perfect picture of domestic bliss, judging from the sheep's eyes Ardra and Little Red were exchanging.

Claire decided to give up trying to work and retire to her room. Reading offered the ultimate escape for her now.

She leaned into Nonna's doorway. "I'm going to read in my room for a while. Let me know if Palmer comes home or I'm needed for a patient."

At first, she had some difficulty concentrating, but eventually, she lost track of the time. It was still morning, though, when she heard an agitated exchange between Ardra and Little Red outside her door.

"I did not. I told *you* to watch her."

Claire frowned and hurried to the door. When she opened it, Ardra and Little Red froze in mid-gesture, their eyes wide.

"Out with it," Claire said firmly. "What's happened?"

Sick expressions claimed both young faces. They looked to each other, then back to Claire.

Ardra spoke a fraction ahead of Roderick. "It's my fault. I thought Roderick was watching her."

"No, it's mine," he said almost on top of her confession. "I thought Ardra was watching her . . ."

"We can't find Nonna," they said in unison.

Claire's heart lurched.

She had been afraid this might happen. In addition to her compulsion for hiding anything and everything, then forgetting she'd even done so, much less where things were, Nonna had taken to rambling, always in search of some elusive person or thing she just couldn't quite describe.

Stark fear twisted inside Claire. "The bathhouse, have you—"

"She's not there," Little Red stated. "I looked there first, then closed the door behind me and shoved a heavy planter in front of it. She'd never be able to move it alone.''

"Good thinking, Roderick." Claire's mind was frantically sorting possibilities, weighing priorities, and discarding nonessential notions.

"We've gone over the rest of the compound twice," Ardra explained. "We looked under every cover, behind every box, inside every trunk. She's not there."

"How long had she been gone before you realized it?"

Roderick and Ardra exchanged another wilted glance. "Almost an hour."

Claire couldn't have been in her room much longer than that. "All right. Ardra, I want you to keep looking. The compound is so large, she might have eluded you and gone back to one of the places you already looked. But don't call out for her. Keep quiet. She may be making a game of hiding from us."

She turned. "Roderick, I want you to check the spring first, then the stream and the pond below the waterwheel at the forge. Make sure she hasn't fallen in. Then check around the outside of the wall. Look for any way she might have gotten out." Since Nonna's wanderings had gotten worse, they now locked all the gates that led out of the compound. But the tunnels . . . "If either of you finds anything, come get me right away. I'll be in my room. Knock loud and long. It may take me some time to get to the door, but don't stop. Not if you find something."

How long would it take to search the tunnels?

Thirty minutes later, Claire had searched every inch of the tunnels, but Nonna was still nowhere to be found. Even the secret escape exit was still locked from the inside. Dispirited and growing more worried by the minute, Claire hurried up the secret stairs to her room.

Once there, she closed the hearth, then raced into the gardens.

A glum Ardra trotted toward her from the storage buildings. "Nothing."

"I just thought of one more place to look," Claire called to her. With Ardra right behind her, she sprinted for the outflow opening where the compound's irrigation system fed into the woodland stream.

Sure enough, two fresh sets of human toe tracks scraped down the slippery, mossy bank beside the opening, and a larger, fanny-sized swath behind them. Nonna must had fallen on her rump escaping.

To Claire's infinite relief, she did not find her good-mother floating in the stream beyond. "Roderick!" she called across the compound.

"Here!" He waved from atop the opposite wall.

"She's in the woods! We have to find her! Meet us outside the wall!"

Careless of her own clothing, Claire followed Nonna's escape route. As before, Ardra was right behind her. The cool water felt good now that she knew Nonna hadn't drowned in it.

They waded the stream. "Look for some sign of where she might have climbed out."

They waded slowly, inspecting every broken twig and frog-slip.

Little Red loped up through the underbrush, his already ruddy complexion mottled from heat and exertion.

Ardra looked to him in desperation. "We have to find her, Roderick."

He slid down into the stream, shoes and all, and held her. "We'll find her," he said with a man's assurance. "We'll find her."

"Aha!" Claire pointed to a series of scrape marks

on the bank. "Fresh toe tracks. She got out here."

The three of them scrambled up the bank, only to find the usual expanses of oak leaves, broken branches, wild brush, and brambles.

No trail. No path of drips to follow. No disturbed leaves or broken branches.

Claire fought down a wave of queasiness. "You two, stay together." She glared at them. "I mean it. Stay together, no matter what, and keep a sharp ear out. The king is hunting in the forest today. The last thing I need is for one of you to get shot or run down by a hunting party."

Ardra nodded. "And you?"

"Nonna used to make pots at the kilns. I'll go look for her there." She gave Ardra a brief, fierce hug. "Neither one of you meant for this to happen. I do not blame either of you. So put any thoughts of blame out of your head."

Ardra's eyes welled as she nodded, and Roderick looked pinched.

"If late afternoon comes and we still haven't found her," Claire instructed, "meet me back at the main gate. We'll send Roderick for the sheriff and organize a search party. Palmer should be back by then."

Blast. She should have left Palmer a note, but there wasn't time to go back and write one. Claire could only hope that by the time he returned, Nonna would be home, safe and sound.

"Now go. Go." Claire picked up her wet, moss-stained skirts and set off at a steady pace.

Claire had to admit, there had been times, as her good-mother had grown more and more confused and unhappy, when she had wondered if death wouldn't be a kindness, a deliverance for poor Nonna. At least it would free Nonna from the prison her body had become. But now, facing the prospect that something might have happened to her . . . Claire came as close to panic as she ever had.

The loss she would feel at losing Nonna—even as she was—loomed huge, terrifying, and all too real.

They had to find her. They had to.

Nothing seemed out of the ordinary when Palmer unlocked the main gates and rode Frieda into the compound. It was still fairly early, but already the sun was broiling, so he was hot as well as hungry and frustrated, yet he did not notice anything amiss as he locked the gate behind him.

After tying Frieda to the hitching ring, he entered the kitchen and laid the still-wrapped sword on the table. Only then did he notice that the house seemed too quiet.

"Claire?"

Silence.

"Ardra?"

Nothing.

"Claire!"

A small tingle of foreboding prickled through him.

"Ardra!"

No need to jump to conclusions. They could be any number of places.

An hour and any number of places later, Palmer gave his mounting sense of alarm full rein.

Something must have happened. Claire never took Nonna with her on calls anymore, nor would she take Ardra and leave Nonna alone.

Suddenly the ball of yarn he'd found on the bedchamber floor took on a sinister meaning, along with the hastily abandoned skein that lay nearby.

Something had happened, and it wasn't something good.

He heard a sound and turned to see Claire limp through the kitchen door, gasping heavily and holding her side, the hem of her usually immaculate white dress sodden and muddy, and great scrapes of green on the back of her skirt.

In the thump of a heartbeat, he had his arms around her. The thought of something happening to her . . . "Are you hurt? What's happened? Where is everybody?"

"I'm fine," she gasped out. "A stitch. In my side. I was running back." She eased down onto the bench. "It's Nonna." Claire heaved several more painful breaths before she got the rest out and Palmer could breathe again, himself. "She's gone. Into the woods."

He spun away from Claire. "I *knew* I should have gotten some dogs." She could hear the self-accusation in his voice. "It's just, she never liked dogs," he said more to himself than to her. "She was adamant. Said she didn't want them in the compound, digging in her gardens and messing on the paths." He ran his fingers through his hair. "I should have gotten them anyway. I knew she'd been wandering. Dogs can find anybody. I should have gotten the dogs. Weeks ago."

"Palmer, it's not your fault. There was a confusion between Ardra and Roderick. Each thought the other was watching her. They never meant for this to happen. Would you blame them?"

"No," Palmer admitted. "Of course I wouldn't blame them."

"Then don't blame yourself." Claire wrapped her arms around him and held on, tight. "We searched the compound twice. I even searched the tunnels. She isn't here. Then we found she'd gotten out where the irrigation runs out into the stream. We found the place where she climbed out of the stream, but there was no sign of her beyond that. She must be in the woods. I looked for her all the way to the kilns, but there was no sign of her." She stood. "I'm frightened, Palmer. The king's men are in the forest. Anything could happen to her. She could be shot, trampled, maimed by a boar—"

Palmer cut her short before she could enumerate any more of the dire perils his mother faced alone. "Where's Ardra?"

"She and Roderick are still looking in the forest. I made them promise to stay together and keep clear of the hunting party."

"They can't, Claire." Palmer unwrapped the sword. "The hunting party split into several groups, and all of them are mounted. There's no way Red and Ardra could escape if they were in the path of the chase. I have to get them out of there."

Claire frowned. "You still have the sword . . . ?"

"I never got to speak to the king. He'd had a nightmare, a portent of blood, and his advisers were all so busy making themselves indispensable, I never had a chance to see him." He hefted the sword. "Ride for the sheriff as fast as you can, Claire. We'll need a large search party. Systematic coverage is the only sure way to find Mother. I'll go after Red and Ardra on foot."

"You take the horse," Claire pleaded. "I can run to the village."

Palmer kissed her, hard and quick, on the lips. "You couldn't run ten more yards, and you know it." His free hand smacked her rump. "Ride, woman. There's no time to waste." Sword in hand, he loped toward the pedestrian gate.

Claire's mind formed a genuine, heartfelt prayer for

the first time in years. "Dear God, if You're out there, please watch over Palmer and Nonna and Red and Ardra. Keep them safe. If You've ever known what it's like to love someone, please bring them all back unhurt. Please."

Then she mounted Frieda and rode.

Palmer was deep in the forest when he heard a distant rustle and turned to see a familiar shade of cream, the same color his mother and Claire wore. "Nonna?"

The cream splotch halted, then the bushes began to quake in earnest until Ardra—scratched, disheveled, dirty, and bleeding slightly from her cheek and hands— emerged from the thicket. "Master Palmer!" She waved, then picked up her skirts and ran for him.

"Where's Roderick?" he asked when they met half-way. "I thought Claire told you two to stay together."

Ardra bit her lip. "We were, but then so much time passed, and we'd had no sign of Dame Nonna . . ."

"Ardra, where is he?"

"I don't know."

Palmer tried to retain his patience, but this was no inconsequential matter. Still, if he had to find one of them, he was glad it had been Ardra. Roderick stood a far better chance of fending for himself in the forest, even with the hunting parties charging about.

"Hist!" Ardra froze.

They both heard it at the same time—the sound of pounding hooves, louder and louder.

Besides the massive oak under which they stood, there were no trees close enough and large enough to climb, and the limbs overhead were too high to reach. They'd have to go to ground.

"Into the bushes, over there." Palmer hurried Ardra into a thicket of ash and hazel. They could see out so clearly, he felt as if they could be seen just as easily, but he knew better. "Find a comfortable position," he whispered urgently into Ardra's ear, "then don't move. Don't make a sound."

The galloping hoofbeats approached, but not from the direction he'd anticipated. This rider reined his mount to a halt behind them.

Palmer pivoted with agonizing care and saw that the rider was none other than Prince Henry. Palmer recognized him from the hunting lodge.

He watched as the king's younger brother sounded the call of a crow.

Another man-crow answered, then a rider seemed to appear from out of nowhere. He was hooded, even in this heat, so Palmer couldn't see his face, but he was dressed like one of the huntsmen.

When the two men met, Prince Henry looked left, then right, before taking two polished arrows from a concealed fold of his saddle. "These are exactly like the ones he gave Tirel. Make them count. Take care, though. Tirel is bound to be close on his heels. You won't have long."

His back still to them, the hooded stranger mumbled something Palmer couldn't make out.

"You just do what you're supposed to do," the prince retorted. "No one will find Tirel's arrows. I'll see to that."

Prince Henry then produced a small, heavy pouch and dangled it in front of the man, but when the huntsman reached for it, the prince palmed it with a dark grin. "Not until the deed is so done."

The huntsman nodded and nocked one of the arrows, the other at the ready.

Palmer breathed a little easier when Prince Henry trotted over behind a patch of alder a safe distance away, but the hooded huntsman lurked behind the very bushes where Palmer and Ardra were hiding.

If he came any closer, Palmer was afraid Ardra would cry out in terror.

Fortunately, the sound of another approaching horse, then another, drew the huntsman's attention.

The thunder of hoofbeats grew louder and louder until King William Rufus, himself, galloped into the clearing, a spear in one hand and a sword in the other. His thighs tightened, bringing his huge stallion to a sliding halt in a cloud of dust. Before the horse stopped moving, the king had launched himself to the ground and stood, legs apart and weapons at the ready.

As the dust settled, Palmer saw another member of the hunting party—Tirel?—rein his horse in at the far side of the clearing, then swing his nocked bow to the ready. "Did you see the boar?" he called to the king.

The king circled, roaring into the forest, "Where are you, you evil black beast?"

As if summoned, a magnificent stag burst out of the underbrush and bounded between the two men.

Palmer's focus leapt from the stag to the archer. Tirel was aiming dangerously close to the king. Before Palmer could do anything, though, the Norman lord let fly.

Palmer saw the arrow shave along the stag's back, scraping away the hair as the glancing impact deflected the arrow's path.

Then he heard the king utter a heavy grunt as a thump of impact sounded from the royal chest.

He looked to the king to see him gazing down in surprise at the deeply imbedded shaft of an arrow to his chest. A stunned look on his face, he grasped the shaft and broke it off, then toppled onto his back.

Ardra, her eyes wide, started to lunge toward the

wounded king, doubtless hoping to offer aid, but Palmer knew a mortal wound when he saw one. He clamped his hand over her mouth and forcibly restrained her. Blessedly, she did not fight too hard or try to cry out. He met her panicked gaze and shook his head, then cocked it toward the dead king whose eyes were still wide open.

As soon as he realized Ardra had stopped struggling, he released her.

The girl knew death when she saw it. The assassin had found his mark.

Where Tirel's arrow had gone was anybody's guess. Only one thing was certain: It hadn't killed the king. Palmer had seen it deflected not toward the king, but up and away from him.

Tirel sat frozen in his saddle, his features a mask of horror.

Palmer heard a soft whicker behind him and turned just in time to see Prince Henry toss the purse to the huntsman, who rode away as quietly as he had come.

A smug smile on his face, the prince reversed his mount with no semblance of stealth and rode into the clearing at a leisurely pace. Ignoring Tirel, he stopped to look down on his dead brother's body.

Only after a long, satisfying look did he lift triumphant eyes to Tirel. "Why, Walter, that looks like the very arrow my brother gave you this morning."

His comment elicited a strangled gurgle from Tirel.

Palmer had to give the Norman credit. Tirel knew how to keep his mouth shut, even in the most alarming of circumstances.

"Doubtless, the arrow that killed my brother will prove to be one of yours," Prince Henry added. "You may wager your life on it."

The distant sound of hoofbeats reached them through the forest.

"Ah. They're coming." The prince smiled. "You realize, of course, that I'm not here, don't you?"

Tirel's dark brows drew together in confusion.

"No." Prince Henry looked again on his dead brother, then he fixed Tirel with a chilling arrogance. "I left some time ago for London. Wasn't even here." He turned his mount toward the London road. "The only place to be, London, if one is to be crowned."

The king is dead. Long live the king.

With that, Prince Henry spurred his horse and galloped away toward the London road.

Palmer saw a hundred fears and possibilities flicker across Tirel's face before the Norman read the writing on the wall and spurred his own mount for the nearest ship across the Channel.

Palmer sank to his rump with a stunned breath, the hair on the back of his neck standing on end.

William Rufus lay dead, one of Tirel's arrows in his chest. Henry was on the way to London to make his bid for the crown. Prince Robert, next in line for the throne, was still in Normandy. By the time he learned of this, Henry doubtless would be on the throne.

The devil himself couldn't have arranged for the king to miss a boar, track it to the very place where the assassin was waiting, then stand in the line of fire between Tirel and a wild stag that just *happened* to have burst through the underbrush at the opportune moment and headed in the exact direction required to make this sequence of events take place just as Henry would wish it.

Palmer crossed himself.

This was no coincidence. Neither was it the result

of Prince Henry's plot, though he had his part in it, as well.

The hand of God had moved today, and Palmer had been a witness.

He had heard the accounts of the king's dream. He had listened as the king had scornfully read, then dismissed, another warning of doom, this one sent by the Abbot of Gloucester. And he had seen the king struck down by a set of circumstances so Byzantine, even a cynic like Palmer could not believe what had happened was anything but the hand of God.

What remained to be seen was where Palmer and Ardra fit into this particular bit of Divine Providence.

"Palmer." Shaking him, Ardra uttered in a semi-hysterical whisper, "I hear horses. We have to get out of here. Now."

In a burst of sheer survival energy, Palmer took hold of her arm and fairly flew out of the bushes, across the narrow clearing behind them, and into the wood beyond. Both of them ran for their lives.

With luck, they would reach the compound before any of the hunting party had the wherewithal to set the dogs on them. Even then, the dogs had plenty of trails to follow: the prince, the Norman Tirel, the stag, the assassin, and two witnesses of no real consequence.

Yet.

Claire was frantic by the time Palmer burst into the kitchen door dragging Ardra with him. "Palmer! Thank God."

He leaned against the door and bolted it. "You don't know the half of it," he gasped as Ardra flew, weeping, into Roderick's open arms.

Claire hurled herself into Palmer's not-so-open arms. "What happened?" Half healer and half distraught wife, she searched him frantically for signs of serious injury.

Palmer took the time to prop his precious sword against the wall before he slid to the floor, panting so hard he couldn't talk.

Claire crouched beside him. He was filthy, soaked from exertion, scratched, rumpled, and panting, but beyond a few wicked scratches, he wasn't hurt.

She was so relieved she went dizzy and sat beside him, her back to the wall.

Nonna chose that moment to enter the kitchen. "Palmer, how many times have I told you not to sit on the floor?" she scolded gently. "Now you've got Claire doing it."

Everyone in the room but Nonna went stock-still for several startled seconds, then erupted all at once in a cacophony of "She recognized you!" "Where *was* she?" "She called you Palmer!" and "Dame Nonna! You're back!"

Meanwhile, Dame Nonna picked out an apple, then padded back to her room.

"Later," Palmer panted, still struggling to catch his breath.

Claire laughed out loud, as much from the break in tension as from amusement.

Father Kendall entered the kitchen, his face strangely troubled considering the circumstances. "After Claire told me what had happened and rode on for the sheriff," he explained, "I went to ring the alarm and found Nonna sitting quietly in her pew." He shook his head. "I tried to intercept Claire and tell her, but somehow, I missed her. I did speak to the sheriff, though. He's called off the search."

The priest shrugged in apology. "I'm sorry it took so long to get her home, but Nonna was in no hurry."

"She was safe all the time," Claire said with relief.

"Well, we weren't," Ardra wailed.

Roderick shushed her gently, holding her in his lap and rocking her. "It's all right, Ardra. It's over, and you're safe. That's all that matters." He stroked her shoulder. "I won't let anything happen to you."

Claire decided that perhaps Little Red—no, Roderick—wasn't as thick as she had thought he was. He seemed to be doing very well at the moment.

She turned to the priest. "Thank you so much, Father, for bringing her home."

Instead of smiling, he said quietly, "If Palmer can spare you, I need to speak with you before I leave. In private."

"Of course." Claire frowned. Word must have reached him about William, and judging from Father Kendall's demeanor, the news wasn't good.

Palmer looked up at her, his own expression grim. "We must talk, as well."

Father Kendall took the hint. "Pray excuse me." He motioned toward the kitchen door. "Perhaps it would be best if I wait for Dame Claire in the garden. I've quite a bit of praying to do," he said solemnly, "so please take your time."

Filling a mug of cool spring water for her flushed, panting husband, Claire aimed a worried look at the door through which the priest had departed, then handed him the mug.

Palmer took a long draught of water, then wiped his mouth and proceeded to tell her exactly what had transpired in the forest.

Even without embellishment, the story was terrifying enough.

Ardra contributed the dramatic embellishments, her

every outburst a good excuse for more soothing and masculine attention from Roderick.

When Palmer's account was done, Claire sat in grim silence, her worries about William overridden at least momentarily by what she had just heard. "Both of you are witnesses," she said just above a whisper. "The *only* witnesses who saw everything." Her blood ran cold. "Palmer, you must speak of this to no one."

She turned to Ardra. "No games, Ardra. If this goes beyond these walls—"

"We could all be killed," Palmer finished for her.

Roderick buried his face against Ardra's neck and held her even tighter.

Palmer rose to his feet and pulled Claire close. "I have a plan, Claire, but it's not an easy one."

Somehow she knew he was not going to share his plan, not even with her.

"You'll have to trust me," he told her.

Claire wished she could, but something in his manner disquieted her.

"Ardra will tell no one," Roderick said emphatically. "I'll see to it."

"Good." Palmer faced him man to man. "Watch over her, son. I'm counting on you for that."

"I will." Roderick stood to his feet, Ardra still in his arms. "This young lady has had enough for one day, I think. I'm taking her to her bed. Then I'd better hie me to our old homestead, or me sire's liable to send a search party after me."

After Ardra was tucked in, Roderick left, his departure accompanied by Palmer's strict cautions about avoiding any contact in the forest on his way home.

Claire turned to her husband. "Father Kendall is waiting. Don't worry. I won't say a word about what you saw, not even to him."

"For his own safety, that would be prudent. But you need not hurry." Palmer shifted uneasily on his feet. "I want to take a bath. And there are a few things I must do before tomorrow."

"Very well," she said, "I'll wait for you in bed." After today's scare, she craved the security of his embrace.

He met her gaze. "Can you stay awake until I get there?"

Claire saw real concern in his eyes, but she also saw pain. And something dark and unspoken. Something important. "I'll be awake."

After making certain Ardra and Nonna were both asleep, she traversed the garden to the secluded bench where she'd known she would find the priest. She waited to speak until he completed his prayer and crossed himself. "It's William, isn't it?"

The priest nodded. "May God have mercy, yes."

A chill went through her as Claire sank to the bench and lowered her face into her hands. "Tell me the truth, and quickly," she pleaded. "I do not think I can bear to drag it out."

"Since your banishment, your son has been held prisoner in a locked room."

Claire winced, her heart contracting. At least he wasn't dead.

"Until recently, the child was cared for reasonably well. His grandmother saw to that. But now her health is failing, and she has openly expressed the fear that her grandson will not long outlive her."

"Dear God. What can we do?" Miserable, she hugged herself and confessed at last. "William is my son, Father, true and rightly born, and heir to his father's title and holdings."

"I know," the priest said gently. "My cousin told

me about your marriage and your son. And your husband's death.''

Bile rose in Claire's throat. ''Without my husband's protection, I was helpless. Sir Robert cast me out, threatening to kill my son if I refused to leave. He swore he'd do the same if I ever returned, as well.''

''Despicable,'' the priest uttered darkly. ''He shall answer to God for that.''

''My only concern now is William.'' Surely she could think of *something*. She must! ''Even if I could leave Nonna, which I cannot, I dare not try to rescue him myself. I am infamous throughout the whole county. Someone is certain to recognize me. And I have no doubt Sir Richard has placed a healthy bounty on any information about my return.''

''I will gladly go,'' Father Kendall volunteered. ''My cousin and his son will help me, I know.''

''I know you would, you darling man.'' Claire squeezed his jaundiced hand. ''But both of us know how ill you are. The journey to Suffolk alone would be too much.''

He sighed. ''I suppose you're right. But there must be *some* way . . . Perhaps Palmer—''

''Palmer would help if he could, but just now . . .'' She could not tell the priest that Palmer was already in grave danger, himself, embroiled in an intrigue that put them all in jeopardy. If that intrigue should follow him to Suffolk, William might be put in even more peril. Claire would not ask Palmer. ''That isn't possible.'' She left it at that.

''Then we must pray,'' the priest exhorted.

''I've *been* praying, night and day,'' she countered, anger blooming inside her where the sick feeling had been. ''And yet my son is still imprisoned, in more danger than ever.''

"God will make a way," Father Kendall reassured her. "God will make a way."

"I wish I could believe that." Claire rose, already grieving for the son she was helpless to save. "We will talk again of this tomorrow."

"May God keep you and your son safe from harm," he benedicted her.

"I pray He shall," she answered, only hoping that He would.

Claire returned to her bedchamber, sponged herself clean, put on a fresh shift, and crawled into bed, but her heart was too burdened for sleep, and her mind spun endlessly, coming up with idea after idea that wouldn't work.

Palmer was gone much longer than she anticipated. Twice, she caught herself drifting into exhausted slumber, only to sit up and take deep breaths in an effort to stay awake.

When at last he came into their bed, he was drawn and somber. Without a word, he looked at her candlelit face for a long, quiet time. Then he leaned across her and snuffed the candle. In the darkness, her husband drew her to him.

She had expected him to make love to her, but he didn't. Instead, he held her close and stroked her hair until she fell asleep. Her last conscious thought was that when he must leave her, she would hope their last night would be this way, sharing the peaceful darkness in the comfort of each other's arms.

She did not know until the next morning that it *had* been their last night together.

Only when she woke in the gray light before dawn did she discover that Palmer had left her, as she'd always known he would.

SEVENTEEN

Claire wasn't certain when she'd stopped listening for the sound of Palmer's voice, his step.

At first, she'd hoped against hope that he would return.

"I have a plan," he had said. "You'll have to trust me."

But he had also said that his witnessing the king's murder could endanger all their lives. And he had told her from the first that he would leave her.

So, after days turned into weeks and weeks turned into months, she began to think that he had left in order to protect them all.

October came, and the pitchman took his family back to their woodland home, completely rebuilt with fine oaken floors and timbers hewn from the very tree that had once destroyed it. Claire missed them, but she understood their hunger to return to the deep woods. Luckily, the verderers, allowing for the circumstances, exacted no fee for the use of the new king's wood, especially since Roderick presented each of them with several fine, smooth, wide planks of oak for their own use.

By November, Nonna had drifted back into a distant silence, leaving the house far too quiet as the cold and rain kept all three of them inside.

It was during those cold, dreary days that Claire had decided she would never see Palmer again. But her brain had failed to convince her heart, so a tiny flame of hope still burned, too deep to be admitted.

That was when she'd started reading the Gospels. To her surprise, she found comfort in them, for the faith she read about, the love she read about, had little to do with the endless rules, rituals, and denials of earthly religion.

Now that the November darkness came early and stayed late, Claire often read the Bible deep into the night, marveling at the earthy practicality of the stories, yet fascinated by the huge disparity between man's perspective and that of his Creator.

But some nights like tonight, when she was tormented by questions about Palmer and her son that had no answers and probably never would, even the Bible offered her no comfort. That was when, weather permitting, she bundled up in her warmest boots and her blanket and quilt, and walked the walls in solitude.

Tonight, the winter sky was particularly clear.

Warmly wrapped against the cold stone, Claire lay down and gazed into the stars for a long time. She was so weary of hoping, of waiting, of worrying.

She wasn't certain how long she had stared into the endless web of light before she finally had the courage to admit that she could not rescue William, nor could anyone else she knew. Silently, she surrendered her son to the God who had made him, letting go at last of all her blame, her hatred, her rage, her grief, her anger, her worry, and her fruitless plans of rescuing him. Even her hope, she offered up to heaven, holding nothing back.

And then she waited quietly for the pain of loss she was certain would overwhelm her. But instead of grief or emptiness, she felt as if a chain had been broken deep within her soul. Amazed, she closed her eyes and soaked in the unexpected peace it brought her.

She knew now that prayer was the only gift she could give her son. And she was grateful for the precious years she'd had with him. Truly grateful, even if that was all that life allowed. Nothing could ever take that away.

Could she let go of Palmer, too?

Even as she stared up at the stars, her mind turned inward, and she knew that she had no choice: To heal, she would have to let him go.

Only then could she treasure what they'd had, not what she'd lost.

It took all her courage, but she rooted out her smallest secret shred of hope that Palmer might return and surrendered it. Harder still, she gave up the question that had tortured her ever since she'd lost William, and then the man she loved: She gave up asking "Why?"

And deep within her soul, another chain was broken.

She would always love Palmer—more than that, respect him. They had shared many precious acts of love and sacrifice. Nothing could take those treasures from her.

Yet there was more to surrender, still. One by one, she made a silent sacrifice to God of all her disappointments, her anger, and her grief—even the tragedy of Nonna's progressive disease. Claire offered up the hurts and losses of her life until nothing remained but love and memories.

And instead of feeling empty, she felt at peace.

Where was Palmer at this moment? she wondered, finally free of pain such thoughts had stirred.

She stretched her fingers toward the sky, taking comfort in the notion that that was where he'd gone. Out there, into the infinite twinkling lights and lives.

Anywhere but here.

He'd tried to warn her from the very beginning, but she had hoped that *she* would be enough to make him stay.

Lying there in the cold, she realized just how arrogant that hope had been.

Her lasting consolation was that she'd given him his freedom.

It was one of the few truly selfless acts of her life.

So now . . . we go on, she told herself, as he once had. But he'd been wrong about the pain. It had ended now, at least for her.

She had her work. She had a home. Security. Respect. Blessings in abundance.

Claire looked into the starlit sky and marveled once again at the matchless intricacy of the pattern of creation.

All right, she said silently into the heavens. I know You're there, God, Christ . . . whoever You are. I'm speaking to You, and I'm grateful . . . that You came among us and showed us how to love. More than that, You showed us how to suffer, yet love on. So I thank You for my life, just as it is. And I love You.

It was all that she could manage, but she knew He'd heard her.

She only hoped He appreciated candor as much as He valued meekness.

Two weeks later, Father Kendall arrived with word that Ardra was needed at home.

"Nothing serious, I hope." Claire had come to rely on Ardra.

Father Kendall dropped his voice so Ardra couldn't hear him. "I'm afraid it is. Corly has taken ill. Quite ill, I'm afraid."

Poor Beta. Nothing was more frightening for a mother than a sick child. "Is there anything I can do?" Claire offered. "Medicines perhaps?"

"You can pray." The priest regarded her with compassion. "Many times, that is all we can do."

Ardra had been gone for a week when a knock sounded on Claire's door at dusk.

To her surprise, she found Beta waiting outside. The warmth in Claire's greeting was genuine. "Beta. Please come in. You must be freezing out there."

The woman had aged ten years. Beta moved past her to the fireplace and stood there, warming her hands, before she turned and spoke.

"Ardra has taken ill. Now both my girls are dying."

Claire put her arm around Beta's shoulders. "Here. Sit." Once she was settled, Claire pulled up a stool and sat facing her. "Please, Beta, let me help. At least let me try." She took Beta's cold, work-worn hand into her own. "I love Ardra, too. You're her mother. No one else can take your place—and I wouldn't want to—but I do love her."

"I've been washing my hands," Beta blurted out. "And all my instruments. Even boiling my clothes between deliveries." Her eyes pleaded with Claire. "My patients don't much like it, I can tell you, but I do it anyway, because it helps them."

"Oh, Beta. I'm so proud of you."

"Proud? Of me?" That baffled her.

"It took great courage to try something you had once dismissed. And it took even more to admit it helped. You're a brave woman." There had been a time, and not so long ago, when Claire might have said those words, but she wouldn't have meant them. Now she meant them, so saying them brought healing. "Now. Tell me what I might do to help with the girls."

"I wish I knew." Beta sagged. "I've tried everything I can think of, but nothing helps. And women still need their midwife, whether my girls are ill or not."

Clearly, Beta was even more drained by her situation than Claire was by hers.

"I have an idea. Why don't we hitch Frieda to the cart, take all the blankets and quilts we can carry, and bring the girls here?"

"Here?" Beta looked around in suspicion.

"All my cures and equipment are here," Claire explained. "I cannot leave Nonna alone anymore." She offered Beta a reassuring smile. "We could put the girls in my bed. I'll sleep with Nonna. You can have Ardra's cot." Her heart went out to the stubborn, exhausted little woman. "With all of us here, I can watch the girls whenever you're called away."

To give Beta time to think, she counted to twenty in her mind, then asked, "What say you?"

"Let's do it." Then Beta hesitated. "But what about Nonna? You said you couldn't leave her."

"True, but both of us need to go get the girls, one to ride with them and the other to drive the cart." Claire wished she had thought this through before she'd opened her mouth.

She said a hasty, silent prayer that God would watch over Nonna and keep her safely asleep. "Come. Nonna is sound asleep. With God's help, we'll be back long before she wakes."

They had almost reached Beta's house when the

midwife turned to Claire and said, "Father Kendall and Ardra were right. Two widows like us . . . I mean, I know you're no longer a widow, now that you're married to Palmer—"

"I might as well be a widow," Claire interrupted wryly.

Both women smiled at the irony of that confession.

"Two women alone like us," Beta amended, "we should have been helping each other all along."

"You did help me," Claire protested. "You allowed Ardra to be my apprentice."

"Aye, well, she gave me not a moment's peace till I said she could." She looked to Claire. "What I'm tryin' to say is, I'm sorry it took me so long to make peace with you. And I'm not just sayin' that because I need your help. I mean it. I was wrong, and I regret it."

"Life's too brief for regrets." Claire urged Frieda toward the light at the end of the road. "We can help each other now."

Beta stuck out her hand. "Friends, then."

Shifting the reins to her left hand, Claire shook the midwife's hand with her right. "More than that. Sisters."

They had both girls safely back at the compound before midnight. As she had prayed, Claire was back before Nonna even knew she'd left.

By the eve of Christ's Mass, both girls had improved so much, Claire had sent them home to celebrate with their mother.

Now that the house was so quiet, after weeks in the community of women, Claire almost wished she'd asked them to stay.

No. That was selfish. She and Nonna could have their own celebration.

Claire bundled up and went outside to cut some evergreen and holly. After arranging that on the mantels, she spent the afternoon making raisin cakes with honey and baking the last of the soft wheat flour and dried apples into a pie.

Once the fires were all well-stoked and the baking completed, the house looked and smelled like magic, despite the cold wind and spitting snow outside.

Claire sat in front of the fire for a leisurely glass of elderberry wine before changing into her best dress and helping Nonna fix her hair and put on her warmest, most comfortable robe.

The two of them were sipping their wine in quiet companionship and staring into the flames when Nonna abruptly lost the dazed look she had worn for so long. "This is lovely, Claire. Thank you."

Claire took Nonna's hand in her own, delighted. "Thank you, Nonna. For taking me in. For teaching me to be a healer. For giving me the joy of reading. But most of all, for showing me what faith is."

"I wasn't worried about you," Nonna said with pride. "You've always known the truth when you saw it. It was just a matter of time before you saw the truth about Him." She pointed up, her blue eyes lively, even if only for a few precious moments. "I knew it would happen."

"It wasn't easy, though." Claire closed her eyes and drank in the peace that not only surrounded her, but lived within her. "The hardest thing was letting go."

"Mmmm."

"My parents. The children I gave birth to who did not live. Palmer. Those were hard, but the hardest was my son. Not knowing . . ."

"Aye. That's the true test of faith: to trust God in the unknown with those we love."

"Like Palmer," Claire prompted, her bitterness replaced now by gratitude and just a touch of sorrow. "And my son."

"And my mind," Nonna said with an absolute clarity that tugged at Claire's heart.

Nonna shifted in her chair. "Speaking of Palmer . . ."

Claire recognized the brittle animation in her voice. The moment of lucidity had ended.

"I told you God promised me another little boy," Nonna said, "didn't I?"

"Nonna . . ." Claire cut her eyes over at her goodmother. "You haven't been chasing Father Kendall again, have you?"

"No," Nonna grumbled. "I can't. He never comes to see me anymore."

"Little wonder." Claire patted Nonna's arm. "Well, if he does come to see us, promise you won't try to drag him into your bed. It undoes the poor man completely."

"Undoes what man?"

Claire chuckled. "Never mind." She was feeling warm and just a little muzzy from the wine.

She stood. "I'm ready for bed. How about you?"

"I'm getting a present, you know." Nonna lurched to her feet. "A little boy, just like Palmer, with beautiful brown curls and big brown eyes."

"Palmer has blue eyes," Claire reminded her. She took the shovel and banked the fire.

Nonna smiled at Claire, her eyes unfocused. "I've seen him, you know. God showed him to me. Such a beautiful little boy."

Nonna saw all manner of things that weren't there,

these days. Claire was simply grateful that her good-mother's nonexistent visions were all benign.

Nonna started for her room, then paused and turned back. "Will he be here when I wake up? My new little brown-eyed boy?"

"Perhaps he'll visit you in your dreams, dearest," Claire offered. She gave Nonna a big hug, then helped her into bed before laying another fat chunk of oak from Roderick's fallen tree onto the fire. "There. That should be enough to last the night."

"Sweet dreams," she said as she closed Nonna's door.

Once in the privacy of her own room, she yawned hugely and laid her robe across the foot of the bed.

It was snowing hard outside, now.

She smiled, anticipating the muffled silence of a snowy winter's morn.

The hot brick she'd put at the foot of the bed was still warm, but just barely.

Claire undressed, then slid under the covers and lay there listening to the hiss and pop of the fire.

"Thank You," she whispered. "For loving me enough to die for me. And for giving me William and Palmer. And Father Kendall. And thank You for Nonna; especially for Nonna. And for Beta and Ardra and Corly. For my life, just as it is."

It wasn't easy letting go, but now that she knew how to do it, she'd begun to understand the way to true freedom.

"—for all I've lost," she whispered, "for all my disappointments. I love You anyway. And I need You."

It was not a poetic prayer, but an honest one that brought her perfect peace.

Claire closed her eyes and slept the healing sleep of surrender.

Sometime in the night, she dreamed of chasing Nonna as she ran after poor Father Kendall, slamming doors as he tried to escape her. Faster and faster Nonna and Father Kendall ran, and faster and faster, the doors slammed.

Claire opened her eyes in the dark of her room, convinced she could hear the echo of the door's last slam.

But all was quiet.

Then she heard it. The distant creak of the pedestrian gate in the wall. Now that it was so cold outside, they no longer had to keep it locked to keep Nonna from wandering. Claire wondered who it was that sought her help at such an hour, and why. She sighed, soaking up one last moment of warmth before she rose.

Sickness and injury respected no schedule.

When she heard the sound of labored footsteps in the snow, she rolled out of bed, pushed open the window curtain, wiped clear a frosted pane, then pressed her eye to the glass.

A big man, half as wide as he was tall, trudged toward the house. She wasn't certain, but his build was similar to Big Roderick's, and he was moving awfully slowly.

Whatever the trouble was, it must be urgent to bring him out on a night like this.

It took little time to dress and scrub her hands. She was waiting in the open doorway with her lamp lifted high before the stranger reached the last curve of the graveled walkway.

Claire drew her shawl closer against the raw night air and tried to find some hint of the man's condition from his labored gait.

A deep-brimmed hat obscured his face, and his billowing cloak could have concealed any number of things.

He did not look up into the light until he was standing at the foot of the stairs. When he did, though, the light reflected eyes as blue as a summer sky.

Palmer!

He was gaunt, stubbled, and exhausted, but she would have known him anywhere.

Her throat tightened so, she could hardly say his name. "Palmer . . ."

"Claire." His smile erased the weariness and grime. "I've come home. For good."

All the tears she had ever wanted to cry but couldn't tried to escape at once. "Palmer!" It was more a sob than a word.

Claire leapt toward him, but he held up a staying hand. "Wait."

Why hadn't she seen his other arm? Was he hurt? Had he lost it in an accident . . . ?

"You told me once," he said, "that your heart was not whole. Mine wasn't, either." His voice was ragged with fatigue, but it was the most beautiful sound she had heard in more than four months. "I knew I could never make restitution for what happened in Hungary."

She had never seen his expression so intense, yet there was peace behind the anguish he was speaking. She saw it in his eyes.

"But as long as there was a chance I could give you back your heart, I had to try." Darkness flickered across his features. "I could not tell you. That would have been too cruel, if I had failed."

He looked to her with love, his voice breaking. "I've brought you back your heart, Claire, and it's made mine whole again."

Palmer opened his cloak to reveal a thin, curly-haired little boy with big brown eyes too huge for his frail little face.

Claire dropped to her knees, her heart skipping, a single word wrung from the depths of her soul. "William."

He turned those deep, enormous eyes to her, but clung to Palmer.

"This is your mother, William," Palmer soothed, ruffling the boy's hair. "See? I told you she wasn't dead. She's alive, and she's been waiting for you, wanting you every day since they took you from her."

Palmer's eyes met hers. "He's a little shy, yet. It's been a long, hard journey. And some hard years before it, poor lad."

Claire wanted to get up, but her legs wouldn't move.

"I can't carry you both, I'm afraid," Palmer said as he struggled up the last few steps.

What was she thinking? They must be exhausted, cold, and hungry. She was on her feet and shepherding them into the house before she stopped to think again.

Palmer followed her into the kitchen and sat heavily in a chair, but William made no move to let go of him.

Claire wanted so desperately to take her son into her arms and hold him that her chest ached as if she had the pleurisy. But she knew her son had been through an ordeal, so she forced herself to heat mulled wine and warm cakes and fry ham.

By the time the food was ready, William had fallen asleep, and Palmer's eyelids were at half-mast. But the smell of food revived him.

"How?" she asked, her voice soft so as not to wake the child, who clung to his rescuer even in sleep.

Palmer downed a swig of wine, then ate a chunk of ham before he answered. "Just as I said in the letter. I had a plan."

"What letter?"

Palmer stilled, crestfallen. "The one I left for you when I went to London."

"Palmer, I found no letter."

"No letter . . ." The full implication of that took a moment to sink in.

"Nonna," they said in unison.

Claire laid her face into her hands. "You left a letter."

"But if there was no letter . . . Great heaven." Palmer's voice tightened. "Then you thought—"

"I thought you'd left me." Claire looked at him with all the love in a whole heart. "But I loved you anyway, because I knew you never would have left us if you could have stayed."

"If Nonna ever had any idea of the pain she'd caused—"

"She'll never know," Claire assured him, "because it doesn't matter. All that matters is that you are here, and you've brought William with you." She kissed his hand. "Tell me what happened."

"First, I bought a horse and rode for London. Once I found Prince Henry, it took only a few carefully chosen words to win a private audience. Though no one was in the room, both of us knew we could not speak candidly. So in the way of the court, nothing was said outright, but both of us managed to come to terms."

"Terms?"

"First, I made certain he knew that I was not the only one who had witnessed his treachery. And I assured him that should anything happen to me or my family, word would reach his brother in Normandy of just what had happened. That was more than enough to convince him. He granted us the same rights we enjoyed under his father. And a few assurances that if things didn't go as I hoped with William, he would place the child under his protection.''

''A murderer's protection?'' Claire was as appalled as she was grateful.

Palmer met her look of challenge. ''A king's protection.''

''And then?''

''Then I took my tools to Castle Compton and hired on as a woodwright. I quickly found out your brother-by-law kept William locked away, under close guard. Only his grandmother could visit him.''

Claire realized he was editing what he told her.

''I tried a dozen ways to get to the boy, but nothing worked. Finally, I had to risk telling the dowager that I had come to rescue him from his uncle.''

''The dowager? But she hated me.''

''Aye. But she loved William. And her health was failing. She was terrified the boy's uncle would kill him as soon as she died.'' He took a bite of cake. ''Mmmm. Heaven.'' Another swig of wine.

''While I was there,'' he went on, ''I kept up my healing, but only in the village, lest I raise suspicions at the castle. I had been trying to save a street urchin. He was older than William, but stunted by starvation. When he died, I realized I might just have a way to rescue William yet leave no one the wiser. I planned to bring the dead child's body secretly into the tower where William was kept, get William out and leave the dead child in his place, then set the tower afire.''

Claire shuddered.

''Dame DePeche got me the key to the room where William was imprisoned. And when the time came, she distracted the guards so I could sneak the dead child inside. But then something went wrong. Before I could make the swap, I heard an argument in the hallway, and when I looked, Sir Robert had arrived and was determined to get past his mother. For some reason, he suspected something."

Palmer shook his head. "He may have meant to kill William then. I do not know." His arm tightened around the sleeping child. "I thought it was all over. Then the dowager pretended to go mad. She screamed and shrieked and fought her son as fiercely as any warrior. She dragged him back down into another hallway, drawing the guards with her.

"That gave me time to unlock the door, lay the dead child on a heap of straw and cover him with the only blanket, grab William, then set the straw on fire. It blazed up right away, so I pulled William close under my cloak and locked the door behind us. Lady DePeche had told me where to leave the key.

"By the time we reached the back stairway, the entire room was ablaze, but I heard them coming in our direction. So we hid behind an arras.

"I'm certain Dame DePeche saw us, but she made sure the others didn't." He took another swig of wine and bite of cake.

Claire was on tenterhooks. "What did she do?"

"She drew them back to the tower, picking up the key I'd left. But when Sir Robert saw the fire, he seemed determined to make sure the body was William's."

Palmer sobered. "Unfortunately, he discovered that his mother had the key. But before he could take it from her, she made certain no one would ever know the child in that room wasn't William."

· Claire knew he was leaving something out. "How?"

Palmer hesitated. His voice dropped. "By locking herself, and the key, in the room with the body, so no one could get in before William's substitute was burned beyond recognition.''

''Dear God.'' Claire went numb.

''She loved William,'' Palmer reminded her. ''Remember that, instead of how she died. In the end, it was love that made the sacrifice.'' Impeded by the clinging child, he kissed Claire's hand, but his eyes told her there were deeper kisses yet in store.

Nonna's voice preceded her into the kitchen. ''I'm up now. Is he here yet?''

Palmer shot Claire a puzzled look, clearly wondering who Nonna had been expecting in the middle of the night, and why.

William stirred, opened his eyes wide for a look at Nonna, her white hair streaming, and promptly clung to Palmer with renewed terror.

Palmer sheltered him with his cloak. ''He's been through a lot. Give him time.''

''Ah.'' Nonna peeked past Palmer's shoulder. ''He *is* here.''

Claire nodded her head in amazement. ''Yes, Nonna. Your brown-eyed boy is here.''

Nonna rounded the chair and crouched low, her bright eyes fixed on William. ''I know who this is,'' she said fondly. Then she looked at Palmer in suspicion. ''But who, pray tell, are you?''

Palmer rolled his lips inward to keep from smiling.

Without waiting for an answer, Nonna turned her attention back to the child peeking from behind Palmer's cloak. ''The very boy God showed me.'' She stroked William's cheek with infinite tenderness. Surprising both Claire and Palmer, he did not pull away. ''I've been waiting for you,'' she said softly. ''Have you been waiting for me?''

William nodded and reached out for her with both arms.

Claire and Palmer were speechless.

Nonna enveloped her brown-eyed boy in love. "Come along, Palmer. It's way past your bedtime."

"My name is William," the seven-year-old protested hoarsely as she carried him toward her room, "not Palmer."

"Well, if you want to be called William for tonight, I suppose it won't do any harm." Nonna kissed him on the cheek. "There's a nice, soft little bed in my room ready for you. How does that sound?"

"I'm hungry," they heard him say.

"That's good," Nonna exclaimed, "because I have some lovely little cakes you can eat in bed, and some nice sweet cider to drink. Would you like that?"

"Will you sing me a song?"

"Of course I'll sing you a song, my sweet, precious Palmer."

A very sleepy, "I told you, my name is William," was the last thing they heard before Nonna's door closed.

"What was *that* about?" Palmer asked, shrugging off his sodden cloak. "Cakes, and a bed made ready, and her waiting for a brown-eyed boy . . . ?"

"It's a long story, but a good one," Claire told him as she rose and took his hands to draw him into her arms at last. "And now, we have all the time in the world for me to tell it."

Palmer's arm circled her waist as he walked beside her until they were at last within the privacy of their room. "I want to hear every detail, but first—" He pulled her close just beyond the threshold and bumped the door shut with his hip. "I want to kiss my wife."

Four long months of pent-up longing made his kiss one Claire would never forget.

She kissed him back just as hungrily, then laid her head upon his chest, the sound of his heart hard and strong in her ear. "Today is Christ's Mass, and you've given me back my only son. A perfect gift for the birth day of the Christ."

Palmer scooped her into his arms and carried her to the bed. "I'd like to give you another gift: a son or daughter of our own ... about Michaelmas, I should reckon. What say you?"

"A child of our own? What a wonderful gift that would be." She grinned. "But a dangerous gift, I'll wager."

"Not if he's anything like his mother." Palmer carried her toward the bed.

"Or if she's anything like her father," Claire countered.

He tumbled into the rumpled covers with her still in his arms. "We'd better get about it, then, hadn't we?" he said huskily, his erection hard against her thigh.

"Aye." Claire nibbled seductively on his earlobe, then whispered, "Consummate, my dear. Consummate."

AUTHOR'S NOTE

As with all my books, the protagonists and their families depicted in *Dangerous Gifts* are fictional, but I have made every effort to be accurate in describing the culture, beliefs, politics, and customs of their times. With the exception of the secret underground tunnels, the fictional Freeman compound is based on actual excavations of Roman forts in Britain.

Tragically, the atrocities committed by some of Peter the Hermit's Christian Crusaders against their Eastern European brethren are well documented, as are those of subsequent Crusades.

At the time of the Norman Conquest of England, the term "royal forest" referred not just to wooded land, but to any specific area set aside for the king in which all wild animals were reserved for royal hunts. Thus, the New Forest included woodlands, meadows, bogs, and fens. The New Forest still exists today in Hampshire, as does the town of Lyndhurst (Linherst).

King William Rufus was, in fact, killed on August 2, 1100, under suspicious circumstances during a hunt in the New Forest. The king's bloody nightmare and the next morning's dire warnings are well documented, but the truth about his death remains a mystery.

In the century following William Rufus's death, many explanations were put forth about what really happened in the forest that day. An account written in 1125 by William of Malmesbury (the most commonly accepted version) attributes the king's death to a freak hunting accident in which one of Walter Tirel's arrows glanced off the back of a running stag and fatally wounded the king. Although Tirel—and all the other huntsmen—fled the area without even attending to the slain king's body, Tirel staunchly denied, even on his deathbed, shooting the fatal arrow. An account written by Oderic Vitalis in 1135 places Prince Henry in the hunting party. Since I am a writer of historical *fiction*, I have drawn my own conclusions and portrayed what I think is the most probable explanation of the king's death.

Survey

TELL US WHAT YOU THINK AND YOU COULD WIN
A YEAR OF ROMANCE!
(That's 12 books!)

Fill out the survey below, send it back to us, and you'll be eligible to win a year's worth of romance novels. That's one book a month for a year—from St. Martin's Paperbacks.

Name _____

Street Address _____

City, State, Zip Code _____

Email address _____

1. How many romance books have you bought in the last year?
    (Check one.)
    __0-3
    __4-7
    __8-12
    __13-20
    __20 or more

2. Where do you MOST often buy books? *(limit to two choices)*
    __Independent bookstore
    __Chain stores *(Please specify)*
        __Barnes and Noble
        __B. Dalton
        __Books-a-Million
        __Borders
        __Crown
        __Lauriat's
        __Media Play
        __Waldenbooks
    __Supermarket
    __Department store *(Please specify)*
        __Caldor
        __Target
        __Kmart
        __Walmart
    __Pharmacy/Drug store
    __Warehouse Club
    __Airport

3. Which of the following promotions would MOST influence your decision to purchase a ROMANCE paperback? *(Check one.)*
        __Discount coupon

        __Free preview of the first chapter
        __Second book at half price
        __Contribution to charity
        __Sweepstakes or contest

4. Which promotions would LEAST influence your decision to purchase a ROMANCE book? (Check one.)
        __Discount coupon
        __Free preview of the first chapter
        __Second book at half price
        __Contribution to charity
        __Sweepstakes or contest

5. When a new ROMANCE paperback is released, what is MOST influential in your finding out about the book and in helping you to decide to buy the book? (Check one.)
        __TV advertisement
        __Radio advertisement
        __Print advertising in newspaper or magazine
        __Book review in newspaper or magazine
        __Author interview in newspaper or magazine
        __Author interview on radio
        __Author appearance on TV
        __Personal appearance by author at bookstore
        __In-store publicity (poster, flyer, floor display, etc.)
        __Online promotion (author feature, banner advertising, giveaway)
        __Word of Mouth
        __Other (please specify)_____

6. Have you ever purchased a book online?
        __Yes
        __No

7. Have you visited our website?
        __Yes
        __No

8. Would you visit our website in the future to find out about new releases or author interviews?
        __Yes
        __No

9. What publication do you read most?
        __Newspapers *(check one)*
          __*USA Today*
          __*New York Times*
          __ Your local newspaper
        __Magazines *(check one)*

_People
_Entertainment Weekly
_Women's magazine *(Please specify:_____)*
_Romantic Times
_Romance newsletters

10. What type of TV program do you watch most? *(Check one.)*
    _Morning News Programs (ie. "Today Show")
      (Please specify:_____)
    _Afternoon Talk Shows (ie. "Oprah")
      (Please specify: _____)
    _All news (such as CNN)
    _Soap operas   *(Please specify: _____)*
    _Lifetime cable station
    _E! cable station
    _Evening magazine programs (ie. "Entertainment Tonight")
      (Please specify: _____)
    _Your local news

11. What radio stations do you listen to most? *(Check one.)*
    _Talk Radio
    _Easy Listening/Classical
    _Top 40
    _Country
    _Rock
    _Lite rock/Adult contemporary
    _CBS radio network
    _National Public Radio
    _WESTWOOD ONE radio network

12. What time of day do you listen to the radio MOST?
    _6am-10am
    _10am-noon
    _Noon-4pm
    _4pm-7pm
    _7pm-10pm
    _10pm-midnight
    _Midnight-6am

13. Would you like to receive email announcing new releases and special promotions?
    _Yes
    _No

14. Would you like to receive postcards announcing new releases and special promotions?
    _Yes
    _No

15. Who is your favorite romance author? _____

WIN A YEAR OF ROMANCE FROM SMP
(That's 12 Books!)
No Purchase Necessary

OFFICIAL RULES

1. To Enter: Complete the Official Entry Form and Survey and mail it to: Win a Year of Romance from SMP Sweepstakes, c/o St. Martin's Paperbacks, 175 Fifth Avenue, Suite 1615, New York, NY 10010-7848, Attention JP. For a copy of the Official Entry Form and Survey, send a self-addressed, stamped envelope to: Entry Form/Survey, c/o St. Martin's Paperbacks at the address stated above. Entries with the completed surveys must be received by February 1, 2000 (February 22, 2000 for entry forms requested by mail). Limit one entry per person. No mechanically reproduced or illegible entries accepted. Not responsible for lost, misdirected, mutilated or late entries.

2. Random Drawing. Winner will be determined in a random drawing to be held on or about March 1, 2000 from all eligible entries received. Odds of winning depend on the number of eligible entries received. Potential winner will be notified by mail on or about March 22, 2000 and will be asked to execute and return an Affidavit of Eligibility/Release/Prize Acceptance Form within fourteen (14) days of attempted notification. Non-compliance within this time may result in disqualification and the selection of an alternate winner. Return of any prize/prize notification as undeliverable will result in disqualification and an alternate winner will be selected.

3. Prize and approximate Retail Value: Winner will receive a copy of a different romance novel each month from April 2000 through March 2001. Approximate retail value $84.00 (U.S. dollars).

4. Eligibility. Open to U.S. and Canadian residents (excluding residents of the province of Quebec) who are 18 at the time of entry. Employees of St. Martin's and its parent, affiliates and subsidiaries, its and their directors, officers and agents, and their immediate families or those living in the same household, are ineligible to enter. Potential Canadian winners will be required to correctly answer a time-limited arithmetic skill question by mail. Void in Puerto Rico and wherever else prohibited by law.

5. General Conditions: Winner is responsible for all federal, state and local taxes. No substitution or cash redemption of prize permitted by winner. Prize is not transferable. Acceptance of prize constitutes permission to use the winner's name, photograph and likeness for purposes of advertising and promotion without additional compensation or permission, unless prohibited by law.

6. All entries become the property of sponsor, and will not be returned. By participating in this sweepstakes, entrants agree to be bound by these official rules and the decision of the judges, which are final in all respects.

7. For the name of the winner, available after March 22, 2000, send by May 1, 2000 a stamped, self-addressed envelope to Winner's List, Win a Year of Romance from SMP Sweepstakes, St. Martin's Paperbacks, 175 Fifth Avenue, Suite 1615, New York, NY 10010-7848, Attention JP.

Haywood Smith

"Haywood Smith delivers intelligent, sensitive historical romance for readers who expect more from the genre."

—*Publishers Weekly*

KAT MARTIN

Award-winning author of *Creole Fires*

GYPSY LORD
_____ 92878-5 $6.50 U.S./$8.50 Can.

SWEET VENGEANCE
_____ 95095-0 $6.50 U.S./$8.50 Can.

BOLD ANGEL
_____ 95303-8 $6.50 U.S./$8.50 Can.

DEVIL'S PRIZE
_____ 95478-6 $6.99 U.S./$8.99 Can.

MIDNIGHT RIDER
_____ 95774-2 $5.99 U.S./$6.99 Can.

INNOCENCE UNDONE
_____ 96089-1 $6.50 U.S./$8.50 Can.

KATHLEEN KANE

"[HAS] REMARKABLE TALENT FOR UNUSUAL, POIGNANT PLOTS AND CAPTIVATING CHARACTERS."

—*PUBLISHERS WEEKLY*

A Pocketful of Paradise

A spirit whose job it was to usher souls into the afterlife, Zach had angered the powers that be. Sent to Earth to live as a human for a month, Zach never expected the beautiful Rebecca to ignite in him such earthly emotions.
0-312-96090-5 _____ $5.99 U.S. _____ $7.99 Can.

This Time for Keeps

After eight disastrous lives, Tracy Hill is determined to get it right. But Heaven's "Resettlement Committee" has other plans—to send her to a 19th century cattle ranch, where a rugged cowboy makes her wonder if the ninth time is *finally* the charm.
0-312-96509-5 _____ $5.99 U.S. _____ $7.99 Can.

Still Close to Heaven

No man stood a ghost of a chance in Rachel Morgan's heart, for the man she loved was an angel who she hadn't seen in fifteen years. Jackson Tate has one more chance at heaven—if he finds a good husband for Rachel...and makes her forget a love that he himself still holds dear.
0-312-96268-1 _____ $5.99 U.S. _____ $7.99 Can.